Love Lies Bleeding

Tightrope Series Book 2

L. Knight

Love, Honor, Betray
By L. Knight

Published by L. Knight
Copyright © July 2024 L. Knight

Cover: Clem Parsons CovertoCover Designs
Editing: https://www.blackopalediting.com
Formatting: https://www.blackopalediting.com

Acknowledgments

Thank you to Clem Parsons designs for the amazing cover.

Thank you Linda Clarkson and Dee Hadrill at Black Opal Editing, as always you made this rock a diamond.

Thanks to all my beta readers—Greta, Maria, Brenda, and Becky D for steering me in the right direction and giving advice on plot line and flow.

Special thanks to Clementine Parsons, my wonderful sister-in-law, for allowing me to bounce my crazy ideas off you and always being there for me.

Thank you to the bloggers that share my books with your readers. Thank you to all the Indie Authors that support each other with advice, support, and just being awesome.

Lastly, my readers. Your love for what I write gets me through writer's block, midnight edits, and plot nervous breakdowns.

1. Cherry

THIS IS THE BEST DAY OF MY LIFE. LETTING MY BODY FALL BACK onto the narrow bed with the pink floral bedspread, an excited squeal of breath escapes me. I can't contain the smile spreading over my face as my reality starts to seep into my bones. I'm here, I'm actually here. I can hardly believe it. I'm at Harvard, about to embark on the adventure of a lifetime.

I sit up and look at the dozens of pictures I've pinned on my board above my tiny desk, a smile creeping over my face that is reflective and tinged with sadness. I wish my dad could see me now, that I could hear his deep baritone tell me how proud he is of me. I love my mom to pieces, but nothing will ever stop me from missing my dad. I miss Lexi, my best friend, too. She and I have been friends since we were in junior high, but we're on different paths right now and I need to let her live the life she wants, regardless of my thoughts or opinions.

Pictures of us are littered across the board and in each one, Lexi and I are smiling wide or behaving like goofs. Pictures of me and my mom, my mom and dad, and me and my dad are also displayed. All

1

the people I love and need are on that board. My circle is small out of choice. I have lots of people I consider friends but none I'd trust with my secrets.

My hand trails over the glossy image of me and my dad just before he died and my heart aches a little. I wish he could see this. I wish he was alive to see me fulfill this dream we'd had for me. Rolling my lips, I push away from the desk, shaking off the melancholy.

I will not be sad today.

This is my adventure, and I'm going to make the most of every second I have here. I worked my ass off to get here and I'm going to relish every experience and get my butt out and meet new people, experience new things. My small window looks out onto Mass Avenue and is a hive of activity. The sounds of people going about their business filters through, reminding me that I'm not alone. I unpack my clothes and hang or fold them away by season. Storage is minimal here so I only brought fall and winter, and some key pieces I could layer. I can always get more when I go home for the holidays. I'm drawn again to the view over Mass. Watching the other students come and go fills me with a sense of belonging.

"I did it, Daddy. I got my dream college just like you said I would."

Being a daddy's girl made losing him so much worse and, every day since, I've vowed to make this happen, to make him proud. I know my mom misses him too. Their relationship had been so full of love, and I worry about her being on her own. She assures me she has the salon to keep her busy, but I still worry. I don't trust or love easily but when I do, I'll go down in a fiery blaze for the ones I love.

My phone pings with a text message and I smile when I see Lexi's name.

Lexi: Have an amazing time. I miss you but you're going to kill it at Harvard. Love you.

Cherry: It's everything, Lex. I miss you too, but I'm going to scope out the local coffee shops and see if I can land a job. This scholarship will only get me so far.

Lexi: Don't forget to scope out the local talent too 😉

Cherry: I'm not interested in boys. I want to get my degree and take over the world.

Lexi: Do both. If anyone can, it's you, babe.

Cherry: Damn right. Talk later.

Lexi: Okay x

Slipping my phone into the back pocket of my skinny jeans, I check my hair, which has faded to a soft pink since my last color, and decide I quite like this shade. It suits my fair complexion, but still gives me some oomph. At five feet tall, I need every advantage I can get and, thankfully, my personality has never been that of a wallflower.

Sliding my feet into pink wedges, I adjust the collar on my pink shirt and re-tie the waist so that a sliver of skin is showing. It's sexy but not slutty, cute but not boring. Style is everything to me. Clothes are armor in more than one way, and I always make sure I show people what I want them to perceive.

Stepping into the small common room that links the four rooms on this entryway, I see a girl with red, curly hair pinning a poster above a desk.

"Hey."

She turns, her foot slipping off the chair she was using to reach, and I dive to grab her before she falls. A giggle escapes her as she clutches my arm.

"Sorry, I didn't mean to scare you."

She regains her balance and waves away my apology. "Don't worry, I'm a klutz. In fact, it should be my middle name."

Laughing, I study her wide smile and the freckles on her upper cheeks. "What's your first name?"

"Marianna. Nice to meet you...?"

"Cherry."

"Hence the pink hair. I love it."

Waving a hand at my hair, I smile. "Pink is my favorite color, which you'll find out, I'm sure."

"I love that. What are you studying?"

"The history of Art and Architecture."

"Wow, that's much more exciting than math."

"Math? That's impressive."

Marianna rolls her eyes. "It would be if it was my choice, but my parents kind of steam rolled me into it."

I could never understand that pressure from parents or the kids that let them do it, but then my mom was the coolest on the planet and I'm far too stubborn to allow myself to be pushed into something I don't want. "That sucks."

Her shoulders shrug. "Meh, I don't really mind. It's a good one to have and gives me options at the end."

"True."

Marianna motions to my bag on my shoulder. "You headed out?"

"Yeah, gonna hit up the coffee shops and try and snag a part-time job."

"Well, good luck with that."

I get a feeling Marianna doesn't need a part-time job to fund this experience for her, but she seems nice.

"You want to come to a party later?"

Inclining my head in question, I ask, "Party?"

"Yeah, my sister's a sophomore and invited me. You should come."

"I don't know." I'm not one to go someplace I wasn't invited.

"Oh, come on. We can go and get to know each other and meet new people. It will be good to have some fun before classes start."

"Maybe."

Marianna claps her hands excitedly. "I'm taking that as a yes."

I beam a smile at her exuberance and head for the door. "We'll see."

"I'll leave the details on the board for you." Her voice echoes down the hall as I head out.

My steps almost bounce with happiness as I head for Mass Avenue, where the bookshop is located. My dorm overlooks this part of campus and I feel immeasurable joy as I take in a big breath of air. The summer is ending, and fall is teasing its arrival but, with the warm air still fighting to hold on, I bask in the feeling of change. Tilting my head high, I can barely contain the grin on my face as people rush around me, clear excitement etched on their faces, too. Freshmen are easy to spot among the sophomores, juniors, and seniors. They have this energy that is palpable.

I'm on my third coffee shop when I catch a break and find a vacancy. I fill in the application then and there and hand it back. The scent of fresh coffee, warm caramel, and the sweet smell of blueberry muffins remind me that I haven't eaten since my mom dropped me off this morning. The manager gives me the quickest interview in history with a bored expression on his face and then nods.

"You start Monday. I'll email your shifts once you let me have your class schedule."

I bounce on my toes, a grin making my cheeks ache. "Thank you. I won't let you down."

Finally, Stewart the manager, cracks a smile. "I hope not, kid."

Quickly I order myself a cinnamon latte and blueberry muffin, adding a chocolate chip cookie to celebrate my newfound employment.

I'm on such a high as I rush through the exit that I don't look where I'm going. My forehead smacks into a hard wall and I reach out to grab something to hold onto and find my fingers curling around a muscular forearm. My coffee survives and I'm thankful I tucked my sweet treats into my backpack. Strong hands grip my upper arms and I lift my head to look at my rescuer or attacker, depending on how you look at it.

Tingles prickle my skin as I look into dark green eyes that make me want to sink into them. His brow is pulled down in concern as he gazes at me. God, he's beautiful; square jaw that must have been chiseled by the gods, thick dark hair with just the hint of an untameable curl, and lips that were made to take a woman to heaven.

"You okay?"

Wrenching out of his hold, I fold my arms and stare up at him. Blinking widely, I shake away all the delicious thoughts and snap out of my lust-induced fog. I fall back on my defense mechanism of sass and sarcasm as I try and ignore the intoxicating scent of this boy in front of me. "Okay? Are you implying I'm average? Because let me assure you, I'm a ten, buddy."

My rescuer's mouth falls open and I can't help but let my gaze wander to his lips for a moment. He really is spectacularly good-looking. I watch as his mouth pulls at the corners and a wide smile transforms his face from handsome to 'Oh my god, have my babies' hot. It really should be illegal to look this good and be smart enough to attend this school.

"My sincere apologies. I never meant to imply such a wretched thing. You're indeed a ten. No, a twelve, and I'm only happy that you allowed such a humble servant to break your fall."

A smile twitches on my lips and I fight to hide it as this boy plays my silly game. Most boys find me too much to handle and that's okay. If they can't handle me, they don't deserve me. I know that, and I live by it, but it's nice to find someone who's met me head-on and gives me as good as I give.

"I accept your apology."

We stand staring at each other as people bustle around the coffee shop, moving around us with annoyed sighs. The sounds of the frothing machine sputtering, the blender whizzing, and the chatter of the patrons fade away. It's as if we're in a sound bubble where only we exist. I can feel the heat from his body as he steps closer, his heady scent wrapping around me and seeping into my skin.

"Seriously, did I hurt you?"

I shake my head. "No, I'm perfect." I lift my hands up to prove I'm uninjured and he smirks, causing butterflies to take flight in my belly.

"You certainly are."

He winces as the words leave his mouth and I can't help the laugh that erupts from me. "Does that line ever work?"

He palms the back of his neck and rubs it awkwardly, his biceps bunching and flexing as he does. His high cheekbones are tinged pink, which I find adorable. "Honestly, it's the first time I've used it."

I drop my head so that he can't see the smile on my face and move around him, needing to get out of there. "Perhaps you should make it the last, too."

"Yeah, I think you might be right."

I pat his arm, not able to stop myself from touching that warm skin again but pull back quickly when I realize that it's a mistake. It makes me wonder what the rest of him would feel like but I'm not here to hook up with boys, no matter how handsome and charming they might be.

"See you around..."

"Jake."

"See you around, Jake."

I head for the exit, but his deep voice stops me. "What should I call you?"

"Bye, Jake."

I'm not giving this boy my name. He's temptation wrapped in the most sweetly edible package I've ever seen and I have a sweet tooth, so my plan is avoidance.

"Bye, Blossom."

I smile as I walk toward my dorm, determined not to be charmed by the first hot guy I meet. I need to get a few more things unpacked and then maybe I can go to the party Marianna talked about and forget about the handsome Jake with the gorgeous smile and the cute blush.

2. Jake

"I'M SORRY, JAKE, I WON'T MAKE IT THIS WEEK. DAD SPOKE TO the Dean and he okayed it for me to start in two weeks."

My head drops as my shoulders droop. "That sucks, man, but if you need anything, give me a shout."

"I can't believe I broke my leg on that damn slope."

I smirked as I looked out over Mass Avenue from my window. "Well, if you have to indulge in those snooty sports, then you get what you asked for."

"Skiing is not snooty, it's skillful."

"Whatever, call if you need me."

"I will and leave those freshmen alone."

A chuckle rumbled out of me as I spy a girl with pink hair walk into the Coffee Corner coffee shop. "I told you, I'm a changed man, no more fuck-boy ways for me. I need to concentrate on my grades this term or I'm going to fail."

"Whatever, like you can say no to fresh meat."

I watched as the pink-haired girl comes out and looks left and then right before walking towards the Mocha Bar, her head held high, a sway in her hips that's confident and sexy as fuck. "Gotta go, Mac, talk soon."

"Yeah, later."

I head out with an itchy feeling inside me that just won't subside. Being here without Mac feels wrong. I can't help the sense that I don't belong, that I'm the misfit in this picture. I didn't grow up with money. I had no silver spoon in my mouth at birth. In fact, I was lucky to eat at all some days.

Yes, I wear the hundred-dollar white tee, the designer jeans, and the trainers that cost more than the rent on my childhood apartment, and I feel like a fraud. Without Hunter McKenzie and his family, I'd be nothing. I am nothing.

"Hi, Jake."

I lift my hand at the sexy blonde who purrs my name and give her a short wave as I keep moving. I'm not in the mood for Candy, Kylie, or whatever her name is today.

I shove my way into the Mocha Bar, my mood is irritated and short, and a pink-haired fairy slams into me head first. My hands fly out to steady her, my fingers closing around slim, toned arms. It's on the tip of my tongue to yell at her to be more careful when she glances up and the air in my lungs dies.

A heart-shaped face gazes up at me, her brilliant blue eyes mesmerizing me as I take her in. She's fucking beautiful, with long dark natural lashes, pink cheeks, and full blushing lips that immediately make me want to bend my head and see if she tastes as sweet as she looks. Everything about her is exquisite, even her pale pink hair is perfect on her. She looks like a princess.

Realizing I'm staring like a weirdo, I open my mouth as my eyes run over her smoking body. She's tiny against my six-foot frame, barely hitting my shoulder and I have this ridiculous urge to wrap her in my arms and protect her. "You okay?"

Wrenching out of my hold, she crosses her arms over her chest and I fight not to look down at her tits. She blinks owlishly and I wait as her lips purse temptingly for her to flirt with me. Minutes ago I was so sure I had no interest in checking out the freshmen but for this little angel, I might be persuaded.

"Okay? Are you implying I'm average, because let me assure you, I'm a ten, buddy."

My mouth falls open in shock at her sass, and attraction runs hotly through me as her gaze wanders to my lips and I wonder if she wants me to kiss her as much as I want to claim those full lips. Her words intrigue me as much as the sexy package it's wrapped in. My mouth pulls at the corners and a wide smile transforms my mood as I see the challenge in her eyes. This girl is something else, she's not falling at my feet like most do, and I feel the excitement of the hunt invade my veins. It's been so long since any girl has given me a challenge and I find I missed it. Deciding to see where she takes this, I play along, finding her confidence sexy as fuck.

"My sincere apologies. I never meant to imply such a wretched thing. You are indeed a ten. No, a twelve, and I'm only happy that you allowed such a humble servant to break your fall."

A smile twitches on her lips and she fights to hide it from me, but I'm the master of details. I tower over her, probably outweighing her by a hundred pounds at least and yet she's facing me like not only could she best me but like I'm unworthy of her attention. I like it, a lot.

"I accept your apology."

We stand gazing at each other as people move around us. I hear my name a few times and know that this interaction won't be missed. Girls giggle and whisper and I wish for a minute that I still had anonymity but being best friends with Hunter McKenzie brings a spotlight, and I'd never trade that friendship for anything. He and his family saved me in every way and I'll always consider myself in their debt.

I let my gaze run over this girl, her coffee balanced in her hand, the button on her shirt undone just enough to tempt you to want more.

"Seriously, did I hurt you?"

She shakes her head, her pink hair catching my attention and giving me the strongest urge to reach out and touch it, to see if it's as soft as it looks, but that would definitely come off as creepy.

"No, I'm perfect."

Her hands lift and my gaze drops down her body, spying a sliver of smooth skin on her flat belly and I find myself wishing my hands could take the same journey, only slower and with far less clothes. "You certainly are."

I wince as the words leave my mouth knowing how fucking corny they sound and my cheeks heat awkwardly. *Awkwardly!* I haven't been awkward since I grew into my height at fourteen.

"Does that line ever work?"

Palming the back of my neck, I wish I could rewind the last few seconds and come up with something better, something to impress her. I'm not used to working this hard, or at all, for attention and my game is in the toilet. "Honestly it's the first time I've used it," I admit, hoping she'll take pity on me.

Her head drops and I see the ghost of a smile on her full pink lips as she moves around me. I have the unexpected urge to reach out and take her hand, to pull her back and keep her here so we can continue this conversation, as awkward as it is for me right now, but I resist; just.

"Perhaps you should make it the last, too."

"Yeah, I think you might be right."

Her tiny hand lands on my forearm for a second before she pulls it back like I scalded her, but that isn't what I feel. I feel electricity pulse through my skin at her touch and if her reaction is anything to gauge, so does she. It makes me wonder what her hands would look like on the rest of my body. Before I can stop her, she's moving to the exit as I stand like a fucking decoration in the middle of the aisle.

"See you around..."

"Jake," I supply.

"See you around, Jake."

I'm not gonna let her leave without getting her number. "What should I call you?"

"Bye, Jake."

Playing hard to get, is she? I can work with that. What this girl doesn't know is that I'm incredibly stubborn and determined when I want something and I've just decided I want her.

"Bye, Blossom."

I hear her chuckle as the door closes and I watch her walk down the street like she owns it, before turning with a smile and heading back to my dorm. Hunger rushes through my blood as I think over our interaction, remembering the sweet scent of honeysuckle on her skin. Somehow it's hotter and more satisfying than sex with any of the nameless, faceless, one-night stands I've had recently. She didn't cower or simper, which is what I'm used to. Girls don't make me or Mac work for it. They just want to say they've fucked either of us. But this girl demanded more from me without even asking. She knows her own value and that's the hottest thing ever.

"Jake, hey."

I stop as Lorelei steps across my path, putting her hand on my chest in a possessive way that makes my skin crawl like an army of ants have descended. I lift her hand and let it drop to her side, but she's undeterred. Her red lips tip up like I've just announced our engagement.

"What do you want, Lorelei?" I ask, folding my arms over my chest in a clear sign that I'm not interested.

She pulls at her top, shoving her tits in my face and I wonder if she realizes how unattractive it is to look so desperate. We've hooked up a few times and, honestly, I can barely remember it, and have no desire to repeat it but she's not getting the hint at all.

"I'm having a party tonight. My parents are away and my baby sister wants to meet some of the other students. You should come, bring Hunter with you. I haven't seen him yet, and some of the girls have been asking."

"Hunter isn't back yet."

"Well, you should come alone. I'm sure I can find a way to keep you from getting lonely without your friend."

"I'll see. I have shit to do later." I know saying no outright would just prolong this nightmare, but I have no intention of going and being pawed at all night. I'm just not in the mood. I have better things to do, like find out more about my pink-haired mystery girl.

"Oh, come on, my sister is stuck in a dorm with some total freaks. One even has pink hair. Surely you can come and help show her how friendly we all are. I've been dying to introduce you to my family."

Uh, what the fuck? I'm not being introduced to anyone's family. We've fucked, that's all. Where the hell does this girl get the idea we're a thing? But something she said does intrigue me and force me to keep my mouth shut about that little statement. There can't be many freshmen with pink hair, and something tells me going to this little party will put me one step closer to my pink-haired mystery girl. "Sure, I'll come."

Lorelei jumps up and down and then throws her arms around me. "Oh, Jakey, I'm so happy."

I unhook her arms from around my neck and hold her at arm's length, stepping back to a safe distance.

Lorelei seems unfazed and completely unaware of my disinterest.

"It's at my place. The pool is heated so bring your bathing shorts... or don't."

"I'll see you later."

"You sure will, Jakey."

She gives me a suggestive wink and I wonder what the hell I'd ever been thinking to stick my dick in her. She's like a praying mantis, only instead of wanting to eat me, she wants to trap me. Thank God I never fucked her without a condom. I wouldn't put it past her to get pregnant and trap me that way. It's funny to me because everyone assumes that, because I live with Hunter in the dorms and we're best friends, I have money too. If they knew I didn't have a pot of my own to piss in, they'd be very different. I'm only here because Hank McKenzie, Hunter's dad, saw something in me, paid for my education, and gives me a generous allowance that I earned over the summer working for him. Sometimes I'm tempted to tell them all that I'm a nobody, that I'm a fraud but I'd never embarrass Hank or Hunter that way. Wanting this encounter over, I make to move around Lorelei.

I avoid the kiss she tries to force on me and sidestep her, walking off at a brisk pace determined to do everything I can to avoid her later and focus on showing Blossom that I'm not just some guy with a bad pick-up line.

3. Cherry

"Oh my God, this place is whacked!" I clutch Marianna's arm as we step into what can only be described as a mansion. We push through the double front door into an entryway that is packed with people.

"It's mad, right?" Marianna giggles. "It's my stepdad's place, really. My mom and I moved in last year when they got married."

"So, your sister is here?"

Marianna shrugs. "Stepsister, I guess. Lorelei likes to call me her sister, but I think that's more because she likes the idea of having someone she can boss around. You'll see when you meet her. She's a lot."

We push through the throngs of drunk people, the scent of pot and beer hanging heavily in the air. "I can't believe your parents would allow this." My mom would skin me alive if I did this to her house, not that we could fit this many people in our home.

"Oh, they have no idea. They're out of town and Lorelei can get away with anything, anyway. Let's grab a drink and head out the back, we have a pool."

I follow Marianna into the kitchen, the sounds of clanking beer bottles mixing with the excited sounds of laughter and screams from all around me. Red solo cups litter the counter, and ice is melting in the sink.

I take the beer she hands me and we knock cups together. "Here's to our first semester. May it be filled with hot guys, high grades, and lots of fun."

I laugh at the toast as Marianna twirls around, her red hair flying around her shoulders. She's fun, I like her and I have a good feeling about this.

We head outside and the scene out there is even more crazy. Half-naked people are dancing to the music, the deep thrum of the bass filling the night air with a sultry beat.

"Oh, I see some friends, I need to say hello."

Marianna tries to pull me forward but I resist. "You go. I'm going to nose around for a bit, do a bit of people-watching."

"You sure?" Marianna gives me a look.

I shove her gently and she laughs. "Yes, I'm sure."

"I'll be back."

I watch her go with a smile. I wasn't lying, people watching is one of my favorite things to do and I don't get to do it often. Leaning against one of the pillars on the steps that lead down to the pool, I watch as a guy in red shorts throws himself off the diving board backward, landing in the pool to a chorus of cheers from his friends on the side.

Around me, couples are in different stages of hooking up, some talking and flirting and others practically having sex in full view and not caring who watches. My cheeks flush as my mind goes back to the boy from the coffee shop, Jake. I might have sworn not to get involved with anyone but boy, was he hot and, worse, he seemed sweet and that's my kryptonite.

Chugging my beer to cool my heated cheeks, I head back inside for another drink.

"Hey, beautiful, wanna dance?"

I roll my eyes at the guy in front of me. He's tall, athletic, good-looking, and off his face drunk. He makes a move to reach for me and I skillfully avoid his touch. "No, thanks, buddy."

With a smile, he shrugs and then winks as he turns and yells at one of his friends to turn up the music. I continue on to the kitchen, passing a line up at the bathroom. A haze of smoke fills the rooms, the sickly sweet smell of spilled beer and marijuana permeating the air. I move to the fridge and pull out a beer, closing it with my hip as I look for a bottle opener. Spying one across the other side of the room, I squeeze past three boys and feel a hand land on my ass.

I straighten, my eyes popping open wide. *Oh no he did not!* I turn and see one with blond hair and an arrogant grin wink at me.

"Hey, gorgeous, wanna suck my dick for me?"

The fucking balls on this guy. I smile sweetly, moving closer and he grins at his friends, clearly believing that whatever the fuck that was, has worked. Resting my hand on his chest, I let it travel over his chest and down. I cup the bulge in his pants and squeeze and squeeze, watching as he winces and tries to move away but I have a pretty good grip on his junk.

"Gentle, love."

I tilt my head and glare up at him. "Oh, I'm sorry. Am I being too rough with your needle dick?"

His cheeks redden and he grips my wrist trying to loosen my grip.

"Fuck you, bitch."

I laugh, my gaze cold. "I'd rather deep-throat a cactus than put your dick anywhere near my mouth."

I let him go and shove away from him, but he grabs my shoulder. I spin, ready to punch him in his jock face when I feel a presence at my back, a warm familiar scent surrounding me.

"Put a hand on her again, Marcus, and I'll break every bone in your hand."

His deep voice is cold and deadly and I watch as the needle dick and his friends pale and back away.

"Sorry, Jake, I didn't know she was yours."

"Well, now you do, so fuck off before I decide to teach you some manners."

Marcus and his friends turn and flee, like the little cockroaches that they are and I turn my attention to Jake. He looks good, his black t-shirt pulling across his chest and tight around his biceps, the dark jeans fitting just right. His hair is slightly damp, like he just showered and the visual is enough to turn my brain to mush, but I won't be dicknotized by his hotness.

"I had it handled."

He smirks and my belly swarms with traitorous butterflies. "Oh I know, I saw, but I know those guys and they won't think twice about putting their hands on a girl in anger."

"Assholes," I sneer.

"Yeah, they are, but they'll leave you alone now."

I cock my head at him as I lean back against the sink and fold my arms. The beer bottle still dangling from my fingers. "Because they think I'm yours?"

"Yes."

"But I'm not. I don't belong to anyone except myself."

Jake reaches out and, instead of the dread or revulsion Marcus instilled, I find myself going still, waiting for his touch, but he merely takes the beer bottle from my fingers and slams the lid against the counter, popping the cap off before handing it back to me.

"What if I said I wanted you to be mine?"

His lips look soft as I fight the urge to trace them with my fingertips. I glance back to his eyes and find him watching me with a hungry look. He wants me, that's clear, and I doubt I'm hiding the fact I feel the same, but something about this boy gives me pause. He isn't some fuck boy, or at least he isn't giving the vibe that he wants just that from me, but that could be my ego talking.

He steps forward and his hand extends toward me, his fingers grazing my cheek as he tucks my hair behind my ear. His touch causes a shiver to skate down my spine, and I resist the urge to lean into him, my breath coming in short pants as my pulse pounds against my neck.

"I'd say I wasn't interested." I lie because it's what I want the truth to be. The thought of belonging to this boy right now is really fucking tempting but I'm not fool enough to believe it's anything more than pheromones.

"What about a kiss?"

His head bends, his minty breath feathering over my skin as he moves slowly closer and I close my eyes, relishing in the heady feeling, before I plant my hand on his chest and push. He moves back easily and that only makes me want him more.

"I'd say you haven't earned it."

Jake chuckles, surprising me. Most guys would have sulked, stormed off, and called me a tease, but he's different. He takes it in stride and it makes me like him more.

"What about your name?"

"Cherry."

He nods as if he's mulling that over. "I like it, it suits you."

"Because of my hair?"

He leans back against the island, shaking his head. "No, although the hair is epic. Cherry blossoms look delicate and fragile but they're actually really hardy and resistant to drought."

"Wow, you're a botanist. I did *not* see that coming."

Jake shrugs. "Not really. I read it somewhere."

"You read, too? Wow, you *are* a catch. Wife me up already." The sarcasm in my tone is flirty and I hope he gets that. I don't want to come across bitchy but I do fall back on it a lot, it's like my factory default setting. My mom is always telling me it will get me in trouble one day.

"You're not like other girls are you, Cherry Blossom?"

"Nope, one of a kind."

"Yes, you are."

"So, Jake, tell me about you? What are you studying?"

"Law."

"Wow, impressive."

"What about you?"

"The History of Art and Architecture."

"We have some beautiful old buildings on campus. Have you seen them?"

I take a swig of my beer, feeling the cool liquid slide down my throat, and then offer him the bottle to share. He takes it, doing the same, his eyes locked on mine as he does. It feels intimate as if we're sharing way more than spit.

"Have you?"

"Have I what?"

"Seen any of the old buildings?"

"I've seen Massachusetts Hall and it's breathtaking. I could study it for hours and still not take in all the details. I want to visit Holden Chapel next."

"They are impressive."

He looks down and then up at me sideways and I can't hide my grin. "So, Cherry Blossom, are you going to let me take you on a date?"

I want to, I really want to but I promised myself I wouldn't do this. And, honestly, Jake scares me slightly. He's too tempting, to perfect almost and it makes me wary. But I like talking to him.

I shake my head and his expression falters before he nods.

"I'm sorry, Jake. I'm just not looking for anything."

"I get it. How about friends then?"

Can you ever be friends with someone you find so attractive? I'm not sure you can but I find I want to try, because this connection I feel to him is addictive. "Just friends," I state as I hold out my hand and he takes it in his and kisses my knuckles, causing my breath to hitch slightly.

"Good friends."

I shake my head, snatching my hand back. "Don't make me regret this, Jake."

"Never."

"Hey, there you are. I thought you'd left." Marianna wraps an arm around me and smiles drunkenly at me.

"You good, Marianna?"

"Yes!" Her arms shoot into the air. "I'm great." She eyes Jake inquisitively. "Who is this?"

"Jake Marshall. Nice to meet you."

"Oh, he's hot and sweet, and I bet those big hands of his could show a girl a good time."

Her stage whisper is practically a bellow and Jake smirks and shakes his head as I slap a hand over her mouth. "Inside voice, Marianna."

A hiccup leaves her and she giggles. "Oops."

"Jakey, there you are."

I turn as a gorgeous blonde with a black fishnet dress over hot pink underwear drapes herself over Jake like a blanket. Her gaze moves to me as he extricates himself from her grip.

"Who are you?"

Her tone is anything but friendly, the mean girl vibes emanating off her in waves as she attaches herself to Jake with a proprietary demeanor that's hard to miss. "Cherry Baker, and you are?"

Her lips purse and she sneers at me. "You have a stripper name. Do you dance?"

"That's enough, Lorelei," Jake states angrily but she just simpers up at him, her bottom lip turned down.

"I was only asking, Jakey."

"No, you were being a bitch as usual," Marianna declares, shoving away from the counter and facing the girl who is obviously her sister.

"At least I'm not sharing a dorm with a little slut."

I place my bottle on the counter with more calm than I feel and turn back to Lorelei. "Are you really so insecure that you need to demean other girls to make yourself feel better?" I hate girls like this bitch and I have no time for that kind of energy in my life.

"I'm not insecure. What would I have to be insecure about? You're nothing."

"Bitch, you don't even know me." I step closer and I can feel Jake watching me, probably regretting his offer of friendship, and thanking the gods he dodged a bullet with me but whatever. This is me.

"I know you're coming on to my boyfriend in my house."

"I'm not your fucking boyfriend, Lorelei."

She doesn't even react to his statement, just carries on glaring at me, her fake lashes batting like spider legs on crack.

"You're right, this is your house, and I'll leave but let me give you a little warning, Lorelei. I play nice. I'm a nice person until you fuck with me, and then you'll find out I'm not so nice."

I shove past her and head for the door as Marianna chases me.

"I'm so sorry, Cherry. She's such a bitch. I never should have told her you were my roommate and I swear I never said that about you."

I rub Marianna's arm as she struggles to stand upright. "It's fine, we can't choose family, right? Why don't you get to bed and I'll see you tomorrow?"

"Why don't you stay here with me? I don't like the idea of you getting back to campus alone."

I'd rather face down a tiger in a meat dress than stay under this roof but I don't say that to Marianna. She's sweet and she can't help it that her step-sister is a total bitch.

"I'll take her. I have my car and I only had a few sips of beer."

I look up to see Jake watching us from a few steps back. He gives me a soft smile that is almost contrite. A part of me wants to say no, I don't need the hassle that comes with his friendship, but I still find myself agreeing.

"Yay. Thanks, Jake."

Marianna hugs me before I can say no and rushes back into the house. I tilt my head back to keep his gaze as he walks closer, his hands in his pockets. "Won't your girlfriend mind?"

He shakes his head in annoyance. "Not my girlfriend. Not my anything. We just hooked up, it was nothing."

"Clearly she doesn't feel the same way."

"Well, tough shit, because I'm not interested."

"Good luck with that. I have a feeling she'll be harder to shift than a Strep infection."

Jake rubs his thumb along his lower lip as he chuckles. "You're something else, Blossom."

"Yeah, so I hear." I roll my eyes, but my shoulders sag a little hearing him say it. I should have known that my personality was just too big.

He lifts my chin with his forefinger and raises his eyebrows. "Hey, it was a compliment."

"Really? You didn't think I was mouthy or too loud?"

"Are you kidding? It was hot as fuck."

I study him, looking for the lie, and find none. "Friends, remember? You aren't meant to find me hot."

"I agreed to friends, I never agreed not to find you hot."

I shrug and turn away so he can't see how pleased that statement makes me. "Using technicalities, Counselor?"

He bends close to my ear as we walk and he steers me towards a sleek, black BMW. "Not a lawyer yet, Blossom, but yes, technicalities and details matter."

Running my hand over the cool glossy paintwork, I wonder how a boy his age can afford such a luxury car. Maybe he comes from money or he's a criminal, but I dismiss that instantly. He doesn't seem like the type to break the law and risk his future, but then I don't know him. The question is, do I want to? The answer is quick; yes, I do.

"Will you let me give you a ride home? I promise no funny business."

"Fine, but I'm choosing the music."

He groans as he flicks the fob on the keyring and the doors unlock. Before I can reach for the door, he stops me, opening my door and reaching over to help me with the belt. I can feel the heat of his body as his hand skims across my belly and latches the clip. My pulse is racing in my neck as he moves slowly, letting his hands linger. Not in an inappropriate way but almost teasing.

"Do you open doors and latch seatbelts for all your friends?" My voice is a husky whisper as I stare at his lips, wondering why the hell I'm resisting him.

"Most of my friends don't look like you. They're only a nine, not a twelve."

I laugh at his reminder of our earlier interaction. "Well, that makes all the difference."

"Plus, I was taught that a real man doesn't let a beautiful woman open her own doors, friend or not."

"Your mom taught you well."

He glances across at me as he buckles his own belt, a look I can't define in his eyes. "Not my mom or my dad, but someone who has done more for me than I can ever repay."

Before I can comment, he turns away and the engine roars to life. There's a story there, one I want to hear. Jake Marshall isn't who I thought he was. He's so much more and it terrifies me because keeping him at arm's length suddenly seems like a monumental task.

4. Cherry

I woke up early this morning, nervous excitement swirling in my belly. It's my first shift at the Mocha Bar today. I'd emailed my class schedule over to my boss, Stewart, and he'd got back to me the same day with my shift roster.

I've been here almost a week now, and my classes and lectures start next week, but I can't deny I feel a little homesick. But new friends like Marianna and Lucy, my dorm sisters, have made it easier. Marianna had banged on my door the night after the party at her house absolutely mortified by her stepsister's behavior and begging my forgiveness.

I'd laughed it off, telling her she wasn't responsible for her sister, and I'd meant it. Lorelei might be a prize bitch, but Marianna is nice, sweet. She quizzed me about Jake, asking how we knew each other. I'd played it down, saying we hardly knew each other and had literally just run into each other at a coffee shop on my first day. She'd divulged that he and his friend were like gods around campus. Everyone knew them, and either wanted to be their friends, fuck them, or were scared by the amount of power and influence they had.

From what she said, they didn't seek people out or go to a lot of parties, and that untouchability just made their stock soar higher.

To say I'd been shocked was an understatement. I hadn't got the vibe off Jake at all. Yes, I could see by the way Marcus and his friends reacted that Jake wasn't to be messed with but this almost god-like status hadn't been obvious to me by his behavior towards me at all, but then maybe I wasn't looking too hard.

I haven't heard from him since Saturday night when he dropped me home, and I haven't seen him around but that's okay. I've battled a little disappointment before deciding it's probably for the best. He'd asked for my number and I'd refused, saying if he wanted it enough he'd find it. Clearly, he hadn't wanted to put the work in and that's okay.

As I dry my hair and style it into soft waves before pulling it into a ponytail for work, my phone buzzes.

> Unknown number: Want to make out....

I blink in surprise, a grin pulling at my lips as I guess Lexi is messing with me. She does that sometimes, or she used too. Pranks are kind of our thing. I can see the dots jumping as the person types again and I wait to see what they'd say next.

> Unknown number: Oops! That was meant to say do you want to hang out, but I'm happy with either 😌

> Cherry: Who is this?

> Unknown number: Gif

The gif was of a cartoon man with an arrow through his heart. I smile, daring to hope that it's Jake but also trying to play down how much this sends a thrill through my blood.

27

> Unknown number: Wow, Blossom, You forgot me already, you sure know how to wound a guy.

My grin widens as my fingers fly over the screen, prickles of excitement making my skin tingle.

> Cherry: How did you get my number, Jake?

> Jake: Aww, so you do remember me. You said if I wanted it enough, I'd find it, and I really wanted it. Now, about that making out…

> Jake: I mean hanging out. 😉

A laugh burst from me at his flirty comment and I let my body fall back on the bed as I quickly type out a response.

> Cherry: Much as I'd love to HANG out, I have to work today.

I place my phone down on the bed, not wanting to be one of those girls who watches her phone like a maniac waiting for a boy to text her, even if he is only a friend. I apply some mascara as the text message alert dings. With more restraint than I thought I possessed, I finish my make-up with some cherry lip gloss because I'm not above that particular cliché and cherry is the bomb.

Picking up the phone, I read the text.

> Jake: How about later?

> Cherry: What would we do?

Jake: Well, as you shut making out down, and we're friends, I thought we could go play crazy golf? As long as you don't get upset with losing. I'm not one to brag but I am pretty amazing, if I do say so myself.

Cherry: Crazy golf?

Jake: Hey, don't judge my little quirks.

Cherry: I'd never and that sounds fun. I get off at five, does that work?

Jake: 😈 I'd love to get you off before but since you shut me down, five works. I'll pick you up from work.

Cherry: How about I meet you there? You can send me the address.

I don't want this to feel like a date and him picking me up feels too much like a date.

Jake: It's a THIRTY-MINUTE drive and you don't have a car.

Cherry: I can Uber.

Jake: Fuck me, you're stubborn.

Cherry: ✅

Jake: Just let me pick you up. I promise I'll let you choose the music

Cherry: Even if it's the Spice Girls?

Jake: Fuck me. Yes, even if it's the spice girls.

Cherry: I don't like the Spice Girls.

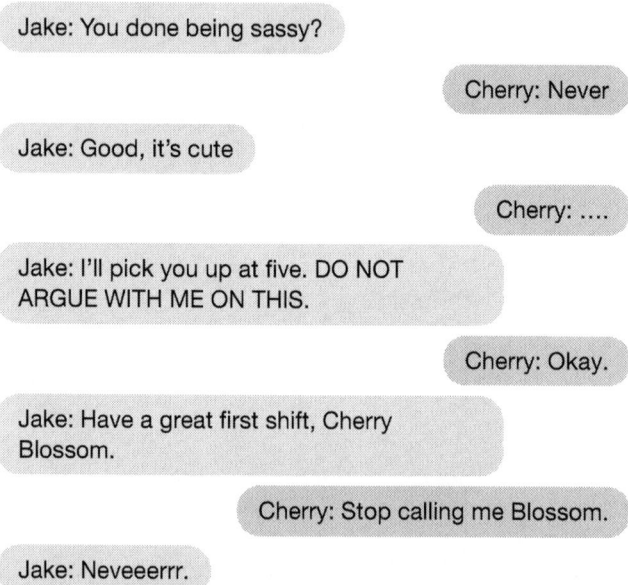

Jake: You done being sassy?

Cherry: Never

Jake: Good, it's cute

Cherry: ....

Jake: I'll pick you up at five. DO NOT ARGUE WITH ME ON THIS.

Cherry: Okay.

Jake: Have a great first shift, Cherry Blossom.

Cherry: Stop calling me Blossom.

Jake: Neveeerrr.

Okay, that's kind of hot. I like a man who takes charge and is sweet at the same time and he's allowing me to be me. I finish getting ready with a smile on my face and then head for the Mocha Bar.

The next few weeks are crazy busy with classes and work as I get my head around work, living away from home, and the demands of my course, but I love it. I'm thriving here and that is in no small part down to Jake. He's been true to his word and hasn't tried anything with me, and I'm kinda bummed over it.

I'd drawn the line in the sand and he's stuck to it, but now I'm wondering if I've been too hasty in friend-zoning him. He's sweet, thoughtful, hot as fucking lava, and he pays attention to me.

Every morning I wake up to a text from him wishing me a good day, but they say more than good morning, they let me know he's thinking about me.

This morning's text had been Good morning Blossom. I hope your day is as lovely as you.

It wasn't too flirty but it was sweet and made the walls I'd erected tremble as each brick began to fall. Lately, he'd even begun to wait for me after my shift and walk me back to my dorm even though it was less than a block away.

"Hey, you. How was your shift?"

I look up as I exit the Mocha Bar and see Jake leaning against a shiny black Yamaha, his arms crossed over his broad chest. My eyes on the bike, I walk towards him and run my hand reverently over the paintwork. "This is a Yamaha R3."

"It is."

I look up to find him watching me, surprise flickering on his face. "You like bikes, Blossom?"

"My dad loved them so I grew up around them."

"Wanna go for a ride?"

Jake holds up the spare helmet in his hand and I grin, a thrill like no other rushing through me at the thought. "Yes."

Jake bends to put the helmet on my head, and buckles it at my throat, his fingers brushing my skin as he does. "If I'd known it would put a smile like this on your face, I would've brought out the bike sooner. I'm about to put her away for the winter and wanted one last ride and thought you might enjoy it too."

"I haven't been on a bike in ages."

His knuckles brush my cheek and I blush at the tender touch and the way he's looking at me. "I won't let anything happen to you, Cherry Blossom."

Our gazes lock and it's like the world falls away, and I believe him when he says it. I trust Jake not to hurt me, or at least I was starting to. He hadn't just given up when I said I could only offer him my friendship. He's shown up every day in one way or another. Even if we don't see each other, we talk or text.

My heart skitters behind my breastbone as I watch his strong throat bob on a swallow. Blinking away the fog as somebody whistles across the street, I look back at the bike. "She's beautiful."

"Yes, she is." The reverence in his tone makes me look up but his eyes are on me, not the bike. How easy it would be to give in and risk it for this boy, to follow my heart instead of my head?

"Okay, let's go before it gets too dark."

Jake swings his leg over the bike, his jeans pulling tight around his powerful thighs. He reaches his hand up and I take it, using him to balance as I swing my leg over behind him. I take a second to settle myself on the seat as he waits patiently. My hands fall to my sides as I hesitate, not knowing where to put them. What I want to do is cuddle up to him, to lay my cheek on his back and wrap my arms around him but I'm not sure he wants that. I turn, looking for the handles at the back as he sits up and reaches back. Taking my hands, he hauls me forward, my chest falling against his back, his heat seeping through my jacket into my skin.

"Put your arms around me, Cherry Blossom."

His fingers thread through mine as he links my hands at his waist and then puts his palm over the top, the other smoothing down my thigh. Awareness prickles my skin, my nipples beading against the cotton of my bra at the way he makes me feel precious.

The bike roars to life, and I feel the power of it thrum between my legs.

"You good?"

"Yes."

"Hold on to me, baby."

I know his calling me that crosses the line of our friendship but I don't have it in me to care as the thrill of being this close to him on my dream bike takes over all thoughts. I grip his shirt, his abs hard beneath my touch as we begin to move.

The rush of the wind is cool on my skin, lifting my hair from my shoulders as we weave through traffic and then we're on the open road. Riding a bike is as close to true freedom as you can get. It's exhilarating, my blood pumps through my veins like liquid ecstasy.

I've only ever been on the back of one bike before this. It was an ex from school and he was so busy showing off he almost wrecked us on a corner. It left me feeling angry and afraid, thinking he'd ruined my most precious connection to my dad. Jake is giving me that back with each mile and he has no clue he's even doing it. I feel safe, like no matter what, he won't let anything happen to me and that's huge because trust isn't a commodity I trade in very often.

After about an hour, he pulls into a rest stop where a food truck is serving. I move to get off, but he places a hand on my leg to stop me. Swinging his leg over the front of the bike, he strides behind me and lifts me off, setting me on my feet, but holding me around the waist as he waits for me to get my legs under me.

"You good?"

I nod, not trusting myself to speak in case my voice comes out husky.

"Okay, you wanna grab some food or just a hot chocolate?"

"I could eat."

We walk side by side to the line at the food truck and I eye the menu. Tacos, burgers, and hot dogs mainly.

"These are the best tacos in the State."

I cock my head, looking up at Jake as he scans the menu. "Wow, that's a powerful statement."

"Try them and you'll see."

"Well okay, then."

We both order tacos and Jake orders some fries to share, and I get a hot chocolate and he grabs a coffee. I reach for my purse, ready to pay my share and he pushes it away.

"Don't even think about it."

The look he's giving me brooks no argument, but I wouldn't be me if I just let it go, so I place my hand on my hip and raise my brows. "This isn't a date, Jake."

He hands some cash to the guy behind the counter who's smirking at us and motions at the bench where we'll wait for our food to be called.

"I'm well aware of that, but that doesn't mean you pay when we're out. I asked you to come here, so I pay."

"So if I ask, I can pay?"

Jake hesitates, before shaking his head. "No."

"That's hypocritical."

"It's not. It's how I've been taught to treat a woman."

"Like a prize?"

He smirks and huffs a laugh. "Do you just like to argue, Blossom?"

"No, I just want to know. I'm your equal. I don't need you to pay for my stuff."

Jake leans in, and I find myself doing the same, his gaze hints that he knows things I don't.

"We ain't equal, babe."

I sit back, stunned, a gasp falling from my lips ready to rip into him when he continues.

"We ain't equal because you're so much better than me in every way. You work your ass off, you're smart, funny, sweet, you are unapologetically you in every way and you're hot as fuck. You are the prize in every way, and if all I can do is pay for a cheap taco dinner, then that's what I'll do."

My entire body softens at his sweet words. Nobody has ever said something so sweet to me before and I want to wrap my arms around him and never let go. "Jake."

He grins and holds his hand up as he pulls back. "Now, don't go soft and fall in love with me. I told you we can only be friends."

I smile, my pulse beating faster, laughter bubbling inside me. "I'm pretty sure I said that."

"Tomato, tomahto."

I shake my head feeling happier and more carefree than I ever have before as he stands to collect our food. Jake gets me, he gets my need for control, my desire for someone to make the effort and show me I matter.

I'm falling for my new friend and it's fucking terrifying and exhilarating.

5. Jake

THE LATE MORNING SUN IS ON MY BACK AS I STARE DOWN AT THE text I just sent to Cherry, a smile trying to fight its way onto my face.

> Jake: I know I haven't seen you today, but I just know you look great.

I watch as the dots jump and bounce as she types. I never know what I'm going to get with Cherry. She can be sweet, but mostly she's sarcastic and snarky and it makes those moments when she reveals her heart that much sweeter. I never tire of being around her because she doesn't give a fuck who I am, she's just herself and I'm low-key obsessed with her.

> Cherry: Of course I do, when do I not?

I shake my head, a chuckle moving through me as my fingers move over the screen.

> Jake: True story. You always look sexy as fuck.

> Cherry: Are you flirting with me, Casanova?

> Jake: Always.

I smirk, imagining her smile as she reads the last one, the roll of her eyes, but the pleased look that makes them twinkle with delight. She's breathtaking and she has no idea just how much she consumes me. Since Cherry and I became friends, the one thing I've learned is that her walls are a mile high. She likes me, she wants me, and our connection is something I've never felt before and it scares her to death.

> Cherry: Dream on.....

> Jake: Every night and twice in the shower.

> Cherry: Really, Jake, you're a sex addict.

That's hilarious because if she only knew I hadn't laid a finger on anyone else since the day we met. In fact, if this continues, I'm going to get a repetitive stress injury in my wrist from jerking off.

> Jake: Correction, I'm a Cherry addict.

> Cherry: Go to your lecture. I have a paper to write.

> Jake: I'll see you later?

> Cherry: Maybe. Depends how this paper goes.

> Jake: Then stop slacking and get to work, Blossom.

I turn my phone to silent and slip it into my pocket as I adjust my rucksack on my shoulder. Time to put on a show and hopefully, while

I'm at it, have a word with a few people about the attitude I've seen toward Cherry. I know Lorelei is behind it and it's time they realized she's under my protection and they've fucked with the wrong girl. If I have to get my hands dirty and crack a few skulls, then so be it. It's all part of the game.

Head up, I move through the hallways of Langdell Hall as I head to my next lecture. I get head dips in greeting from some, and others avoid my eyes. The respect I get around here is still so strange to me, but it's a role I play and one I'm damn good at. Power is a delicate balance and every day there's someone waiting to shift it to their favor, to challenge mine and Hunter's position here, but one I work twice as hard to keep while he's away dealing with his broken leg.

Name alone isn't enough in this new world, it requires a balance of respect, fear, and adoration. I keep my circle incredibly small. In fact, until Cherry, I'd say the only person I trust in this place is Hunter. Everyone else seems to want something from me.

A favor, prestige from being seen with me or Hunter, and some just have this weird hero worship which I'll never understand, but I play the game and I play it well. People move aside as I stride down the middle of the hall before slipping into the lecture hall.

I stop short as the room falls silent, excited murmurs falling away as I look at the boy sitting in my seat. It's a dumb thing but nobody sits there, it's where Hunter and I sit and every fucker knows it or is told. I lift my chin, slowing my gait as I walk up to the kid who's smirking and joking with his friends.

I don't know him, so he's probably a transfer, but that's no excuse. He knows what he's doing, and he fucked around so now he's going to find out. There are no second chances or giving someone the benefit of the doubt. That's just a weakness in our world, and I'll never let myself be weak again.

He doesn't even look up as I approach, further disrespecting me, and my blood flushes with heat as I drop my bag, at his feet, and plant my legs wide. "Move."

Finally, the asshole looks up, his gaze running over me arrogantly, as if he's trying to provoke a response and he's going to get his wish.

"No, I don't think I will."

The murmurs behind me grow and I crack my neck as he once again turns back to his friends, dismissing me. He's got balls, I'll give him that, but his friends seem to notice what he hasn't yet, and that he's a big dog but he just picked a fight with a fucking Tiger.

"Move or I make you, and you don't want that."

I feel people at my back, wannabes and hangers-on who want to believe they're my friends and I let them, but we all know I don't trust them.

"You should move, Brian."

Brian thrusts back his chair and faces me. I have at least two inches on him and at least twenty pounds in muscle but he doesn't seem to notice.

"I don't see no name on the chair, asshole."

A few people suck in breaths of shock behind me and I can feel my pulse pumping my blood faster as the thrill of stalking ignorant prey moves through me. "I don't need a name tag, asshole. Everyone knows who I am and everyone knows this is my seat. So move."

"No, I'm not moving for some pussy hanger-on who fucks freaks with pink hair."

I can take insults toward me with no emotion at all. I've learned to let any jabs slide off me because I know who I am, but nobody, and I mean nobody, gets to bad mouth Cherry and get away with it. Not ever.

I shake my head and look away before my hand darts out and I grip his throat tight. I step forward, backing him up as he struggles to loosen my grip on his throat, his feet falling over the bags at his feet.

"Now listen to me once because I'm not going to repeat myself. Nobody, not anyone in this fucking room, gets to speak about her like that. She's worth a hundred of you and every person in this room. Do you get me?"

Brian is turning a funny shade of purple as he tries to speak before giving up and nodding.

"Sorry, I didn't catch that?" I cock my head, releasing my grip slightly so he can suck in a breath and answer me.

"I understand."

I turn and look around the room, my gaze zeroing in on Lorelei and her friends as she watches me with lust in her gaze, which makes me sick. "Do I make myself clear? Cherry Baker is off-limits. You fuck with her, you fuck with me and I think we all know nobody wants that."

Nods of assent mix with murmurs of agreement and I know I just got my point across, but I still feel this simmering rage that anyone would dare to take a swipe at her. Come at me, I don't give a fuck, but not her.

Releasing Brian, I step back and then let my fist fly out at lightning speed, catching the asshole with a jab to the nose. He gasps, clutching his nose as blood pours from him and his eyes water.

"Motherfucker, you broke my nose."

"No, you did that when you decided to try and be the big dick and challenge me by going after someone who matters to me."

"You won't get away with this."

Clearly, he has memory issues because not thirty seconds ago he was nodding like a dog to everything I said.

I look around as the door opens and Professor Ackerman walks into the room. I don't try and hide what I did, I own everything I do. His eyes scan the scene in front of him before he shakes his head and focuses a glare at Brian and his cronies, who are looking smug, thinking I got caught.

"You, what is your name, boy?"

"Brian Wills, sir. This boy just attacked me completely unprovoked." His voice is nasally as he speaks through the blood and broken bone.

Professor Ackerman walks closer, his eyes landing on me as his lips purse in displeasure, before he focuses back on Brian, his gaze moving over him before dismissing him.

"But he attacked me."

Ackerman claps his hands behind his back and sighs. "Mr. Wills, do you really think I care about silly student squabbles? I'm here to teach the next generation of lawmakers and leaders of this country and if I have to referee ridiculous petty fights between adults, then I fear this country is doomed. Now get out and decide if this course is for you before you come back. You're bleeding on my floor. Get yourself to medical and don't come back until you learn to conduct yourself and learn the rules, Mr. Wills."

Brian glares at me and I smirk, holding his stare until he drops his gaze and rushes from the room.

"Mr. Marshall, see me after class."

"Yes, sir."

"Now open your books. Today we're learning the nuances of a plea bargain."

People groan as they take their seats and get to work. The lesson is boring and I'm lost in thought as I half listen and take notes. I might rule this school but I also work hard because I want to be the best at what I do. I want to prove to Mr. McKenzie that I'm worth his time and belief in me.

As Professor Ackerman wraps up, chairs begin to scrape and he has to raise his voice over the noise as students begin to pack up. I smell the sickly sweet scent of her perfume before I can avoid her.

"Hey, Jakey."

"I don't have time for this, Lorelei." I'd planned to talk to her but all I want to do now is talk to Cherry and tell her what happened before it spreads around school. Knowing Cherry, she'll be pissed that I did what I did. She won't appreciate me standing up for her, or laying claim to her, but I'll never be okay with someone bad-mouthing her and she needs to learn that about me. I'd rather it was me who told her though.

"How about you come over later and we can talk?" Her fingernails dance over my shoulder as I clench my teeth to stop the shiver of disgust from rolling over my body. She'll more than likely take it as desire.

I turn, letting my gaze rake over her, and Lorelei preens, lifting her shoulders and shoving her tits in my face. "Lorelei, I need you to hear me." My voice is low, sweet even as I lean in and she follows. "I will never be yours. I don't want to fuck you or speak to you or even look at you and if I hear that you're bad-mouthing Cherry again, I'm going to ruin you. Do you get me?"

It's like it takes a moment to register my words as her smile falls and her lips pinch in anger. Her expression loses the sweet doe-eyed look and the hardness beneath is revealed. Lorelei likes to come across as cute and sweet but she's rotten to her core, the fake sugar she laces her act with having poisoned every little thing.

"Whatever, Jake. You're making a huge mistake but if you want me to play nice with your little pet, I will for now. I have bigger fish to fry, anyway. Hunter will be back soon and I can move on from the likes of you." She gives a little sniff and tosses her head in the air as she prances off on her four-inch stilettos.

I'd wish her luck in going after Hunter but she doesn't need luck, she needs a goddamn miracle.

"Mr. Marshall, have you finished?"

I spot Professor Ackerman waiting for me at the podium where he stands for his lectures, his expression bored.

"Yes, sir."

I move toward him, ready to take my punishment. I might lord it over the students because that's how it works here but I have respect for most of my teachers.

"Marshall, I understand that you have a position here you wish to maintain but in future, keep your issues out of my classroom. You're an exceptional student, with the potential to go to the very top of any profession you choose, but I will not tolerate you disrupting my class. Do you understand?"

"Yes. It won't happen again."

"Good."

He lifts his chin to the door, dismissing me and I rush out, wanting to get to Cherry and not just so I can get my side of the story over first but because the air in my lungs feels easier when I'm around her.

6. Cherry

"Hı, Mom."

"Cherry Pie, oh, I've missed you. How are you? Are you eating properly?"

I smile to myself as I sink back against the pillows on my bed. "I'm good, Mom. I miss you too. How's the salon?"

Closing my eyes, I let the sound of my mother's voice, as she brings me up to date on everything happening at the salon she owns, drift over me like a warm hug. There's nothing like the sound of her voice to settle me.

Ever since Jake rushed over here last week to tell me what happened with the student from his class, I've felt rattled, uneasy, unable to think about anything else. It's not because of what he did, I'm not some pacifist, unwilling to throw a punch, it's that he did it for me. No, it's not that either, it's how much I liked that he'd done it.

I'm not that girl, I've never been the girl, happy or accepting of someone claiming me like property, but with Jake, it feels different. He isn't trying to own me so he can control me, it makes me feel protected and cherished and that scares the crap out of me because I don't trust it.

"Hey, Blossom, I need to talk to you."

"I have to get to my shift. Can it wait?"

I'd been halfway out the door when Jake showed up at my dorm, looking gorgeous as always but also slightly sheepish. His entire demeanor had my stomach knotting in dread and my voice coming out warily when I responded. I was already in a pissy mood from spending my entire class on the Gothic Influence of Modern Architecture, listening to the four girls behind me going on about how hot Jake was and how they'd heard he was just dreamy between the sheets and could get a girl off multiple times. It had taken everything in me not to turn around and claw their eyes. Jake wasn't mine but, increasingly, I was finding I wanted him to be.

"No, because I need to explain my side of things."

"Okay, this sounds bad."

I stepped back into my room and closed the door before putting some distance between us and folding my arms. I should have known Jake wouldn't allow that, he was the most tactile person I knew, and he pulled me down onto my bed to sit next to him, holding my shoulders in his big hands so I had to look at him.

"I punched Brian Wills and broke his nose."

"What?" I could hear the slight screech in my voice and winced, trying to tone down my reaction as he stroked the bare skin of my arms as if to try and soothe me. *"Why the hell would you do that? You could get thrown out?"*

His smirk almost made me want to slap it off his dumb, hot face.

"Blossom, nobody is throwing me out, believe me, and he had it coming. He challenged me and then made the fatal error of bad-mouthing you."

"Don't call me Blossom. I'm mad at you. You don't need to defend me, Jake. Do you think it's the first time someone has talked shit about me? Look at me!" I threw my hands in the air in frustration, knocking his hands from me. *"I don't fit in. I'm the freak with pink hair that looks like her mommy lost her."*

His expression turned thunderous at my words and a hum of

energy shifted in the room as his jaw feathered and ground, his eyes closing before he opened them and pinned me in place with his gaze.

"Let's get a few things straight, Blossom. Nobody, and I mean nobody, talks shit about you, not now and not ever. You are not a fucking freak, you're damn near perfect and if small-minded assholes can't handle that and choose to voice that ugly jealousy, then they'll find themselves facing a fist to the face too."

I shook my head and fought the urge to lean into him and accept his words. "Jake, you can't hit every person who doesn't like me. I'm kind of an asshole sometimes, and I rub people the wrong way. I don't need your protection."

"Tough shit, you have it anyway and I made it very clear to everyone who was in earshot that if they messed with you, they messed with me. You're mine, Blossom. Even if you won't admit you want me, we're friends and I protect what means something to me."

"That's actually kinda sweet." Jake ducked his head to catch my gaze a grin on his too handsome face. "You're still a dumbass for doing it. I'm not worth it."

Jake pinched my chin between his thumb and finger and forced my head up. "Don't let me hear you talking bad about yourself again. You're worth that and so much more. I've never met anyone like you, Cherry Baker."

"Yeah, well, if you're lucky, you never will again."

Jake bent so fast I had no time to back away before he nipped my lip and dropped a light kiss there before I could even respond. "I warned you, Blossom, no talking shit about my favorite person or I'll punish you."

My heart rate spiked, my nipples hardening as my body tingled at the swift assault on my senses. Jake smirked at my reaction before he stood and walked to the door.

"When is your friend coming back to school?" I'd heard a lot about Jake's friend, Hunter, but hadn't met him yet and perhaps Jake needed him back to distract him from me.

Jake frowned, his lips pursing. "Why do you ask?"

"Because then maybe you can bother him instead of me."

A chuckle rumbled through his chest as he shook his head. "I'll always bother you, Blossom, and don't get your hopes up. Hunter needed a second surgery on his leg, so he's out for another three weeks."

"Well, damn. I guess I need to keep you entertained for another few weeks."

"Just looking at you entertains me, Blossom."

I shook my head, trying to hide my smile at how secretly pleased his words made me, and pushed him out the door. "Go, I need to get to work. And stop calling me Blossom."

"Never."

"CHERRY PIE, DID YOU EAT DINNER?"

I sit up, shaking the thoughts and memories away as I focus on my mom's voice. "Yes, Mom, I had a slice of pizza for lunch and I'll grab some chicken noodles later."

She tuts, and I brace for the lecture I know is coming.

"Cherry Baker, that isn't food. You need fruit and veggies and protein or you're going to get sick."

"Fine, I'll have noodles and some veggie sticks and hummus as a snack later."

"Better, but try and lay off the junk. I don't want you to get sick. I can't bear the thought of you so far away and needing me."

My heart constricts with love for my mom, and I hear the worried tone in her voice. "I promise, Mom. Have you seen Lexi?"

I haven't heard from my friend as much as I'd like, and I miss her. I want to tell her about Jake and all the feelings I have around this weird friendship we have that feels so much more but for some reason, I haven't. Our calls are always short because she's in a hurry or I am.

"She came in for a trim last week."

"How is she?"

"She seems.... Fine."

I sit up straighter, my instincts hearing more to my mom's words. Fine is never good. "What aren't you telling me, Mom?"

"Nothing, she just seemed in a rush to get back to that boyfriend of hers. I don't like him, Cherry. He gives me a bad feeling in my stomach."

My mom is the gentlest person I know, and she likes everyone, so for her to say she isn't keen on Dean, Lexi's boyfriend, says a lot.

"I know, Mom, me neither, but when I even broach the subject, she shuts down on me. She's so into him."

"Then don't broach it, sweet girl, just be there for her, be her friend."

A frown pulls at my brow as I fight my instincts to be submissive about any situation. "Wouldn't a good friend be honest?"

"Sometimes yes, but sometimes part of being a good friend is being that soft place to land and for Lexi to know she has you, no matter what. If you criticize him and she isn't ready to hear it, all it will do is cause her to push back or shut down, and then when she's ready to talk, she won't."

I nod my head slowly, even though she can't see me. "Smart or sneaky, I'm not sure which."

"Both, sweetheart. You don't raise a headstrong daughter without learning a few tricks."

"I love you, Mom."

"I love you too, Cherry Pie."

"Are you okay?" I know she won't tell me if she isn't but I need to ask anyway. Since we lost my dad a few years back, our relationship has changed. We were always close, but now there's this sense of protectiveness I feel too. We're a unit, we literally held each other together when he was taken so suddenly.

"I'm fine. Stop worrying about me."

"You first."

"Never, I'm your mom. It's my job to worry."

I know that's our role in life but I can't help but worry. She fell apart when dad died, she was a mess. They adored each other to the point they were nauseating sometimes. It always embarrassed the hell out of me to see them acting so sappy and romantic, but secretly I loved how much they loved each other. I wanted that for myself until the day he died. I realized in that moment that loving so hard is such a monumental risk, because at any time that love can be ripped away and leave you struggling to mend the broken pieces.

"Have you met any cute boys yet, sweetie?"

"Okay, time to go. I love you, Mom."

I'm smiling as we hang up, but my thoughts linger on home. Harvard is my dream, but even living this dream, which is everything I'd hoped for and more, doesn't stomp out the homesickness.

Grabbing my bag, I head out, knowing that staying here will only make that worse. I lift my head, closing my eyes for a second as I suck in a breath of the cool fall weather. I adore this time of year when all the colors of nature are so rich and vibrant. Marianna and I had spent the last Saturday shopping for cute fall clothes. She'd become a good friend, but I knew I was holding back with her a little, too. Not because of her but because I found it hard to trust and her sister made it harder, but I was here and loving Harvard. I still pinch myself every time I get to walk into the library at Harvard. I made it, I actually did it.

The smell of books is comforting as I find an empty space at one of the large tables and get my books out. The smooth wood under my fingertips holds so much history and I wonder what it would say if it could talk, what stories it holds within the grain.

I notice a few students watching me, but as soon as I try and catch their eye they look away. It doesn't bother me, not really, I've always been that person, the one who is either loved or hated and I'm okay with that. I'm myself and if people don't like that, then fuck them. But this doesn't feel like that, it feels different as if they're looking at me because of who I am to Jake Marshall.

His reputation around school, along with that of his friend Mac, is almost God-like. They're revered or feared, sometimes both. I get it, in some ways. Jake has this aura, this presence that instantly commands a room when he steps into it. An energy about him that makes everyone sit up and take notice no matter their age or gender. I can imagine him in the courtroom, in a few years' time, making the jury eat up every word he utters like it's candy. He's going to go places and do amazing things with his life, I know it. I just don't know if I have a place there or if I even want one.

We're friends, our connection over the last few weeks having a depth to it that I never expected when we first met, but simmering below it is the attraction I feel for him, and I know he feels it too. Jake could easily swallow me up if I let him and a part of me wants to let him. Yet he doesn't act like he wants to consume me, he treats me with respect and kindness. He's sweet and sexy, and sometimes, when I catch him staring at me, the look in his eyes makes my belly flip over with need.

He's my friend but he could be so much more if I let him. I just don't know if that's the smart choice. But then smart isn't living, and I promised myself I'd live every day like it could be my last without fear or doubt, at least I try, but that promise never included Harvard, and now the risks seem so much bigger.

Knowing I won't figure this out today, I sigh as I get stuck into the task of researching monolithic structures, my brain falling down the rabbit hole of history. My eyes are gritty when I look up to find that dusk has fallen while I read and made notes. The library is almost empty, save for a few students on the far side, who seem to be having some kind of study session.

Raising my arms, I stretch my back, arching out the kinks from being hunched over. My phone vibrates on the table and I turn it over, my mouth spreading into a grin when I see Jake's name on the screen.

> Jake: I'm glad I brought my library card because I'm totally checking you out.

Laughter bursts from me, causing heads to lift towards me, but I'm too busy looking at the boy in the corner who's grinning at me. He lifts his hand and crooks his finger at me and something about that movement that is so sure, so confident has me packing my books away and walking towards him. His eyes sweep a slow path over me before coming back to my face and I feel it everywhere.

"Hey, you."

His voice is soft and deep and hits me between my thighs, making me want to hear him whisper something dirtier in my ear. "You stalking me, Jake?" I hold my bag in front of me as he reaches out and hooks his finger into the loop of my waistband, pulling me just enough for me to lose my balance and step closer, so I'm standing between his thick thighs.

"You got a problem with that, Cherry Blossom?"

I should have a problem with it, nothing about that comment should turn me on, but it does. "No."

His gaze is so intense, the smile he gives me now having none of the sweetness I'm used to. Everything about it is predatory and I crave it.

"Good answer."

"Yeah, why is that?"

His fingers are still hooked in my belt loop, and his thumb sweeps out and skims the skin of my hip beneath the pink sweater I'm wearing. Every nerve in my body sings at his touch. It's innocent in the grand scheme of things but it feels like he's stripped me down naked. The hungry look in his eyes only fueling the desire. We stay locked in this moment, his thumb on my hip, his gaze drinking me in like I'm the only oasis in a million-mile desert.

Then, as if a button is pushed, he grins and pushes to his feet, hooking an arm around me in an almost head lock. "Wanna watch a movie or grab a coffee?"

My brain takes a couple of beats to catch up with the sudden switch in him before I nod. The air leaves my lungs in a whoosh from holding my breath. "Sure, dealer's choice. I'm easy."

Jake lets his gaze trail over me, lingering on my hip for a second as if he can feel the phantom touch still, too. "You're anything but easy, Cherry Blossom."

Holding out his hand, he ushers me out of the library, then takes my bag from me, despite my assurances that I can carry it.

"I know you can, but why should you when I can carry it for you?"

"You know feminists will be crying right now."

"It's not anti-feminist to let me carry your bag for you, it's just good manners."

"Well, it feels wrong."

Jake wraps an arm around me, pulling into his side. "That's because you've never been treated properly by a man."

"My dad would have loved you. He was just like this with my mom. If she even tried to carry the groceries, he'd lose his mind. I used to think it was silly but now I miss seeing it."

We walk side by side in silence for a bit before he speaks again. "Tell me about him?"

I don't talk about my dad often, not to Lexi or anyone really. Not because I don't want to but because it hurts, and I don't want to drag anyone down with my grief or my guilt. Yet as we walk past the historic buildings, Jake gives me the space to decide if I want to answer or not.

"He was old-fashioned, some would say. He believed a man should work and provide for his family. He loved his bikes and would spend hours on the weekend tinkering with old bikes. Yet when my mom gave him a look, he'd pack it away and give her all of his attention. He helped me learn to ride a bike. He showed me how to make pancakes on Mother's Day and, more importantly, he taught me what it was to be loved unconditionally."

"You miss him."

"Every single day. He was my hero, and my biggest cheerleader."

"He sounds like an amazing man."

"He was, and do you know the worst thing, Jake?"

He stops us outside my dorm building and turns me to face him, tipping my chin up to look at him. I could drown in his eyes, so many flecks of color that it's hard to know sometimes if they are green or blue.

"Tell me."

I look away, knowing I'll see judgment in his gaze when I admit this next part. "I never cried when he died. I didn't shed a tear and I still haven't." What kind of daughter does that make me that I can't cry over the loss of the man who gave me life?

Jake's palm cups my cheek and I close my eyes not wanting to see the disgust, instead letting the callouses on his hands scrape against my skin.

"Tears don't mean you loved him and no tears don't mean you didn't. Emotion, especially grief, is complex and just because you don't wear it like a shield for the world to see, doesn't mean a fucking thing. You loved him, Cherry, anyone who hears you speak about him knows it and he knew it too."

My eyes open and all I see in his gaze is sincerity as he holds me captive. "You don't think I'm broken?"

His thumb sweeps over my cheek, in a soft caress and I fight the desire to lean into him.

"I think we're all a little broken, Cherry Blossom, but do you want to know what I see when I look at you?"

I nod, my lips parting as I try and suck in enough oxygen.

"I see a beautiful girl who fights for those she loves, who's strong and fierce and brave. Who's smarter than even she knows but is afraid to trust in case she gets her heart broken. I don't know if it's losing your dad or something else, but I do know you're special, and you'll succeed because you're brilliant and you're a survivor."

I drop my head into his chest, my fingers clutching at his shirt. Jake makes me feel things that frighten me, but he also sees me. Not the mask I wear for the world, but me, inside where a little girl still wakes, calling for her father and knowing he will never be there to hug her again.

It's too much, my chest feels like it will explode and I want to admit to him how right he is, to tell him how broken I feel, how afraid but being that open is a risk. What if I show him who I am, let him see my fragile heart, and he leaves or dies, or takes my heart and breaks it? I'm not sure I could survive another loss like that, so I fall back on coping strategies of old.

"Did you just call me a cockroach, Jake Marshall?"

His arms come around me and I feel his laughter against my cheek, before I lift my head and step away, forcing him to let me go.

"Only you would turn a sweet moment into a perceived insult, Blossom."

I shrug as we walk up the stairs to my dorm room. "Sweet rots your teeth."

"I'll win, you know."

I throw my bag on my bed as Jake slumps across my bed like he's done the few times we've spent time here already. Nothing has happened between us that is overtly sexual, not even a kiss. He's respected my friendship boundaries with grace, but now I wonder if he's been breaking my defenses one brick at a time. Little familiar touches of his hand on mine, his fingers kneading the knots in my neck after a long day. All of it lowering my defenses against him as he wages war on my reasons for keeping him at a distance.

"Win what?"

"Your trust. One day you'll see that I have no intention of hurting you. Not now, not ever."

My breath hitches in my chest at his words, spoken softly and with so much certainty. "Nobody intends to hurt someone, Jake. It just happens."

His fingers skim my cheek with the whisper of touch and I feel my heart stutter, wanting him to kiss me and yet afraid that if he does I'll give up my heart without any more fight.

"I won't hurt you, Cherry. You can trust me on that."

"Choose a movie, Jake."

I can't answer him because I want so badly to believe he means it, but then my dad promised he'd always be here, and he's gone. Every boy I've ever liked in school, every friend I've shown my true self to, except Lexi, has gotten bored with my abrasive attitude and proved me right. Why would a boy like Jake Marshall be any different? He could have anyone, why would he stick around for me?

The rest of the night we spend arguing the merits of action movies versus chick flicks and perversely, he's the one arguing for the chick flick.

"Seriously, it's like the men's guide to what a woman wants. Why would men not watch them?"

I shove more pizza in my mouth and mentally say sorry to my mother. "So you're saying it's more of a how-to guide for men?"

"Exactly."

"Well, if you want to deep dive into this then you should really be reading the books women read."

Jake frowns as he folds his slice of pizza in half and hangs it over his mouth to catch the melting cheese. He chews, his brows pulling in as he nods. "Why?"

"Because they'll give you the biggest insight of all. Most movies are written, directed, and produced by men, but books, especially Indie authors, are written by women for women. So they sell the universal fantasies that all women want. Even the dark ones we don't want to admit to."

"And you read these?"

"Of course."

"Can I read one?"

I pop my eyelids wide. "You want to read one of my dark romance books?"

"Dark romance, what is that?"

I can feel my cheeks heat as I try and find the words to explain dark romance to him. "Well, the MMC in the book is usually a walking red flag, like a stalker, or a bad boy, or someone the FMC should not be attracted to, like in a bully romance."

"MMC, FMC, and bully romance. What the hell is that?"

Crossing my legs, I study him as he lounges back on my pillows waiting for my answer. He takes up most of my bed with his broad muscular shoulders and long, thick legs. My gaze rakes over him in sweatpants and a white tee and I can see his hard length, outlined by the fabric, and he is big, bigger than any I've had before and my mouth waters at the thought of him. He has it all, looks, attitude, and he treats me like I matter. He could definitely be a hero in a book.

"You're staring, Blossom, and I suggest you stop before I say to hell with all my good intentions and take you on this bed and make you come with my name screaming from your lips."

Fuck. Me. That visual has my panties soaked, my body screaming at me to let him, but my head wins out, and I look away with a laugh. "Okay, an MMC is a male main character, and FMC is a female main character, so that's all pretty simple."

"And bully romance?"

"That's where she falls for her bully, or in some scenarios, bullies."

"And you want that? You want a man who treats you like that?"

I can tell he's confused by the stunned look on his face. I laugh and shake my head. "No, but it's a fantasy and a safe way to live it. I'd never entertain it in real life, but in a book, the MMC is so obsessed with her, that he only sees her. He craves her, would kill for her, die for her, and break any rule to have her. A lot of girls crave that undivided attention but we aren't dumb enough not to know it's unhealthy in real life. Books allow it to be safe."

"So how would reading it help me understand what a woman wants?"

"Because if you break it down into the basic fantasy, you can see it. So, for example, a stalker trope is the fantasy of having someone so in love with you that they will do anything to have you. With a bad boy, it's about him hating everyone and being deadly to all but with her, and only her, he shows his soft side."

"Okay, I think I get it. It's about being his whole world."

"Exactly. Every girl wants to feel like they are cherished, but they don't want a doormat either. At least that's how I interpret it."

Jake sighs and runs a hand through his hair. "Women are fucking complicated."

"Yes, we are, so maybe don't try and understand us because, honestly, I'm not sure it's possible."

"That feels like a challenge, Blossom."

"No, just a fact."

"Wanna hear another fact?"

I shrug. "Sure."

"I'm going to take every fantasy you've ever read and blow them out of the water. That's a fact you can take to the bank."

My breath is trapped in my lungs at his words and I have to fight the desire to throw myself across the bed at him, especially when he looks at me with such heat in his stare.

"Good, I have you speechless, so why don't you give me the name of your favorite books so I can expose these book men as frauds and show you what the real thing can do?"

"Book boyfriends," I squeak.

"What?" Jake frowns as he lies back on my bed with his phone in his hand, ready to start downloading books.

"They're called book boyfriends, not book men."

His gaze holds me captive, and I have the strongest urge to crawl to him and demand he follows through on the promise his body is making but I stop when he growls.

"Cherry Blossom, the only boyfriend you're gonna have is me, so get used to it, because I'm running out of patience waiting."

With that, he goes back to his phone, and I'm left wondering if perhaps he's every book boyfriend I ever had rolled into a real man. It's time for a little distance. Maybe going home for the holidays is exactly what I need to combat my homesickness and give me some space to think about whether I can keep seeing Jake as a friend.

7. Jake

"IT'S GOOD TO HAVE YOU HOME, SON."

I glance across the table decorated for the holidays at Hank McKenzie and dip my head. "It's good to be here, Mr. McKenzie."

I still marvel at the way he took me in when he'd had every right to turn his back on me that night. This man, this family, changed my life in so many ways and I'll never be able to repay it. When I'm not at College, my home is here. I have my own room, my own space, and people who love me like I'm one of their own.

"Jake, how many times do we have to tell you, it's Hank and Vivian."

I scratch my neck, feeling awkward as I glance at Hunter for some help. He smirks and shoves more turkey into his mouth. "Yeah, sorry."

"Nothing to be sorry for, son. Now, tell me about school. How are you finding it?"

"Good, I'm enjoying the legislation and corporate stuff a lot."

Hank nods, as he eats, his focus on me, showing me that he really cares. His question isn't just one to fill the time. "You think you might want to go into corporate law? We can always use another smart mind in the office."

Honestly, I'm not sure what I want to do, but I'm leaning towards corporate, and working for Hank would be a dream. "That'd be an honor, sir."

Hunter groans. "Jake, stop with that shit, call them Hank and Vivian, for fuck's sake."

"Hunter McKenzie, watch your language at my table."

I smirk at my best friend as he hangs his head at the reprimand from his mom. Vivian is a sweet woman, but she has a core of steel running through her and everyone I know adores her, but most especially her husband. I watch as Hank lays his hand over hers and links their fingers before bringing them to his lips.

"Tell me more about your classes, Jake?"

My shoulders relax a little as I tell him about my classes and we discuss a few of my professors. Dinner is a relaxed affair considering Vivian and Hank McKenzie are two of the richest people in the United States. You wouldn't know it, dinner isn't catered for, or filled with unnecessary talk of work or politics, or pompous guests milling around. It's fun, food, and family, something I can hardly remember having.

Even before the day that changed my whole life, my family was nothing like this. My mom worked every hour of the day to keep a roof over our heads. My father, or sperm donor should I say, left before I was six. Then tragedy struck six years later and everything fell apart and it was all my fault.

The pecan pie in my mouth turns to dust as I allow the memory to break through the wall I normally keep erected, but I choke it down, knowing that Vivian only made it because it's my favorite. Reliving those memories always leads me down a dark path. It's why I never let myself go there, but for some reason this weekend they've crept up on me.

Instead, I try and think about the night Hank saved my life.

"Hey, wanna watch the game in the den?"

I look up to see Hunter watching me with a careful look on his face. He knows me better than anyone and he can see me walking down that path that leads to destruction and guilt. "Sure, sounds good, but let me help your mom clean up first."

"You boys go catch up. I'll clean up dinner with Cassie."

"Gee, Dad, thanks for volunteering me."

Cassie rolls her eyes as she begins to collect plates from the table. Cas is a few years older than Hunter and I, and she just started working in the family business. She's cool, but being around her is a reminder of what I lost, so I tend to avoid her when I'm here.

"Can't a dad find an excuse to spend time with his favorite daughter?"

"I'm your only daughter."

I watch Hank kiss his daughter on the cheek with so much affection, and it makes me think of my Cherry Blossom. After our discussion about books, she's put some distance between us. She hasn't been overtly cold with me, just unavailable and I don't like it.

I was so close to kissing her that night, to throwing caution to the wind and saying fuck it. I don't want to be her friend, I want to be her everything. I want to consume her, to kiss every inch of her body, and watch her eyes go dark when she comes with my name on her lips.

What stopped me was the thought that more than any of those, I wanted to lie with her in my arms all night. Sex was one thing but I want to protect this girl. I want to be the person who makes her smile, who lets her cry over her father and be herself in every way, and that shit was scary.

"What the fuck's going on with you?"

I glance up from the black leather couch I'd flopped down on to see Hunter watching me. This den has become our haven, the place we come to when we want to be left alone and just hang out. Hunter has been my best friend since the day we met. I'd gone looking for a fight, the chip on my shoulder so big it was crushing me. I'd seen his wealth and privilege and decided I hated him, but it was never him I hated, it was myself, and still is to some extent. When Hunter had bumped my shoulder on the way to our first class, I'd thrown down with him, causing a fight that had left us both bloody.

We'd both been hauled in front of the Principal, me still spitting fury and anger from every pore. I'd been ready to see my scholarship ripped away, to be thrown out of the prestigious school where I'd never belonged. My future lay before me, leading in only two directions, prison or dead and, in that moment, I'd realized I just didn't care. Life in the system was worse than I ever imagined, but it was the loneliness for me, the sense of having no place to call home and nobody to give a shit if I lived or died.

Then Hunter had done something I hadn't expected. He'd taken the blame. He said he'd started the fight when we both knew it was me. My mind drifts back to that day; the day my life changed direction.

"Why the fuck did you do that? I don't need no fucking charity, rich boy."

"Fuck you, asshole. I didn't do it for you."

"Then why?"

"What the fuck do you care?"

"Because I don't want no help from the likes of you."

"Get fucked. You don't know me."

"I know you hit like a pussy."

"Yeah, tell that to your broken nose, pretty boy."

"I've had worse."

"Then maybe you should learn not to be a cocky cunt."

"So why did you lie?" I didn't even know why this was bothering me, but it was. I needed to know, so I could figure out my next move.

"Honestly, I just didn't want to lose sleep tonight thinking of poor orphan Annie losing her scholarship."

An involuntary laugh burst out of me at that comment. "You're a real asshole making fun of an orphan."

"Yeah, well, like I said, you don't know me."

He was right, I didn't know him, but for some reason, I felt a kinship with this boy. He'd fought me hard but he'd also stood up for me when my future was on the line. "Well, thanks. This place is my ticket out of my shit life."

"Whatever."

Hunter turned to leave and I moved to head back to the group home that made a mockery of the word 'home'.

"Hey, you like hockey?"

I shrugged, not wanting him to see any kind of weakness or give the impression I cared too much when the opposite was true. "Sure, it's okay."

A lie, I loved hockey, football, soccer, tennis, all sports, really. Not for the sport but from the sense of team camaraderie that jumped off the screen.

"I have tickets for the game this weekend. Wanna go with me?"

I wanted it more than my next breath, but I held my emotions in check, not trusting this feeling or the hand of friendship Hunter McKenzie was offering. He wasn't just a rich kid, he was the rich kid. Everyone wanted to be his friend, to say they knew him, and yet he kept to himself.

"Sure, why not?"

Hunter shook his head and smirked. "You're alright, Jake."

The lesson I learned that day was that you may never know where the lifeline would come from, or if it would, but for me, it had been the friendship he offered.

"Jake, are you even listening to me?"

"Yeah, I'm fine."

"Bullshit, but whatever."

That was the other thing about Hunter, he let me have my space and never pushed me to open up about my past. Calling Hank the night I'd been arrested had been a stupid move. At that time, I'd only been his son's punk friend, but even then he'd been kind and shown me respect.

To this day, I don't know why he was my first call from jail, but it had saved my life. Hank had driven down to the station and had his best attorney represent me. The prosecution wanted to make an example of me, and the kid I'd been with that night had money and power on his side.

I'd taken all the blame for what we did, making the attorney's job harder, but Hank hadn't given up. He'd stood by me, offering me a home, a family, and given me back my self-worth and all he'd wanted in return was a promise that I'd work hard to become that man he knew I could be.

I'd made that promise and he kept fighting until I was released into his and Vivian's care. He'd believed in me when nobody else did, including myself, and I'd spent every waking hour since showing him he'd been right to believe.

"Do you think your dad meant what he said about working for Lungo Tech?"

Hunter propped his legs onto the coffee table and rubbed his abs as he winced in pain. Hunter had broken his femur skiing a black diamond slope. "You know Dad, he never says shit he doesn't mean."

I nod, knowing there and then I was going to pursue corporate law and legislation as my specialty. I would be the best damn attorney he'd ever seen and make good on the promise I'd made him.

"You good, Jake? I know you've had some shit to handle with me away. This damn leg is a gonna need another operation by the looks of it, so I might be doing online from here for a bit longer."

"Yeah, it's all good. You know I hate this time of year."

"You visit them yet?"

I nodded. "Yeah, went before I came here." Every year on Thanksgiving I'd visit my mom's and my baby sister's graves and lay flowers down. I couldn't go more often, the crushing weight of losing them was always so fresh after I visited that I had to limit it or I'd lose myself.

"It wasn't your fault, Jake."

"Wasn't it? It was my fault Tiffany got a hold of the matches."

"You were twelve years old, and you got her out. You saved your entire block from burning down."

"It doesn't matter though does it. She still died from the smoke she inhaled. I should have been watching her better. My mom trusted me and I let her down. I killed them both."

"Again, you were twelve years old and your little sister wasn't your responsibility. She was your mom's."

"Mom had to work."

"Come on, Jake, you know she wasn't working. She was out with her boyfriend getting wasted."

I shake my head, hating that he's right and hating the resentment I felt towards my mom for what happened. She'd never forgiven me, and was gone six months later from a drug overdose.

"It doesn't matter, Hunter. They're gone and it's done. I just have to make sure I don't let your family down."

"You won't, Jake."

"How do you know?"

"Because you're my best friend and I know you."

"Yeah, I guess you do. I'm gonna be the best damn lawyer your dad ever had."

"We're gonna fucking kill it, Jake."

"Dream team, bro."

We bump knuckles then settle down to watch the game.

I should have told him about Cherry then, but for some reason, I wanted to keep her all to myself for just a little bit longer. She was mine and I wasn't ready to share her with anyone, even the people who'd saved me.

8. Jake

"Fuck, I missed you."

Wrapping my arms around her, I haul her close to my body and inhale her sweet fragrance. Her arms come around me and she buries her nose in my chest like maybe she missed me too, but won't admit it. Her chin comes up and I find those gorgeous brilliant blue eyes that I can't stop thinking about twinkling up at me.

"We spoke like yesterday."

I pinch her side and she giggles as she jumps away from me. "Hey."

"Well, stop being so lippy, or I might just bend you over my knee and spank the sass right out of you."

I watch Cherry's eyes go wide before they take on a deep slumberous look, her lips parting in invitation. "What if I want that?"

Stepping forward, I grip her hips, feeling her silky skin beneath my fingers. I hadn't been expecting that, but it seems like my girl has finally made a decision to trust me, but I need to be sure. She's stripped my brain of any thought but her and the thought of having her makes my whole body buzz with adrenalin. "Don't play with me, Blossom. My restraint is on my frayed leash."

She looks away, toward her bedroom window that faces Mass Avenue, as if she needs a moment to get her words together and I practice a patience I didn't know I had as I wait. This girl has had me since the first second I laid eyes on her. I never dreamed I'd fall in love, let alone get taken down so hard by someone who doesn't seem to want it, but here we are. She could ask me for the world and I'd kill myself to hand it to her on a plate.

Her gaze finds mine as her chin tilts up with determination.

My brave little fighter.

"No playing, Jake. I'm done fighting this. I don't want to. Just don't hurt me, okay?"

Her voice trails off on those last five words and I want to hunt down every person who has ever hurt her and rip them apart with my bare hands. I might be refined now, dress well, and act the part but, deep down, I'm still a kid from the wrong side of the tracks who fought his way out with blood and tears.

My hand shakes as I thread my fingers through her hair and grip her neck, my thumb forcing her bottom lip open. "I promise I'll never hurt you, Cherry. You own me. Every single part is yours and every piece of yourself you allow me to have, I'll cherish."

A shudder wracks through her body and I can feel her relax into me, trusting me, and I won't break that trust. "Gonna kiss you now, Blossom, so open that pretty mouth for me."

Her lips fall open and I bend in, taking her mouth in a hungry kiss that consumes us both. Her nails scrape against my scalp as I grip her ass and pull her closer so she can feel how fucking hard I am for her.

"Jake, please."

Her hands move over my chest, and down, her fingers quick and desperate as I lift her by her ass, her legs coming around my waist, as I sink to the bed, Cherry straddling me. I can feel her everywhere, her tongue in my mouth, her hands on my skin, her hot, wet heat pressed against the thin cotton of my t-shirt. There are just two layers separating us.

"Please what, my sweet Cherry Blossom?"

"Fuck me."

I chuckle, pleased by her need for me. "Not yet. First, I'm going to make you come screaming my name for all to hear so that everyone knows just who you belong to."

"I don't belong to anyone."

Fuck, I love how much she challenges me. I kiss down her neck, letting her feel my teeth as I slide my hand up her soft thigh to her drenched panties. "Fuck, you're soaked for me."

Cherry squirms on me as I run my thumb up her slit over her soaked panties, and skim her clit. Her groan makes my cock harden even more. I could listen to the sounds she makes on repeat for the rest of my life and never get bored. The thought should scare me, but it doesn't. All I feel when I'm around her is alive, and excited for the future.

Pushing her panties to the side, I slide my finger along her slit and hear her hum with pleasure as I stroke firm circles over her clit.

"More. I want to feel you."

"I make the rules, here, Blossom. You get what I give you because you're mine and I'll always satisfy what's mine."

"Fuck me. You read the books, didn't you?"

A dark chuckle rumbles through me as I continue to play with her swollen clit and slide two fingers into her tight wet pussy. She's so tight I can barely move my fingers and I know she'll grip my cock like a fucking vice when she takes me, but we need to work up to that.

"Yeah, Blossom, I read the fucking books."

I had to, but this is also just who I am. Or at least who I am with her.

Her hips move as she begins to ride my hand, her juices running down my wrist. I bury my nose in her neck, my tongue flicking the pulse that beats so wildly for me. Her hands lift to her hair and I feel her nipples pressed against my chest. Lifting my head, I cup her high, round breast in my hand, hating the fabric between us but determined to take my time and unwrap her like the gift she is. As I pinch her nipple through the cotton, her muscles tighten around my fingers and I curl the tips, finding that soft spot inside her that makes her detonate like a wild storm, sucking every bit of pleasure from me.

I let her ride out her pleasure, my fingers still inside her, and I can't take my eyes off her. She's fucking magnificent and she's all mine. Her gaze falls on me and she looks satiated and soft. I pull my fingers from her pussy and bring them to my lips and she watches hungrily as I suck the sweet taste of her climax from them.

I groan as my dick jumps at the taste. "Fuck, you just became my favorite dessert."

"You've got a dirty mouth, Jake."

I smirk as I run my hand over her straining tits, and she arches into my touch like a flower seeking the sun. "Yeah, and if the mess on my lap is any indication, you like it."

A blush stains her cheeks, and I let my gaze move her skin, following the perfect pink color until it disappears under her pink dress. "I've never come so hard before."

Her admission spurs me on and I grind my cock against her pussy, making her moan. "That's because you were always meant for me, Blossom." Leaning in, I nip her earlobe and she tilts her head, giving me better access.

"You didn't get off, Jake."

"Who says we're finished? We have all afternoon, and I'm going to spend every second of it giving you pleasure."

"What if I want to give you pleasure?"

"You want that, Blossom? You want my cock in that pretty mouth or in your hungry cunt?"

"Jesus, Jake."

"You want me to stop?"

"Hell no."

"Good girl." I find the zipper on the side of her dress and slide it down, before pulling the offending fabric over her head and dropping it to the floor. Her skin is like silk, the winter light from the window touching her like it wants to worship her.

"So beautiful."

I love how she wears pink all the time, with zero fucking apologies. She does what she wants and it's so refreshing. Her hot pink lace bra matches her panties and teases me with the view. I want to go slow, to savor her but I also want to rip it from her skin and mark her as my own.

Before I can decide, Cherry slides off my lap and sinks to her knees, her hands resting on her thighs as she looks up at me. I widen my legs and lean back on my hands as I take in the scene before me.

"I want to taste you, please."

Her please breaks my resolve and I feel pre-cum leak from my dick. Lifting my hips, I dragged the sweatpants off my thighs and kicked them away, before lifting my hand behind my neck and doing the same with the t-shirt. We'd already kicked our shoes off when we came in, so all that stood between us was our underwear.

"Pull the cups down on that pretty little bra and show me those sexy tits." I knew I was pushing her a little, demanding things from her that might seem base and crass, but I could read her and her body loved it.

She did as I asked and the pink lace framed the prettiest tits I had ever seen. My mouth watered and I wanted to get my mouth on her so bad I ached with it, but my girl wanted my cock, and what she wanted she got.

Crooking my finger at her, I motioned her forward and she shuffled closer, her eyes on my dick restrained by my boxers. Her small hands landed on my thighs and I was so turned on I feared embarrassing myself.

"Hands behind your back, Blossom."

Her gaze flashed to mine and she frowned. "But I...?"

"If you want my cock, you'll do as I say."

"Bossy, much?"

"Yeah, baby I am, and if I put my hand between those pretty thighs would I find your pussy soaked because of it?"

She doesn't answer but glares at me with attitude shining

through. She's fighting an inner battle with herself to do what she wants or what I want and get the reward for it.

Pulling my cock out, I grip the head and stroke slowly down, then up as her eyes widen, watching me with hunger.

"Open your mouth for me, Blossom."

Her lips open and I cup her neck, pulling her forward and feeding her my length. The first touch of her tongue against my crown has me ready to come so I have to fight it back so hard that sweat drips down my neck. My fingers leave her head as she takes me further into her mouth, but I know she can take more.

"Relax your throat, baby." I feel her do as I ask and take more, my cock hitting the back of her throat and making tears run down her cheeks. My hands wander from her hair over her shoulders before I cup both her tits and tease her nipples.

"I can't wait to taste these."

Cherry moans around my cock and a shudder runs through me, as she inches me closer to my orgasm. Pleasure zings through my entire body, my thighs shake and I know I have to warn her.

"I'm gonna come. Decide where you want it."

Pulling out of her mouth will be torture, but I'll never force her to do something she doesn't want, and tasting me was different from my coming down her throat. Luckily I didn't have to pull out as she doubled down, taking me deeper, and laving my length like she'd die without the feel of me on her tongue.

I come hard, my whole body tingling as I spurt down her throat and she takes every drop I give her, lapping it up like she's starved for me. Pulling her off my cock, I grip her head between my hands and take her mouth, tasting our combined pleasure on my tongue.

"Now it's my turn to taste you."

9. Cherry

"Now it's my turn to taste you."

My confidence wavers at his words, and I look away from his handsome face and god-like body. I want that but I've never let a man do that to me before and I'm unsure if he really wants that or is just returning the favor. I once had a boyfriend tell me men didn't enjoy it, but did it because they had to and it has stuck with me.

Yet, for some reason, I trust Jake. I'd spent a lot of time over the holidays thinking about him and us, and the way he is with me. Never in my life has a boy treated me like I was special like being around me feeds his soul and that's Jake. Every morning, a text comes through to let me know he's thinking of me. Some have been flirty, others funny but they're always there waiting to greet me when my eyes open. Not just that but throughout the day he sends me funny videos or memes and when we hang out he respects me. Even with all the girls on campus fighting for his attention, he only has eyes on me.

It's why I'd decided to take this leap with him, to take this for myself. I hadn't discussed it with Lexi, hardly seeing her over the break thanks to Dean. I'd always regret my part in getting them together. I see it now, that side of him that blew up every red flag alert in my brain, but my best friend didn't, and any attempt to talk to her resulted in her shutting down. So I'd decided to just be there when she needed me and, in the meantime, have my own adventure with Jake and see what happens.

"Blossom."

A blush heats my skin as I look at him to find him watching me intently.

"I've never.... You don't have to do that. It's fine, really." I go to move away but find myself on my back with Jake hovering over me, as he tackles me, rolling me beneath his big body.

"What the hell?" My heart beats faster at being pinned. Not in fear, but excitement. Something about not being able to get away makes my breath hitch with passion, my blood zing with it. I trusted Jake not to hurt me, and perhaps that's why my body is reacting this way.

Embarrassment is making me waspish and defensive as I squirm beneath him. Jake smirks knowingly before he leans in and kisses me slow and deep, drugging my senses. I try to resist, keeping my mouth closed, but he nips my lip and I gasp, giving him the access he needs to seduce my body and mind. When he pulls away, I feel more relaxed as he studies me. He really is so fucking handsome it should be illegal, and I tell him so.

"Your face is like a damn work of art."

Jake smiles, his dimples making him otherworldly beautiful. "Then your thighs should frame it."

I laugh despite myself and shake my head at him. "Subtle and cheesy."

Still, he watches me like he can't quite believe we're here, that I'd disappear if he blinks. He has such a sweet side to him, which I adore, but also a dominant, dark side which I want to explore more.

"Has nobody tasted your pussy, Cherry?"

God, this man and his filthy mouth will be my undoing. I shake my head and glance away.

"Eyes on me, baby."

I want to defy him but the need to please him seems to win out and his gaze is dark and intense as he stares at me like I'm the lamb and he's the wolf.

"That's my good girl."

God, I'm fighting the urge to purr at his praise, my entire body tingles with it. I'm not this girl, I do what the fuck I want and fuck everyone else, and yet I want to be his, and only his.

"Do you have any idea how fucking hard I am right now to think that I'll be the first man to put his mouth on your pussy?"

I shake my head and he hums. "So fucking hard. Feel."

Taking my hand, he wraps our fingers around his cock, and it's like steel. Thick and long, silky smooth with ridged veins that I know pulsed when he came.

"But I thought men didn't really like it."

Jake's demeanor seemed to change, his eyes darkening, dangerously. "What fucking moron told you that?"

"Just some ex-boyfriend."

"Well, he's a fucking idiot. Real men live for the taste of perfect pussy and yours is the most perfect I've ever had. I'm salivating at the thought of you riding my face and letting me drink down every drop of your pleasure."

Hearing he'd done this with other girls causes a lump to lodge in my chest. Jealousy burns hot and fast, as I try to push it down.

"Really? You're gonna bring up other women's pussy while I'm naked?"

"You brought it up, baby, but you're right. I shouldn't have said that. I have a past like you do, but that's all it is, a past. All that matters to me is you."

"Fine."

"Am I forgiven?" He kisses his way down my neck before his teeth tease my nipple and then he sucks it hard, making my back bow in pleasure.

"Yes, yes."

"Good. Now, be quiet and let me eat."

And God does he.

His lips skim my ribs, my belly, my hips, before his scruff grazes my thighs and he takes a big inhale, running his nose up my slit.

"Fuck, you smell like heaven."

Then his tongue is on me as he takes a long swipe through my folds, and I've never felt anything like it. He fucks me with his tongue as his thumb rubs firm circles on my clit. My legs shake as he forces my body to submit to the pleasure of his mouth on me. Sweat slicks my skin as my back arches and every nerve in my body lights up. I'm so close to that peak, to that high, that I'm terrified I'll detonate so hard that it will leave me a fragile shell. Yet still I chase it like my life depends on it.

Before I can fall over that edge, he switches it up, flicking my clit with his talented tongue as he finger fucks me. The wet sounds of his fingers in my pussy turn me on more, knowing he's doing this to me. He teases and tortures me in the most beautiful, soul-defining way and I know nothing will ever feel as good as Jake Marshall's mouth. He holds my orgasm just out of reach, backing away each time I come close. Until I'm begging, panting, writhing on his face, my desire coating my thighs and his chin.

"Fuck, I could live here and die a happy man."

"Please, Jake, let me come."

"Not until you tell me you understand."

I shake my head, not understanding his question and half out of my mind with wanting him. "Understand what?"

"That you're mine, and that I'm yours. No other woman matters to me. They never have and never will. Only you, Cherry. Only you exist for me and I need you to understand that."

God, I want to, but I've never been enough before. Why would he be different?

"I can do this all day, baby, and it would be my pleasure."

"Fine, I understand."

Jake shakes his head, as he holds my clit between his teeth, the sting of pain only making me wetter. My climax is so close it borders on pain at this point but a pain so good it feels like nirvana.

"I don't believe you."

His finger hooks inside me and teases that secret place that no man before Jake had found. A moan slips from my lips as every cell in my body screams for the release he holds hostage.

"I understand. Nobody but me. Not now, not before."

"Or ever again, Blossom. You're mine."

"Yes. Oh, yes."

He must be satisfied because he takes me over the edge, and I scream his name until my throat is sore and I'm sure the university is going to throw me out for making a spectacle of myself. Jake holds my thighs as he laps at me, drinking down every drop of my release like it was the water he needed to survive.

When I look down at him, my body limp from the climax he'd given me, I see his hooded eyes watching me with a smirk before he drops a kiss on my clit and I wince.

"Sore?"

I shake my head, as I feather my fingers through his hair and he lays his head on my inner thigh and almost purrs, as his eyes close. "No, just sensitive."

His eyes pop open, and he grins at me. "I should probably give you a break before I fuck you then."

God, his mouth is deliciously dirty and I find I like this side of him as much as the sweet caring one. "I feel like you've been holding back on me, Jake Marshall."

"How so?"

"Well, you've shown the sweet, devoted, protective, hot guy, but this is the first time I've seen the dirty-talking sex god."

"Does it scare you or put you off?"

He looks vulnerable as he asks the question and it reminds me that maybe I'm not the only one taking a risk. He has a reputation here and being with me might change that for him. I'm not the cute cheerleader or the girl next door, I'm different and loud sometimes, and abrasive and I've never felt the need to blend in, and yet he's brave enough to want to do it anyway.

Sitting forward, I cock my head, as I palm his face, the stubble scraping my skin. "Nothing you could do would put me off you, Jake."

"Nothing? What if I said I killed a man or I had a secret cross-dressing fetish?"

I study him, as he holds my gaze and I wonder if perhaps he does have a secret that he's afraid for me to find out but it's neither of those things. He's just testing the waters around me. He has things in his past he's ashamed of or have wounded him, just like I do, and that's okay. We're all a little broken in some ways, aren't we?

"Not even those things." And I found I meant it. "There are only two things that would make me walk away from you, and that's lying to me or cheating on me. You do those, then we're done, no matter how good the orgasms are."

"I would never cheat on you, Blossom, and I don't lie. I won't say I haven't in the past because I have. I was a punk, but I'm not that man anymore."

I kiss him quick, worried I'll blurt out my feelings for him if I don't. He kisses me back lazily before pulling away. "How about we get some food and bring it back here and watch a movie?"

"Sounds perfect to me."

10. Jake

This is what it feels like to walk on air. Knowing that Cherry is mine, that I can walk up to her and kiss her like I want to. That I can touch her, hold her, it feels like victory and redemption all in one.

We still have a lot to learn about each other. I still have secrets that she'll need to know one day but not yet, not until she trusts me enough to hear them. I need her to know who I am now, so she can forgive the sins of my past later.

Snow falls, blanketing the ground as I walk towards the coffee shop where she's working the late shift. I hate her closing up on her own and always make sure I'm there with her. I might rule this campus but, as evidenced by Brian Wills, there is always an asshole looking to make a name that will push his luck.

I've been around dickheads like him since I was a teen and went to that private school where I met Hunter. They thought they were special because of Daddy's money or the name they were born with, but they weren't. Yes, money gave you power but you only held power if you could wield it. Hank McKenzie has taught me that, he was the one to save me after I almost fucked up my life by falling in with Nicholas Kendrick the Third when Hunter and I were still in the early days of our friendship.

I'd been a stupid punk who hadn't trusted that Hunter was who he said he was and followed Nicholas down a dark path, stealing a car for fun, which ultimately led to an innocent man's death. I'd regretted it the moment I set foot in the car but I was wild and untrusting, surviving my own demons as best I could.

When the car crashed, I got arrested. Nicholas walked away without a scratch, even though he'd been the one driving. His father gave him an alibi and I'd been left to hang. Only Hank stepping in had saved me from the year in juvie that I'd been sentenced to for grand theft auto. We hadn't killed the owner of the vehicle, not directly, but stealing his car had left him walking along the dark road that night where he'd been hit by another vehicle.

So many lives were ruined by one stupid act that I'd never forgive myself for. Three months had been hard enough to set me straight and I still had nightmares about juvie and the accident of the nameless, faceless victim to this day. Hank refused to tell me who the man was, or any details and begged me not to go looking. I knew he was protecting me and, out of respect for everything he did for me, I complied, but even now I thought about it, dreamed about it.

As if thinking about that time had summoned the demon, my cell rang. I glance at it, seeing an unknown number, a feeling of dread runs over my skin like a warning. Shaking it off, I press accept. "Yes?"

"Jake, my man. Long time no hear."

Revulsion races through my body at the voice from my past, spewing into my present. My muscles brace as if ready for a fight because I'd never run from him. I wasn't the weak boy he pushed around and manipulated before.

"Not long enough. What do you want, Nick?"

"Can't a friend catch up with another friend without it being because he wants something?"

I huddle back against the building for shelter as snow falls harder, my shoulders hunching against the cold, but the cold was coming from the inside this time, not the temperatures outside.

"We aren't friends. We never were."

I have no time for this asshole, and want him off my phone as quickly as possible, but I also want to know what he wants and I know ignoring him will make it worse.

"I guess not." His tone changes from cajoling to cold in a heartbeat.

"Well, why are you calling me?"

"You need to do something for me. A favor, if you will."

"I don't need or want to do a fucking thing for you."

A dark laugh comes down the line and I want to reach through it and grab him by the throat and squeeze until he ceases to exist.

"You've changed, Jake."

"Yeah, I've changed and you're wasting my fucking time."

I'm seconds away from ending the call when he speaks again. "Your girlfriend's a pretty one, isn't she? Feisty too. I bet she's a handful in the sack."

My hand tightens on the phone and my vision turns red at the insinuation he's making. "You stay the fuck away from her or I'll rip every limb from your body."

"Don't be so defensive, Jake. I just need one little favor and you'll never see me again."

I grit my teeth so hard, I swear I crack a molar, but I hold my silence, not daring to speak in case my temper gets the better of me.

"Good. Now I have your attention, I need you to get into the Dean's office and steal the final exam for the Art of Gothic Architecture."

"Fuck that. I'm not stealing shit for you."

"That's a shame. I'd hate for Cherry to find out about your past."

"You really think holding that over my head is gonna work? Cherry knows me. That won't matter to her."

A laugh that causes the hair on my arms to shift falls down the line. I hate this man with a vengeance.

"No, she doesn't and thanks to Daddy McKenzie coddling you, neither do you. Have you any idea who it was you killed that night, Jake?"

I swallow, my throat dry as my heart rate kicks up as if it knows something I don't, my animal instinct sensing a trap. "I didn't kill anyone. I never stole that car, you did. I was just your scapegoat."

"Semantics. Just steal the paper and give it to my cousin, Brian, and you'll never hear from me again."

"Is that what this is? That piece of shit got his feelings hurt and now it's time for payback?"

"Something like that, Jake."

"Yeah, well, you and Brian can go fuck yourselves because I'm not stealing shit for you or him, and if anyone goes near Cherry, they will live to regret it. Or maybe they won't live at all."

"No, Jake, it's you who are going to regret it, but don't say I didn't warn you."

As the line goes dead, the feeling of sand falling through my fingers falls over me. Like I've set something in motion I don't understand, and I want to reach out and grab it back.

"Hey, why are you huddling in the doorway like a stalker?"

Glancing up, I see my Cherry Blossom walking toward me with a smile that rivals the sun. My belly twists, my heart beating faster at the sight of her huddled into her pink puffer jacket and pink earmuffs over her head.

Reaching for her, I drag her close and bend my head to kiss her, inhaling the sweet scent of her and letting it soothe me. Never in my life had someone settled my soul like she does. The second we met, I knew she was the one for me. It felt like the world sighed in relief when she grinned up at me. I knew I couldn't tell her I loved her yet, but I did. I think I did from the first second. I'm going to marry this girl one day, she just doesn't know it yet.

I just have to get past my fear of showing her who I really am. Nick's threat hangs in the back of my mind as I drag her closer, fisting her jacket as I take her mouth, tasting her sweetness. I need to stop

Here

worrying she'll run when I show her who I am, and maybe I can start by telling her about my family, and the heartbreak that set me on this path.

Lifting my head, I look into her bright blue eyes and grin. "Only woman I want to stalk is you."

"Is it wrong I find that kind of a turn-on?" Her admission makes my dick harden and I hiss in a breath. I grab her hand and start towing her toward my dorm room.

Cherry laughs. "Where are we going?"

"My place so I can show you just how hard that comment made my dick."

I glance back to see her eyes widen in delight before she jogs to catch up to my longer strides.

We fall through the door of my dorm, our hands tearing at each other's clothes, as a growl slips past my lips when I feel her cool hands reach inside my pants and grip my dick.

"Fuck, your hand feels good."

"I want you inside me, Jake."

Since the day I'd eaten her out like my favorite meal, we hadn't done much more than kiss and fool around, mostly because her period had started the next day. While I didn't give a fuck about a little blood, Cherry did, so we held back. Now it seems all bets are off and I'm desperate to feel her pussy tighten around my cock.

"I'm gonna fuck you so good, Blossom."

With the lightest of shoves, I push her back onto my king-sized bed, the mattress bouncing as she laughs and throws her arms above her head onto the dark green comforter. Smirking, I turn to put some music on, finding the right playlist from my library. Then I flick a lamp on low and close my curtains to keep out the cold.

Turning around, I expect to find her watching me, and I do, but I wasn't expecting to see her on her knees on my bed completely naked, looking like a fucking siren. I want to rush at her and bury my cock inside her, and fuck away all my self-doubts, to exorcise all my demons on her body, but this was too important for that.

With my eyes still on her, I peel off my coat, and let it fall to the ground before shucking my sweater and t-shirt in one move and dropping my jeans and boxers to the floor at my feet. Her hungry gaze wanders all over me and my dick flexes in appreciation.

"Open your legs and show me what's mine."

I'd hesitated to show Cherry this side of myself, but after the way she'd responded to me before, I know she likes this. My Blossom doesn't hesitate to do as I command, sliding her lithe thighs apart and leaning back on her hands. Her skin is flushed pink and I want to kiss and caress every inch of her perfection.

Fisting my hand around my cock, I pump my length slowly as her gaze follows every movement. Her teeth bite down on her bottom lip and I almost lose it. She's like every erotic dream I've ever had come to life.

"Show me how you make yourself come, Blossom."

Her hand slides down her belly, over her hip and I watch, my cock rock solid in my hand as she pushes two fingers inside her wet cunt, and moans. Her juices glistened on her fingers as she slides them out and rolls her clit in tight circles.

"Feel good, baby?"

"Yes, but you feel better."

"Damn right, I do. Now, get that cunt nice and wet for me."

Putting a knee into the bed, I climb between her thighs and kneel there watching as she fucks herself with her fingers as I drag my hand up and down my cock. The scent of her desire fills my nostrils and I want to taste her so badly. I knock her hand away before she can come, forcing an annoyed snarl from her pretty lips, which makes me grin.

"Don't worry my good greedy girl, you'll get your orgasm."

Before she can respond, I grasp her thighs and lift her cunt to my lips and feast. Her body half on the bed, the rest at my complete mercy, I eat and eat, as her desire coats my face and her moans drown out the sounds of the bass of my playlist.

Forcing two fingers inside her, I scissor them as she rides my face and hand with complete abandon, chasing her release like nothing else mattered and I fucking love it. I feel the muscles in her pussy contract, her clit pulsing against my tongue as her climax races toward her.

"Jake, I..."

Her hands scrabble for purchase on the bed and then I bite down on her clit and she detonates. Her legs clamp around my head, like a vice, her hips bucking and her cunt squeezing my fingers so tight I know my dick will be in heaven inside her.

My name is a scream from her lips and I drink down her release like it's nectar. Her legs fall limp and I squeeze her ass before kissing her inner thighs and letting her go. Reaching for my bedside drawer, I draw out a condom and Cherry watches as I roll it down my length.

Bracing my arm beside her head, I kiss her deeply, her fingers tunnel through my hair, dragging her nails across my scalp. Her nipples rub my chest, and I lift her leg around my hip as I stroke my cock through the evidence of her climax.

"I need you, Jake. Make me yours."

"You've always been mine, Cherry Blossom." Then I push inside her, her pussy walls hugging the tip of my cock like a glove as I work my way inside her. She wriggles and I look down at her.

"You okay?"

She nods. "Yes, you're just big. I don't know if I can take all of you."

I smirk at her words but I know she can take me, she was made for me. "You can take it all, Blossom. You're my good girl." I push in another few inches and she moans, her cunt squeezing me. Dropping my forehead to her shoulder, I wait, giving her a minute to adjust to my size before I push the rest of the way inside her.

"Jake, move. Please."

"Impatient minx."

My hand slaps her ass and she yelps but it turns to a moan when I shove my cock into her to the hilt and my pelvis rubs her clit just right. She feels like the tightest fist hugging my cock, warm, wet perfection.

"Fuck, you feel good, Blossom."

Cherry holds my face in her hands and locks her gaze on mine. "Fuck me like you hate me, Jake. Don't be gentle, I won't break."

God, could she be any more perfect? I don't question her, just take her at her word and withdraw my hips before slamming back into her, hard. Her pussy sucks at my dick like it doesn't want to let go. Her hands claw at my back, her legs lock around me as I suck a nipple into my mouth and bite down, making her cry out in pleasure.

"Harder."

A growl slips from my lips and I lift her leg from around my hip and push her thigh open and up so I can see my cock pounding into her pink pussy. Her juices coat my cock, and slide down my balls as I slam into her.

"This what you want, Blossom? You want my huge cock to destroy that sweet pussy for any other man?"

"Yes, make me come."

Her small hand goes to her clit and I knock it away with a snarl. "Nobody makes you come but me."

An angry snarl rolls past her lips and she glares at me, all fight and fire and I fucking love it. "Then stop dicking around and do it."

God, this woman.

Bending, I take her bottom lip between my teeth and bite down hard enough for her to gasp before I lick my tongue over the tender spot and kiss her like she's the most cherished thing in my life and she is. I run my hand from her ankle all the way up her thigh, over her hip, and belly before cupping her breast and rolling her nipple.

"You come when I say you come, Blossom."

Sweat slicks our skin as my hips move with power, the headboard crashing against the wall in time. I know others will hear and don't give a fuck, I want them to hear, to know who she belongs to, to know that she is mine and I'll incinerate anyone that tries to hurt her.

Tears leak from her eyes and I wipe them away gently with my thumbs, as I slow a fraction. "Blossom?"

"Happy tears, Jake. Just don't stop."

My lips kiss her eyelids, my tongue swiping away the tears on her cheeks. This is more than fucking, more than lovemaking even, this is a claiming and she's claiming me just as hard as I claim her.

My balls tighten, an electric buzz running along my spine as I roll her clit with my thumb, and then lift up so I can angle her hips up and hit that sweet spot inside her that makes her see stars.

Her breath hitches as I run my hand up her belly and grip her throat lightly, her hand covering mine and she squeezes it tighter, showing me what she wants. I've never been so turned on in my life and as I squeeze her delicate neck, her body flails and then I let go and command, "Come all over my cock, baby."

Her keening moan is pleasure filled with pain and her cunt grips me so hard I can hardly move, as I fuck her once, twice, before I come, shooting my seed inside her on a roar that leaves my throat raw.

Rolling off her, I quickly tie the condom off before chucking it in the trash. Cherry is lying just where I'd left her when I roll back, her eyes hooded and slumberous as she watches me. She looks so vulnerable, so stunningly beautiful, and so mine. Tugging the comforter from under her, I settle us in my bed and hold her close, pulling her thigh over my hips. My dick twitches with interest but I shut that shit down. I need to care for her now, to show her how much she means to me, not go at her again like a horny dog.

"I'm making a mess on you," she mumbles against my skin.

Squeezing her thigh, I kiss her head. "I like your mess all over me."

"Weirdo."

I chuckle as I stroke her hair through my fingers. "Are you okay? Did I hurt you or frighten you?"

Cherry pushes off my chest so she is leaning over me, her tits resting on my abs. I can't help but look at her, she has amazing tits, and my hand reaches for her nipple, rubbing it through my knuckles.

"You didn't hurt me, Jake. I liked what we did, I want to try every-thing with you."

Her eyes are soft, the blue of her irises, darker than usual as she offers up that admission with a shy shrug. I want so badly to tell her I love her, to admit that she holds my soul in her palm, but that call has shaken me. Have I destroyed us before we even begin? I don't know but I suddenly have the gut-wrenching feeling that our time is finite, that I have to cram a lifetime of loving her into the short space of time before my secret comes out and it will. Even if I agreed, and I don't want to, and steal those papers for Nick, my time with her is coming to an end. "Go on a date with me."

Her fingers draw patterns on my chest as she cocks her head in question. "Why?"

I roll us so she is beneath me, and see the way her eyes flare wide with desire when she feels me between her legs.

"Because I want the world to know you're mine."

Cherry rolls her eyes. "You pretty much pissed all over me a few weeks ago. I think they know."

"Then how about we do it because I want to spend every second making you smile and I think you'll like what I have planned." I nuzzle her neck as I run my hand up her thigh, making her arch into my touch.

"Fine but if it's a boring dinner, you're going to pay me back with orgasms."

Smiling against her neck, I feel her pulse flutter before I lick her skin, tasting the salt. "You get those either way, Blossom."

"Well, okay then."

"Tomorrow, after your morning shift?"

"What should I wear?"

"Is nothing an option?"

She smirks at me. "Only if you don't mind everyone looking at your naked girlfriend."

A growl leaves my lips and I want to rip apart anyone who's seen what belongs to me.

"Yeah, not happening. Unless you want me to kill any man who looks at you."

Cherry shrugs. "Hey, this was your idea, not mine."

"Wear whatever you want, baby. I don't mind smashing a few skulls for you."

"Animal."

I nudge her folds with my cock as I suck her nipple between my teeth and the rest of our words are forgotten as I fuck my girl until nothing else can penetrate the fog of my brain except her.

Little do I know that it's the last time I get to have her like this before our world implodes.

11. Cherry

I'VE GIVEN JAKE A HARD TIME ABOUT THIS DATE BECAUSE IT'S MY default to try and find the bad in any good. I know that about myself and I know I need to stop doing it or I'll push him away.

His thumb rubs over my knuckle, our fingers linked as we walk around the campus. I hadn't known what to expect when he said date, but today so far had been perfect. We'd met up with a historian at Massachusetts Hall, who'd regaled us with facts and details about the oldest building on campus, going into great detail that I absorbed like a junky.

I adore history, always had, and knew I got that from my mom. But my love for buildings and the stories they held was from my dad. After Mass Hall, we went to McKinlock Hall and spent some time admiring all the details.

"This must be boring for you." I cock my head up at Jake who is gazing up at one of the ceilings. His head snaps down and he grins at me, as he turns me in his arms, and pulls me close. I can feel the hardness of his body against mine, smell the cologne he wears mixed with the scent of his shower gel and I want to drown in it.

"You think watching you get all fired up and excited by seeing these old buildings is boring for me?" His lips quirk and I blush at the way he makes me feel. Wanted, special, like I am the center of his world.

"Isn't it?"

"No, Blossom, any time spent watching you smile is the best time, and knowing I've had a tiny part in putting it there makes me happy as fuck."

Right then and there the words 'I love you' stutter on my lips, but as if sensing it, Jake bends and takes my mouth in a kiss that is hungry, deep, and full of the words he stopped me from saying.

When he pulls back, his hand caresses my cheek, and he looks at me with so much unspoken love, I think I'll burst.

"I have one last surprise before we head back."

"Jake, you're overachieving already. How will I ever come up with a date as good as this one for you?"

His arm tightens around me as we walk and he chuckles. "You don't, Blossom. It's not your job to impress me. You do that just by breathing."

God, he makes it impossible not to love him when he says things like that. "Jake, that isn't how it works."

He stops us in the middle of the path that leads to University Hall and cups his hands around my cheeks. His eyes are more green than blue today as he gazes at me, his tongue wetting his bottom lip, before he shakes his head. "Blossom, you don't seem to get it. You're mine, and I don't mean I want to own you, although God knows I do. Perhaps the better explanation is I'm yours. You've owned my heart and my soul since the day you ran into me. You said you were a ten but you're so much more. You're my reason and it's my fucking pleasure to make you smile and treat you like the princess you are. I fucking love you."

My heart feels like it will beat from my chest as he says those words. Tears blur my vision and I let my head fall to his chest as emotions overwhelm me. I might only be young but I know right here and now that I'll never love another person like I love him.

Gently, he tips my head up and I blink away the wetness in my eyes as he studies me.

"I love you, Jake."

He shakes his head. "Blossom, you don't have to say it back."

Laying my finger over his lips, I stop him. "I know I don't, and I wouldn't do that. I'm saying it because it's true. I love you and it scares me and excites me, and makes me want to experience everything with you beside me."

"It scares me too, Blossom, but I promise you I'll never hurt you."

He kisses me again then and it is sweet and full of promise. When he pulls away, I smile so wide my cheeks almost ache. "So what's this surprise?"

Jake waggles his eyebrows. "Follow me."

He leads us to the University Hall building, which is very different from the other buildings but also more familiar, as I'd been in here a few times already for admin stuff. It is where the Dean has his office and student services have offices here too. It's the weekend so it's pretty deserted inside with most of the doors locked.

"Where are we going?"

Jake smiles. "Do you trust me?"

I roll my eyes because I might be in love but I'm still me. "Of course. You had your hand around my throat last night."

A growl slips from Jake's throat as his eyes skim my neck and a ferocious, dangerous look that makes my pussy ache sweeps over me.

"Don't tease me, Blossom."

"It wasn't a tease, it was a statement."

He mumbles something I don't hear before he pulls me behind him to the door of the Dean's office. My heart beats fast as I watch him look around before picking the lock on the door and swinging it open.

"Jake, what the hell?"

Pushing me through, he closes it behind us and smiles. "I want to show you something."

"And we had to do a little breaking and entering for you to do that?"

"Babe, you do know my past is more than a little murky right, and we aren't stealing anything. We're just looking."

"Your past doesn't matter to me, Jake. I see who you are now."

I mean it too, everyone has a past, and although Jake hasn't told me much about his or really anything, I'm not in love with past him, I love the man before me now.

He walks to a glass cabinet and once again picks the lock as I peer over his shoulder. The cabinet is lined with old books, photographs, trophies, and a few antique bottles. Stepping back as Jake opens the door, I watch him gently lift a book from the shelf and place it on the table beside us.

I gasp in awe as I look at a first edition copy of *A 1669 CLASSIC OF ARCHITECTURE, INCLUDING DESIGNS BY MICHELANGELO.*

"Wow, this is amazing."

Stepping forward, I touch the cover with reverence, knowing just how much a book like this is worth. But it isn't the monetary value, it's what's inside.

"I thought you might like it. We can't stay long but I thought you might want a few minutes to study it."

"Thank you."

Jake leaves me then to study the book as he goes to look at the photographs behind me. But I'm enthralled, taking in every detail of every page and sucking up the knowledge of the artwork inside.

Before long, I feel Jake beside me. "We need to get going."

Taking the book, he places it back in the same exact spot and locks the cabinet before checking the coast is clear so we can leave.

Walking back to the dorms, I talk nonstop about the designs, the lines, and the influence of art on architecture. Jake listens as if what I'm saying is the most intriguing thing he's ever heard.

"Sorry, I'm waffling."

"You're stunning when you're like this."

I'm about to laugh when my phone rings. Frowning, I take it out and see it's work. "I need to take this."

"Hey, I need you to work. Two of the other girls just called in sick."

I listen as my boss begs and, although I don't want to end my day working, I know I'll say yes. Hanging up, I look at Jake with an apology on my lips only to see understanding on his face.

"You have to work."

"Yeah, he's in a tough spot. Sorry."

"Hey, it's fine. I have a few things I need to do anyway. How about pizza at my place tomorrow night?"

"I can't. I have that paper due and I need to study for that exam on The Art Of Gothic Architecture."

I see Jake's shoulders tense before he smiles and I can see he's disappointed. "How about I help you?"

I shake my head. "No, you're too distracting."

"Tuesday then?"

"Perfect."

He kisses me deeply when he leaves me at the door to the coffee shop and I feel hope like never before, my steps filled with happiness. I never expected it to crumble into dust like it does.

12. Cherry

I'm hovering on a cloud as I daydream about my date with Jake yesterday instead of listening to Professor Castle talk about the way World War II influenced architecture. I'd woken to a morning text from Jake saying how beautiful I was and how he missed me already and then opened the door to find him holding my favorite blueberry muffin and a vanilla latte in his hand.

We hadn't had time for more than a quick kiss hello as he was headed to an early lecture but it set me up for the day, knowing he was thinking about me.

"Miss Baker, a word please?"

I glance up from my doodle to find the deputy Dean of the school addressing me. My heart jumps to my throat as I nod and stand to gather my things. Why does he need to speak to me? Is something wrong? Is it my mom or Jake?

Panic grips my windpipe, cutting off air, as I try to force the hammering in my heart to a normal level. "Is something wrong?"

"Follow me."

His stern response does nothing to temper my racing emotions as I follow him toward the University Hall building where just yesterday it felt like all my dreams had come true. Every thought flies through my head, each one worse than the one before.

My hand is on my phone as I walk my finger moving over the letters as I type a quick text to Jake. I watch the two ticks turn blue to show he'd read my text asking if he was okay and waited for him to type something but he goes offline.

Dread sits like lead in my belly as a dark twisted feeling looms over me like a cancer ready to steal my joy.

"In here."

I'm ushered inside the Dean's office, where he sits tall and forbidding behind his desk. My glance flickers to the cabinet where the book I'd been so enraptured with yesterday sits.

"Take a seat, Miss Baker."

My hand shakes and I curl it into a fist as I lower my bag to the floor and take the seat he indicated. "Is something wrong?"

"Yes, Miss Baker. Something is very wrong."

"Is it my mom?" The thought of losing my last remaining parent makes me want to throw up there and then.

"No, Miss Baker. As far as I am aware your mother is perfectly fine."

"Then what is it?"

The Dean clenches his hands in front of him on the desk as he regards me down his nose. "Yesterday afternoon, the exam paper for The Art of Gothic Architecture was stolen from this room."

My entire body loses all feeling as the unspoken accusation sits on the desk between us.

"Would you happen to know anything about that?"

I swallow the bile rushing up my throat and shake my head. "No. I have no idea."

Deny, deny, deny that was all I can do. I know I hadn't taken that paper, but I was sure nobody else would believe me.

The Dean turns his monitor toward me and presses a button on his keyboard.

"Then would you care to explain this?"

I watch in absolute horror as the camera shows me standing by the table hunched over a book before I turn and walk to the Dean's desk and jimmy the lock. No, that isn't right. Yes, I'd been in here and looked at the book but I'd never gone near the desk. My fingernails dig into my palms as I watch myself open the drawer and take out a large envelope before shoving it into my jacket and leaving.

I look up at the man across from me, who holds not a single flicker of sympathy on his weathered face.

"This isn't right. I didn't do this."

"Are you saying you didn't break into this office?" His head cocks as he watches me like a cat toying with a mouse. I know lying will make things worse, but the truth will condemn Jake too, so I have to be careful. If I say I broke in, I'll get in trouble but Jake could lose his ability to practice law.

"I just wanted to see the book."

"So you admit you broke into this office?"

I hang my head and nod as my eyes flood with fresh tears. "But I didn't steal those papers. Someone is trying to frame me. Ask Jake Marshall if you don't believe me. I saw him straight afterward." I'm weaving a web of lies and I hope Jake will support me.

"We will be speaking to Mr. Marshall next."

"Okay."

"Miss Baker, I cannot tell you how disappointed I am in you. You have great potential and you threw it away to become a cheater."

A sob escapes my throat and I try to force it down, to hang on to my composure. "I didn't take the papers."

The Dean shakes his head and sighs. "Miss Baker, the papers were found in your dorm this morning when we searched it."

"What!" I jump to my feet with a screech, hardly able to comprehend what he is saying. "That's impossible. I didn't take them."

"Evidence doesn't lie, Miss Baker."

"Well, clearly it does."

I'm getting angry now, furious that my future is being stolen before my eyes and I can do nothing to stop it.

"Miss Baker, getting angry about being caught won't help anyone."

He stands and walks toward another door that leads to a waiting area accessed through the reception area.

"Please wait here while we speak with Mr. Marshall."

I sink into the chair but my gaze swings around the room, looking for Jake. Needing him to hold me, to tell me it would be okay, but I don't see him.

For twenty minutes I wait before the deputy dean comes out and speaks to me.

"I'm sorry, Miss Baker, but Mr. Marshall does not corroborate your story. He insists he saw you take the papers, therefore we have no choice but to expel you and ask you to leave immediately. Someone will escort you back to your dorm and watch you pack."

"What? No! Jake would never do that. He knows I didn't do it. He was with me. I didn't touch the desk."

"Miss Baker, please stop. You're only making this worse. You're lucky Mr. Marshall has some very influential friends with very deep pockets and has persuaded us not to press charges against you."

In a daze, I step out of the reception area into the hall. A door opens further up and I see Jake walk out of the Dean's office with a smile before turning back to shake the man's hand.

In that moment, my heart hardens into the clearest diamond and splinters into a million pieces inside me. There is only one reason Jake would lie, and that was if he'd taken the papers.

As the man I thought I loved, who I thought loved me, turns to look at me, I die a little inside. His gaze holds mine with sorrow and grief etched into every pore before he schools his features and a cold hardness takes over as he smirks and turns and walks away, leaving our love bleeding on the floor of his lies.

13. Jake

Present Day

"Hɪ, ɪs Mʀ. McKᴇɴᴢɪᴇ ᴀᴠᴀɪʟᴀʙʟᴇ?"

My ears prick up as I stride across the wide reception area, on my way to meet with Hank, to discuss my best friend's sudden departure to China. He had been totally blindsided when a woman he'd had a one-night stand with had told him she was pregnant with his child. Against my advice, he'd believed her and fallen head over heels for her, until it had all come crashing down when he'd found out it was a lie.

Anger surges through me as I turn to see a heavily pregnant woman and the bitch that hurt my friend standing there demanding to see him.

"Do you have an appointment?"

I stand back as our receptionist tries to handle it waiting to see how far Lexi will take this.

"No, but I really need to see him."

"I'm sorry, Miss?"

"Lexi. I'm Lexi."

I can see sympathy marring Molly, our receptionist's, face, and hate the way this woman has everyone under her spell. I can't see her face from this angle but I've seen enough to know that I won't stand for this shit anymore.

"Well, I'm sorry, Lexi. He isn't here."

Moving quickly, I come up behind her and spit her name with all the malice I can muster. "Lexi?"

She spins to look at me, hope rising in her eyes and I take in her appearance through the red mist of anger. "Yes?"

"So, you're Lexi," I sneer, letting all of my distaste for the way she's treated my best friend show as she flinches slightly at my tone. "What do you want?"

"I need to speak with Hunter."

"You can't." I thank God that Hunter is away and not here to deal with her doe eyes.

"Please, I need to talk to him."

"I'm sorry, you can't. He and his fiancée have gone to China for six months." I'm not sure why I add that extra detail, especially as Lana isn't his fiancée. At least not yet or maybe ever, but I want this woman to feel a fraction of what she's put my friend through.

She staggers back at my words and it's then that I really look at her and see the bruises marring her skin. The fragility surrounding her and my stomach takes a nosedive in dread. Something isn't adding up here. My intuition, which is usually so good, is screaming that I've read this wrong, that I've made a mistake here.

"Lexi." I move to grab her arm, calling her name as she goes sheet white, her hand resting on her bump as pain that I can hardly look away from moves across her face.

Then she's falling, her legs buckling under her and her body going down. I dive to catch her, breaking her fall with my arms, before I lay her gently on the ground.

"What the hell is going on out here?" I turn from where I've dropped to my knees at the side of the pregnant woman who broke my friend's heart and see Hank McKenzie striding towards us with a furious expression on his face.

"She fainted."

Staring at Lexi covered in bruises and looking as broken as Hunter had the last time I saw him, I have the horrible feeling that I've just made a huge mistake. I'm ashamed to admit how much pleasure I took in telling her Hunter had gone to China with Lana, referring to her as his fiancée when she's nothing of the sort.

Seeing the devastation and defeat on her face should have given me satisfaction, but all it did was make me feel like a shitty human being.

"Out of the way."

I move back as Hank sinks to his knees beside her and takes her hand. I wonder if he knows who she is and how much she hurt his son. I stand and move back, not really knowing what to do.

Hank turns to me with a glare. "Do you know who this young woman is?"

"Yes, she's the woman who tried to dupe Hunter into believing he's the father of her baby."

Hank hums, his lips pursed in an angry line as he looks at Lexi as her eyelashes flutter. His touch is gentle as he strokes her hand before looking up at me, seemingly having made a decision.

"Call my son and get him back here immediately."

His demand leaves no room for argument, so I step back and dial his number but it goes to voice mail. I dial Lana and the same thing happens. Knowing Hank won't take failure as an excuse, I call the airfield and I'm told the flight has left.

"Get them back."

The woman on the other end of the phone goes quiet. "We can't, sir."

Frustration fills my veins at her response. Can't isn't a word I accept. I'm more than just the lead attorney for Lungo, I'm a fixer and there's nothing that can't be handled given enough encouragement. When that doesn't work, I'm happy to shade outside the lines of legalities to make things happen. Ruthless is my middle name, I owe this family everything and I'll do anything to protect them.

Glancing at Hank, I see him speaking to Lexi in a quiet tone, her lips moving slowly. Hanging up on the flight control, I move closer, wanting to hear her excuses, but none come.

"No. Honestly, I just need to go home."

She looks exhausted and the bruises on her skin, which I hadn't noticed in my anger before, mock me and turn my stomach with fury that someone has put his hands on her. I might be morally grey, but there are lines I'll never cross and that's one of them.

Moving closer, so I'm standing in front of them, I address Hank.

"It's already left."

Hank might be in his sixties, but he's formidable and there's no man alive I hate to go up against more than him. The air around us cools as his quiet displeasure permeates the air.

Standing up, he glares at me, clearly having overheard my part in what happened here today and not happy about it. Yet, all I was doing was protecting his son.

"Then see that my son gets the message as soon as he lands," he growls, and gone is the patient man who placed his hand on my shoulder as I stood in court and shook with fear so many years ago. In his place is a force of nature—a man you don't cross.

"Yes, of course, Mr. McKenzie," I respond with forced politeness, my jaw rigid with tension.

Lexi begins to rise to her feet, and I resist the urge to reach out and help her, knowing I'm the last person she wants near her right now. Her balance is so unsteady she almost falls, reaching out blindly and grasping onto Hank, who places a hand on her back and eases her down.

"Please, Miss. You need to sit."

I see the worry pass over Hank's face and feel a sense of anxiety crawl up my throat, making my collar tight. Lexi looks exhausted, crushed, and broken and I know I should have done more research on her situation before I spoke. If something happens to her or that child, whether it's Hunter's or not, I won't forgive myself.

I'm about to offer her a ride to the hospital when the door to our reception flies open and my past blasts in like a hurricane, taking my feet from under me. In stupefied silence, I watch as the only woman I've ever loved drops to her knees beside Lexi.

"Honey, are you okay? What did that asshole say to you? I'm going to kick his ass," she demands before taking a breath.

God, she's just the same, a stunning, wild whirlwind that is untamed perfection. Her hair is a softer shade of the pink she loves. Her curves are a little more pronounced, making my mouth water and my hands itch to explore every one of them.

Anger and determination tinge her pale skin the slightest pink and my dick hardens at all that fire inside her. I always loved Cherry for being so unapologetically herself. She was captivating, untamed, and I'd loved her beyond reason.

Even in a pink flowery skirt and a white, off-the-shoulder top, she looks like an avenging angel ready to slay anyone who hurts her friend. Lexi holds tight to her hand and Cherry doesn't let go.

"I'm fine. Cherry, can we just get out of here? Please?" Lexi allows all the anguish she'd tried to hide from me and Hank show, and Cherry nods.

"Of course we can, sweetie." Cherry looks up as she goes to stand, and I watch in fascination as recognition barrels into her. First shock and then anger cross her pretty features.

"You!"

"You!" We both say at the same time as we stare at each other.

Ignoring me, Cherry turns back to Lexi and gently helps her to her feet, her posture so rigid I can practically see the hackles prickle along her spine. I have the almost overwhelming urge to stroke my hand down her delicate spine and see if I can make her purr instead. "Come on, Lex. Let's get you out of here. I don't like the smell in here," Cherry says as she helps Lexi toward the door.

Suddenly the thought of her leaving leaves me feeling untethered and desperate to hold on to her attention for just a few more seconds. "Cherry, hang on."

Cherry goes stiff before she whirls on me, fire licking through her gaze as she rakes it over my skin like a brand. "No, Jake, I won't hang on. I should have known you were involved. Breaking people is what you do, right?" she hisses as she turns to leave again.

I deserve that. I deserve everything she throws at me, but it still hurts to know that the woman who still holds the only living piece of my heart hates me.

My attention is yanked away by Hank as he moves to stop them. "Lexi."

Hank places his hand on her arm and I see Cherry move in closer, like a mama bear ready to throw down with anyone to protect her young.

"Here's my number. If you need anything, please call me. I have a feeling there's been a huge misunderstanding between you and my son. Despite everything you've heard and seen this morning, Hunter is a good man, and he cares about you a great deal."

Lexi cocks her head with a sad smile. "Thank you, Mr. McKenzie, but I think Hunter has made it clear what he wants, and I'll respect that. I won't stop him from seeing his son if he wants to, but I won't contact him again, either. I'm afraid I'm all out of energy where men are concerned."

I feel Cherry's eyes on me, hatred so strong it is palpable aimed my way. Yet, all I see is the beautiful girl I loved. She has every right to feel the way she does, but there's so much she doesn't know, so much I still can't tell her. But the thought of her walking away and me never having the chance to try and explain some of it or make things right makes every muscle in my body rebel.

As they reach the elevator, I know I can't let my Blossom walk away. My hand shoots between the closing doors, and they bounce open, allowing me to step inside. Seeing the cold indifference on her face, I suddenly doubt if this is a good idea. Cherry ignores me like I'm nothing more than a bothersome fly and it makes me want to push her, to make her admit that she feels more. That I'm someone to her.

Pressing the button for the ground floor, I turn to her, but she's looking at her feet like her shoes are the most interesting thing on the planet. Honestly, hot pink stilettoes are sexy as fuck, and on her they're lethal, and she wears them like a queen.

"Cherry, I—"

My little Cherry Blossom rounds on me so fast that I have to fight the urge to smile at her. Fuck, she's magnificent.

Pointing her finger at my chest she pokes hard, and my whole body heats at the first contact from her in over a decade. In those seconds, everything falls away except the memory of her hands on my skin. Cherry and I weren't just hot between the sheets, we were burn-the-world-down lava hot, and I remember every single second of it like it was yesterday.

"No, you don't get to speak to me. You're nothing but a lowlife, lying asshole. Stay away from me and stay away from my friend or you won't like what I do," she snarls and I have the strongest urge to bite that bottom lip until her tirade turns to moans of pleasure.

In the past, I would've backed away from an argument with my Blossom. I would've been patient, but she isn't the only one who was changed by what went down between us. I stood back instead of pushing when we were at Harvard, and look where that got us. Now I have no intention of letting Cherry call the shots or blame me for everything. Yes, I am to blame for a lot, but she walked away without giving me a single chance to explain.

"Me? I'm a liar? You're the one who promised me forever and then left, not the other way around, Blossom."

Cherry looks like her head is going to explode, her jaw tight, her face red, her breath heaving. I can't look away, from her fury, it's so fucking hot.

"Fuck you, Jake. You can't even be honest with yourself, and don't call me that," she growls as she turns back to face the elevator doors.

I'm half expecting her to stomp her tiny foot, and the image makes me hard. She's being a brat, and I'd give anything to take her over my knee and redden that delicious ass of hers. She'd hated Blossom at first, or so she said, but I knew then, just like I know now, that she loved it. And even if she doesn't, it gets a reaction from her.

"If I recall, *Blossom*, you loved me calling you that. Admit it. Even now you're wet for me." I give her a confident grin as she glares daggers at me. I see the change in her instantly, the metaphorical sound of her patience snapping as her friend sucks in a sharp gasp. I glance at Lexi and only see the fist coming toward me at the last second. I could dodge it easily, but she deserves this one. She'd earned it so I let it happen.

For a little thing, my Blossom lands a hefty punch and I feel pride in her as I rub my chin and jaw to hide the grin. The doors open and Cherry quickly pulls her friend into the lobby. I could follow her but Cherry needs some time to regroup and I need time to plan my next move.

I watch from the lobby, my hand in my suit pocket as she speeds away on those ridiculously high heels that make her ass wiggle seductively. My Cherry Blossom got away from me before, but I won't let it happen again.

Not when for the first time in ten years I feel alive again, and she's the reason.

She was, and will always be, my reason.

14. Cherry

It's a week later and I'm still vibrating with the anger and shock of seeing Jake. I always imagined that if I ever saw him again it would be when I was looking glamorous and put together, my confidence and success like a shield around me. Instead, I'd been caught completely unprepared at a time when I was worried sick and filled with guilt over everything that had happened with my best friend.

It didn't help that the selfish jerk had gotten more devastatingly handsome in the last ten years. Was it too much to ask that he'd developed warts on his face, or perhaps a beer belly and receding hairline? But, of course, his suit fit him like a second skin, his broad shoulders filling out the custom fabric, his biceps visible when he moved his hand to rub the spot where I punched him. Of course, the letter I got in the mail this morning doesn't exactly help my pissy mood.

"Hey, sorry I'm late."

Glancing up, I tip my head for Frankie's kiss and note the bruises on his face are almost gone. Lexi's asshole ex had beaten him and left him for dead for no other reason than he was a fucking sociopath. Nobody had known just how deranged and dangerous Dean was until it was too late. I'd known he was manipulative and borderline abusive since the day he hit on me while dating Lexi, and then black-mailed me over it, saying he'd tell Lexi it was all me.

Still dealing with my shattered heart after what Jake had done, I'd kept quiet and never said a word. It's something I'll regret until my dying day and one more thing in the 'why we hate Jake Marshall' column.

"It's fine. I just got here. I ordered us Mojitos."

Frankie bats his eyelashes dramatically, and I thank God he hadn't had his light dimmed by that asshole.

"Girl, you read my mind. I just had my last doctor's visit and that nurse I was telling you about was there, and I found out he has a boyfriend."

"Aww, I'm sorry, honey. I know you liked him."

"It's fine," He waves it off as he takes a huge sip of the mojito, his eyes closing before he grins. "He's old news. I saw one of the peds doctors and asked him out instead. We have a date on Friday."

"Wow, good for you."

"Damn right, good for me. I'm not gonna let that homophobic bastard ruin my sex life."

Even as he said it, I see a shadow of pain move over his face. Dean hadn't just hurt Frankie, he'd beaten Lexi unconscious, almost stran-gling her to death. He was the worst human being alive, with Jake the devil a close second.

Any man who can hurt a pregnant woman should be shot in my book, but unfortunately, he can't be found anywhere. Police had put out an APB, but until then, we're all on edge and watching our backs. Luckily Hunter is back and he and Lexi seem to be working things out. Another thing Dean had tried to destroy, but I really hope he'd failed. I was team Hunter all the way. I see the way he looks at my friend like she invented the wheel. I swear if she wanted the moon framed in her living room, he'd get it for her. I'm happy for her, but seeing Jake again reminds me of how, once upon a time, I'd thought I had that too.

"Uh oh, someone looks glum."

"I'm fine, just tired."

I think I've gotten away with my deflection when the waitress comes to take our order, but Frankie is tenacious as hell and as soon as she leaves he pins me with a probing look. "Spill."

"It's nothing."

"Cherry pie, do not make me break out my ABBA routine here in the middle of this fine restaurant."

I squint at my friend, giving him a look that scares most people away, but he just rolls his eyes and begins to stand. He'd do it too. He has no shame and I love him for it.

"Okay, sit down." I shoot him a look full of annoyance.

"Oh, please. I've been perfecting the bitch face since I was fifteen, and yours doesn't scare me."

"Has anyone ever told you you're annoying?"

"Yes, but not today, so thank you for the compliment. I do try not to hide all this greatness under a bushel."

My lips twitch with a smile; it's impossible to be angry with Frankie. I sigh and bang my head on the table and the cutlery jingles from the impact of my despair. Looking up, I see a server looking our way, but he just shakes his head and goes about his business. We're regulars here at The Atlas, a fresh restaurant that serves food from all over the world. Each week we come here, sometimes with Lexi and my mom, but mostly just me and Frankie, and try a different dish.

"Do you think we'll like the French Onion soup this week?"

Frankie bangs the table and lifts one perfectly plucked brow. "Stop stalling and start talking."

"Urgh, fine. Do you remember when I told you about that guy who broke my heart and lost me my place at Harvard?"

"Yes. You were as drunk as a skunk and told me he framed you for stealing exam papers after telling you he loved you. But he was still the best lay you've ever had, and ruined you for all men."

My nose wrinkles at my irritation over his memory of that night being so good. "Yes, well, the asshole is back."

I watch with some satisfaction as Frankie's eyes go wide. "No, he is not."

"Yep, and what's worse, he's Hunter's best friend, so there's no way I can avoid him."

"Is he cute?"

My scowl deepens. "Oh my God, is that what you took from that?"

"It's a valid question."

"Frankie, focus. He broke my heart and betrayed me. He ruined my life."

Frankie takes my hand in his across the table. "Do you want me to hunt him down and put itching powder in his pants? Set up a Tinder profile and list some weird kinks he's into? Maybe go to his office and tell everyone he gave me syphilis?"

"Of course not, although the image of Jake jumping up and down with itching powder around his junk is tempting. Then see how hot he looks with his balls red and scabby."

"So, he is handsome?"

"Disgustingly so," I admit with a sigh.

"So like an eight or a nine?"

"More like an eleven or a twelve," I admit grudgingly, "but his personality puts him at a two."

"What's his surname? They have two Jakes at Lungo."

Frankie is tapping away on his phone and I reach across to swipe it from him. There on the screen is Jake Marshall, my nemesis, and the boy who I'd once thought was the love of my life. He looks good, powerful, and confident with a slightly dangerous air that he hadn't had ten years ago.

"That's him."

Frankie swipes the phone back and smirks. "Oh, yeah, I'd definitely let him get all up in my business."

"Yeah, well, unlucky for you, he's straight."

"Shame."

"Frankie, what am I going to do?"

My whiney tone must have convinced Frankie how dire my plight is because he sobers, placing his phone on the table face down. "What did, Lexi say?"

"She doesn't know. I never even told my college roommate, I just left the same day and cut ties with everyone."

"Why not tell Lexi? I can understand you losing touch with your roommate, she's a reminder of everything, but Lexi is your ride-or-die. She must know why you came back from Harvard after putting so much work into getting in in the first place."

I shake my head, wondering why I haven't told her and knowing deep down it's because I'm ashamed for falling for his lies. "She thinks I was homesick. She knows nothing about Jake. Only you and my mom know the truth."

"What happened when you saw him again?"

I toy with a loose thread on the napkin in front of me as I let the memory of seeing him again flood through me. "Lexi had just fainted on the floor of the Lungo office building and I wasn't expecting to see him. To be fair, he seemed a little surprised too, but then he started to push my buttons with his bullshit so I punched him in the face."

I flex my fingers as I speak, my hand still aching from making contact with that rock-hard jawline.

"O. M. G. I'd pay good money to see that. I bet it was hot. What did he do?"

Frankie lives for the drama, and he's practically bouncing in his seat now, clapping his hands in front of him. "Nothing. He just rubbed his jaw and watched me leave with a stupid smirk on his face. Honestly, I walked away from our encounter feeling like he had the upper hand and it doesn't sit well with me."

Frankie frowns, confused. "And Lex didn't ask about it?"

"She did, but I put her off. Told her we'd talk when she felt better, but that was before Hunter came back. Now they're going to end up married and living a perfect life and I want that so badly for her, she deserves that."

"But having that means you have to face Jake over and over again."

"Exactly. I don't know if I can do it."

"Now you listen to me, girlie. You're fierce, you're strong, and you can do anything you put your mind to. You'll face him and you'll make him regret ever even thinking he could treat you like he did. You'll have that man crawling on his hands and knees begging you to take him back and forgive his fine ass before the summer is out."

I wish I could agree, but Jake is the one man who made me feel cherished, who made me feel like I could be myself without judgment. He'd been the calm to my storm, but now things are different, he's different. I hadn't seen the boy who broke me when I looked at him. I'd seen the man who has ice in his veins, who calculates every single detail and knows the end result before the game is even played.

His power had dominated the room, and I'd fought to stop the feelings he evoked from overpowering me. But I can't let him. No matter how attractive he is, or how much my body remembers and craves his touch, he's the enemy now. One I won't let come between me and my friend.

"I'm gonna downplay it for Lexi. She doesn't need the drama. Fuck knows she's had enough already and I don't want her in the middle of this. I'm a grown woman and I can handle it. I'll be polite and cordial and avoid the jerk as much as possible."

"Sounds boring, Cherry Blossom."

My back snaps straight at the sound of that deep, sexy baritone. Shooting daggers at Frankie for not warning me about his presence, I turn and look up at the man who is now haunting my waking hours as well as my nightmares.

Goddamn, he looks good in a suit. Deep navy and custom-made for his fine form, a crisp white shirt, which probably cost more than my house, and a bright blue tie that brings out the green in his eyes. Even his tan brown shoes look good, making him look untouchable. His jawline holds no evidence of the right hook I'd inflicted, only a light stubble that makes me squirm in my seat as the ghost of feeling it evokes between my thighs assaults me.

I give him a cool withering glare that doesn't match my inner feelings. "Well, a Neanderthal like you would find politeness and cordiality boring."

Jake bends close, his lips so near I can smell the mint on his breath as his cologne floods my senses with memories. Goosebumps spot my skin, and I use every acting skill I possess to portray how unaffected I am by him.

"If I remember correctly, you quite liked my primitive side."

How dare that asshole throw our past in my face after what he did to me. My insides quiver with anger as I fight to keep control. "Honestly, Jake, I barely recall anything about you. You're just a distant mistake from my youth. I've moved on and so should you."

His eyes crinkle as he places one hand on the back of my chair and the other on the table in front of us, pinning me in place with his dominance.

"Who said I hadn't moved on, Blossom?"

My heart is pounding in my chest so loud I'm sure he can hear it. His words sting, in a way they have no right to. This is what I want. For us to pretend that at one time my heart hadn't only beaten for him.

I wave my hand at him. "This little display of yours."

He chuckles as he slowly steps back, giving me some space to catch my breath. "So I take it you've moved on then? There's a man taking care of you?"

"Really, Jake, it's none of your business and I've never needed a man to take care of me, and especially not one like you."

"Meaning?"

I watch his jaw feather as he grits his teeth and almost smile knowing that my barb landed. "What we had was a lie. I was a pawn in a game I didn't know the rules of. You won. Move on and leave me alone."

"Three things. One, you'll always be my business, little Cherry

Blossom. Two, you were never a game to me. What we had was the most real thing I've ever had, and three," he lets his gaze run over me and does nothing to hide the hunger he feels, "I'll never leave you alone."

I stamp my foot as I jump from my seat to face him, my head barely hitting his chin. "Do not call me that. I am not your Blossom or anything else. You say we were never a game but the evidence suggests something different. Leave me the hell alone or I'll make sure everyone knows what an asshole you are."

"Wrong. You'll always be my business and you'll definitely always be my Cherry Blossom. Do your worst, I don't care what people think of me. Let them believe I'm an asshole. I am to most people, but never to you, Blossom. I never intentionally hurt you." His hand lifts as if he means to skim my cheek, but I step out of his reach, not sure I can cope if he touches me with tenderness. The softness in his voice on that last line almost undid me.

"You're insufferable."

"And you're a liar."

My temper flares white hot at his accusation. "How dare you." My hand swings out towards his face before I can even consider what I'm doing, but he catches it in a firm grip, just inches from his cheek.

Heat flashes between us as everything else in the room falls away. Sound becomes muted as I glare at him, my breath heaving in and out like I've run a marathon. His thumb caresses the pulse in my wrist and it's like a brand of pain followed by the most exquisite pleasure.

I lick my dry lips, and Jake's gaze follows my movements, his eyes darkening with heat and desire. God, whatever we'd had still burns between us in some fucked up muscle memory.

"You get one free pass, Blossom. Next time you throw hands at me, be prepared for me to redden that sweet ass of yours."

Visions of me bent over his knee as he spanks my delicate flesh make heat and need flood my pussy. I try to school my reaction but even now he knows my body and reads me too well.

"I see you like that idea." He cocks his head, bending so his lips skim my neck near my ear and I shiver uncontrollably. His thumb continues to rub slow circles on the skin of my inner wrist as if he's soothing me at the same time as torturing me.

"Tell me, Blossom, does your pussy miss my cock?"

His words are what I need to break this spell he's woven around me. I yank my arm from his hold and step back, my butt bumping the table. "Stay the hell away from me, Jake."

He shakes his head slowly. "Not until you let me explain."

God, his words are like knives in my chest, the pain so fresh I expect to see blood pouring down my blouse. "Nothing you can say will excuse what you did."

"And what is it you think I did, Blossom?"

"Do not make me say it, Jake," I beg, hoping he'll leave me in peace to shore up the defenses around my heart. "You already tried to break me once, Jake. Don't think I'll let you have the chance to do it again. Just stay away from me."

"No can do. Hunter loves Lexi, and Hunter is my best friend, and you're hers. I think that means we're going to be seeing much more of each other so get used to it."

With that he spins on his expensive heel and walks away, his back straight, head held high and proud. He commands the room effortlessly. Every eye is on him as he leaves, including mine.

My legs give out as I realize every person in the room has been caught up in our interaction. Sinking into my chair, I grab the alcohol and chug it down like it's my job. Before I can summon the waiter, Frankie has already done it, ordering us two more cocktails and the check and telling them we'd be in the bar.

"We're gonna need shots for this, not food."

He gets me, my friend gets me, so I follow him into the bar area, where we find a spot in the back corner.

"I'm not sure all the liquor in the world is gonna help this situation, Frankie."

"Well, not with that attitude it won't. You gotta put some effort into it, girl. So down the hatch and when you're good and drunk, we're gonna discuss what the hell just happened between you and sexy suit."

"Can we skip that bit, please?"

"Oh, there is no chance on this earth we're skipping that. I almost orgasmed on the spot from the sexual energy buzzing off him."

"Eugh, Frankie. Don't be gross."

"Oh, please, don't tell me it didn't get your lady garden all of a flourish with his dominance. I'm pretty sure he turned half the straight men in here, he was so hot. Seriously, tell me, is he the sex god I think he is?"

As the shots hit, my lips and brain give up the fight and blab all the details. "Better, even ten years ago he could make me come so hard I almost blacked out, and that was before he put his hand around my throat and choked me."

Frankie squeals so loud we start to get annoyed looks from others in the bar.

"I just knew a man who looked like him would be a freak in the sheets."

"That's the problem though, Frankie. He ruined me for other men. He used me, played games with my heart and body, and left me with nothing."

Frankie grips my hand tight as the weight of my words fall around us. "You're not ruined. He may have banged your heart up a little, but you're the strongest person I know."

"I don't feel like it right now. Lexi could have died, Jake is back, and I got this in the mail this morning."

I sober up fast as I pull my bag close and dig through to find the letter I'd been doing everything in my power to ignore since I opened it. I hand it over to Frankie and watch as his eyes widen before his head lifts and he looks at me.

"What are you going to do?"

"Hire a lawyer I guess, but I can't imagine me winning a compulsory purchase order against a company like them."

"Does your mom know?"

"No, and I don't want her to, either. The salon is in my name, and I'm going to handle it on my own."

"You know I hate to say it but Jake is a lawyer."

"Absolutely not. I'd rather lie down in the street and let the bull-dozer roll over me than ask him for help. I'll find a lawyer who can help me. There has to be someone willing to take this on."

Frankie doesn't look convinced but I am. I have to be, I won't let Jake break me, not again and I sure as hell won't let a company like KLM Holdings take my mother's livelihood. It's time to pull up my big girl panties and go to war.

15. Jake

Three Months Later

SCRUBBING MY HANDS OVER MY FACE, I TRY AND FORCE SOME OF the exhaustion from my body. The last few months have been grueling, partly because this deal with China is so important to Lungo, but also the intricacies involved. At least I'd managed to get it done in under three months, working my team to the bone to get it done. Hunter should have been there, but his priority is his very pregnant girlfriend. I understand it, and I know the part I'd played in making things harder for them.

I'm not a man who regrets much in my life, but the way I'd treated Lexi was one of them. It seems like I'm doomed to fuck up with the women who mean something to me. My sister, my mom, Lexi, and most importantly, at least to me, Cherry.

I've never forgotten her, never gotten over her, and always assumed I'd spend my life living the Playboy lifestyle because I knew there was no replacing her. She'd been it for me, and it had gone so badly wrong, I hadn't known what to do at first. Now, though, I knew. I have to make her see what I did was for the best for both of us. The only issue with that is I'll have to lay myself bare for her and pray like hell she can forgive me.

Pulling up outside Hunter's penthouse, I look up with a feeling of doubt I've never experienced around my best friend. We've had countless calls in the last few months and I've apologized for what happened with Lexi, but some things need to be handled in person and this is one of them.

If I'm going to get back on track with Cherry, I need to fix things between me and Hunter first. I nod to the doorman as I stride toward the elevator, but I'm stopped when my card doesn't work.

Nausea rolls through me at the thought he doesn't trust me like he used to. Turning to the concierge, I wave my keycard and raise my brows in question.

"Sorry, Mr. Marshall, all visitors have to be announced, without exception."

"Well, announce me then." I wave my hand in irritation, trying desperately not to take my rising temper out on him.

Nodding, he makes the call and gestures at me as the doors open and I'm admitted into the private elevator.

The ride up feels interminable and makes me angsty. This family means everything to me and knowing that I've hurt them makes me sick. The doors finally open admitting me into the lavish entryway, where Hunter is waiting for me.

Usually, I'm greeted with a slap on the back and a smile but all I get is a cordial head nod.

"Welcome back, Jake."

"Yeah, thanks."

As he turns and heads into the kitchen, I follow him, suddenly unsure of my place here. Lexi has taken over, and her stuff is strewn around everywhere. Her influence in every corner I can see. I'm the outsider looking in and it's not a good feeling.

Hunter holds up a beer. "Drink?"

I nod, taking it from him.

Popping the lid on his, he takes a sip and leans back on the island.

"So, what do you need, Jake?"

"We need to clear the air."

He waves the bottle at me. "Floor's yours."

I can tell he's still fuming about what I did. Sighing, I run my fingers through my hair. "I'm sorry, okay? I was a dick. I never should've said what I did to Lexi. I had no right, and it was out of order."

"Did you even look at her before you spouted your bullshit at her? Did you see the state she was in from the bastard's hands before you kicked her when she was already down?"

"Honestly?"

"No, Jake, lie to me! Of course, fucking honestly."

"I didn't even notice until I saw her start to go down. I was so angry with what she'd done, I didn't see past that. I just wanted to lash out."

I can see the anguish on his face as I paint the picture for him, which I'm sure his father has already done. Hank was furious with me too, but at least he'd understood why I'd done it.

"He strangled her, Jake. He beat and kicked her on the ground and when I was on the other side of the fucking door. He strangled her until she passed out and left her for dead. She could have died. My son could have died."

I've never seen Hunter so distraught, but I can see now his anger isn't just toward me, it's toward himself, too. "But she didn't. Lexi is strong and so is your son."

"She is but nobody is unbreakable, Jake. She came looking for me when she was desperate. When she was on the edge of the cliff with nothing left to give I wasn't there. And, worse, she was met with open hostility from my best friend. The man I would've trusted with my life."

"You can still trust me, Hunter."

Hunter shrugs and sets his bottle down. "Can I? Because I know I can in business. I can sign over every share I hold and know you'd never let me down, but with her, with Lexi, I don't know if I can."

Moving closer, I fight the need to beg, the loss of his trust is like a gut punch. Gripping his shoulder, I force him to look at me. "Mac, you know me. You know I'd never hurt someone you love. I was trying to protect you and it backfired. I was out of line but it won't happen again."

"No, Jake, it won't."

His cool delivery feels like the beginning of the end of our friendship. "So that's it? Decades of friendship done? Finished over one mistake?"

"You don't get it because you've never felt this way but she's my life, Jake. Without her, nothing matters."

"I have felt that."

"What?" Mac looks up at my soft confession, a question in his dark gaze.

"I've had what you have. I felt like my entire world only turned for one person. That she was my sole reason for existing."

"Why am I only just hearing about this?"

I spin and begin to pace, I hadn't planned on revealing this to anyone but if he needs this to forgive me, then so be it. "When we were sophomores at Harvard. You broke your leg and were away. She was a freshman and she was..." I stop, trying to find the words for the way Cherry had bowled me over and stolen my heart. "Everything. She was funny, smart, beautiful, vivacious and she was unapologetic in who she was. I loved her from that first meeting. She was the one that got away."

"Wow, I had no clue."

"After it ended, I didn't want to talk about it. I'd fucked it up so badly there was no way back and it hurt too much to dwell on so I threw myself into life." I look up at my best friend, the man who is more brother than friend, and let him see the pain I still feel. "I get it, Hunter. You want to protect Lexi but I can promise on my life, I'll never let you or her down again. I'll protect her as hard as you do. You have my word."

Hunter blows out a breath and I can see my words have made an impact. "You apologize to Lexi. If she forgives you, then so do I."

I dip my head, knowing that's the best I'm going to get. "Thank you."

"Don't thank me yet. Lexi is stubborn and she has a secret weapon in Cherry. That woman is fierce."

My lips tip in a smile as I nod. "I'm aware."

"So now that's sorted, tell me about China?"

I spend the next half hour telling him the details and gossip from my trip, including a few prospects I'd heard about that might be of interest.

"What about KLM? They still sniffing around looking for an investor?"

My lip curls at the mention of the KLM. Kendrick, Lamar, and Morrison. A company I'll gladly see sink into the pits of hell.

"Apparently they have one and a plan to build a shopping mall with a huge hotel and Casino right here in our city."

Mac shakes his head. "Not happening. Kill it."

"I'm already working on it."

"Good."

Mac walks toward the fridge, and opens it, before tilting his head at me. "You staying for dinner?"

I shake my head. "Nah, I came straight from the airport. I need a shower and about ten hours of sleep before I do anything else."

"Okay."

I don't want to bring it up again as things have evened out the last hour or so, but I need to know when it's a good time to speak to Lexi and from now on, I'm taking Mac's lead. "When do you want me to talk to Lexi?"

"Let me speak to her. She's at the shop but will be home soon."

Lexi and Cherry have a design shop where they sell antique and upscaled furniture, and also offer a bespoke design service which is thriving.

The frown on his face tells me all I need to know. "You don't want her working?"

"Honestly, if I had my way she'd be wrapped in cotton wool but she says Cherry needs help."

"What does Cherry say?"

"That she can handle it, but Lexi needs to feel helpful and not like she's leaving her friend to do all the work. She feels guilty."

"What if someone else helped Cherry out? Lexi wouldn't have to feel guilty then."

"No, but then we're potentially putting someone else in Dean's crosshairs."

"No word on him?"

Mac shook his head. "Nope. Not a word. Hopefully, he jumped off a cliff."

"What about me?"

Mac's brow furrows, not understanding.

"I can spare a few hours now the China deal is done. I can help in the shop a couple of hours a day or even work from there so Cherry has some help."

Mac regards me with his head cocked. "You sure? This doesn't seem like your kind of gig. I'm not sure customer relations is in your wheelhouse."

"Yeah, I can handle it."

"Let me speak to Lexi but I'm in favor. If nothing else, it will humble you."

His smirk loosens something in my chest and I know it's going to be okay. "Says the boy born with a silver spoon wedged in his ass cheeks."

"Fuck you, asshole."

Leaving Mac's place with a sense that something was healing after months of doubt gives me a thrill and the drive to go after what I want next and that's my Cherry Blossom. Later, I get a text from Mac saying Lexi thinks it's a great idea and thanking me.

I grin as I get ready for bed thinking of the look on my Blossom's face when she meets her newest member of staff.

16. Cherry

My hips and butt swing side to side as I sing the lyrics to Cindy Lauper's classic, 'Girls Just Wanna Have Fun'. The shop is always quiet between nine and ten on a Monday morning and I take the time to get my head on straight for the week ahead, and it will be a busy one. I have a thousand things to do here, as well as finish planning the baby shower for Lexi and fend off KLM from trying to steal the salon from my mom.

Monday mornings for most people are the beginning of a long week packed with stress, demands, and little fulfillment, but not for me. After Harvard ended so disastrously, I'd thrown myself into making this venture with Lexi work and it has. More than that, it's thriving and I know a lot of that is because of the drive I have to prove to Jake that I could triumph despite him.

The thought of him sours my mood slightly, but I dance through it, twirling my arms above my head. After our little showdown in the middle of The Atlas, I'd been primed for him to become a thorn in my side but through some subtle probing, I'd found out Hunter had sent him to China to handle a deal there for him, so he could be with Lexi.

The knowledge should have left me feeling relieved, but I can't deny the twinge of disappointment that came with that revelation. Which only annoyed me and made me hate him more. Doing one final hip wiggle as the song winds up, I spin again and scream as my heart tries to jump out of my chest in surprise and mortification.

Lounging against the antique writing desk that I still haven't found the right home for is none other than the bane of my life, the devil himself, only he wears Brioni, not Prada. My gaze falls over him hungrily, taking in every muscular inch of his body before finding the smirk on his face that makes me want to commit violence. I become instantly aware that this is the first time I've seen him alone since the day he told me he loved me. Since the day he made me believe in something that was all a fairytale, and I don't mean the ones with hearts and flowers but the Brothers Grimm type with blood and heartbreak. Even on that last morning at Harvard when he dropped my coffee and breakfast to me, others had been around us, so now that was my lasting memory.

Crossing my arms over my chest, I jut my hip and raise a brow, not wanting to show him how much his presence affects me. "What the hell are you doing in my shop?"

Jake takes his time pushing off the desk and prowling toward me like some big jungle cat surveying his domain, but this is my jungle, not his and he doesn't belong here in my safe place. Jake lets his eyes sweep over me, not hiding his hunger in the least as he lets his desire for me show. My nipples bead and I curse my body's reaction to him.

I'd worn a cerise pink and white floral mini skirt, which shows off my legs, and a white sleeveless blouse which is cinched at my waist. Hot pink six-inch sandals finish my look as my hair falls around my shoulders. I'd likely pay for the heels later in life, but while I can wear them and feel sexy doing so, I'm going to do just that. My clothes are part of my armor and with Jake here, I need it more than ever.

"You greet all your customers like that, Blossom?"

I can feel my temper bristle at the name that holds so much pleasure and pain for me now. Reminding me of what a fool I'd been to fall for him. "You're not a customer, you're an irritant I could do without. So kindly show yourself out, I'm busy."

Jake smiles at my words, walking closer until we're breathing the same air, his exhale my inhale, but I don't step back. I won't show this man my weakness, even as he crowds me, forcing me to tip my head back to him. Being five feet tall you get used to looking up to people, but mentally he won't break me. Not ever again.

"That's why I'm here, Blossom."

"To irritate me?" I snort because that, I believe.

Jake smiles and I hate that my stomach flips at the sight. "No, because you're busy. Lexi asked me if I could help you for a few hours a day while she's laid up resting and I'm happy to help."

My gaze raked over his ten-thousand-dollar custom suit in disgust. "Lexi would never do that without talking to me first."

"She said she'd text you." Jake shrugs one of his big shoulders as if he doesn't give a fuck either way. Turning from him, I let my hair fan out and brush his chest as I stomp over to my phone and check. Sure enough, there's a text from Lexi.

> Lexi: Hey, you. I've managed to sort some help for you in the shop this week. I can't tell you how much this takes the pressure off me.

Any other time I would've told her off or told Jake to shove his help up his bitable ass, but knowing this eases my best friend's stress after everything she's been through, leaves me with nowhere to go. I already adore the baby she carries like he was my own, and I'd let Lexi down time and again. I won't do a single thing to add to her stress.

"She send it?"

I tense as Jake comes up behind me, his breath on my neck, the warmth of his body making me want to lean into him even as I recognize the danger he poses to the life I've built here. Moving around the counter, I put distance between us and give him what I hope is a look of disinterest.

"For the record, I don't need your help. I don't need anything from you, ever. But if it eases my best friend's mind, I'll tolerate you being here but stay out of my way."

"That's your problem, you don't need anybody. You never did. It's why you're so closed off."

"Fuck you, Jake. I am *not* closed off, and not needing people isn't a bad thing. It shows I can stand on my own two feet."

"It shows you don't trust people, that you're still a broken doll deep down inside."

How could this man gut me so quickly and with so few words? My chest aches and my belly feels hollow as he peels back my skin and exposes the raw wounds festering beneath. He spoke into existence the fear I live with. That I was broken, that somehow I'd lost something crucial to who I was when he betrayed me.

"And who's fault is that?" I bite the words out in an angry whisper, pain making me shake inside.

"Mine. I fucked up and I own that, but it was never because I didn't love you, Cherry Blossom. What we had was real."

I hold up my hand to stop him, I don't want to hear it. I deserve answers, I need answers but not here, not now, when once again the only man to make me cry is pushing my buttons.

"Don't. Just don't. You have no right to bring that up. You played your games and won whatever sick prize my destruction cost, so don't try and make out it was more when it wasn't."

Jake slams his hands down on the counter and leans into me, his jaw clenching as he tries to hold on to his control. Anger, like a living breathing beast, consumes us both, but underneath it is that simmering attraction that has always been so natural between us. "You were never a game to me, Blossom."

"Then what was I?"

I brace, waiting for him to admit I was just a fun distraction, a toy for him to play with and ultimately destroy, but what came next was so much worse.

"Everything. You were the oxygen in my lungs, the blood in my veins, and the only person who mattered to me."

"No, you don't get to say that after what you did."

Jake shook his head, slowly. "I know I hurt you, Blossom, but I never meant to."

"Then why?" I ask the question I'd spent so many nights torturing myself over.

Jake looks wrecked as he backs up and then blinks away his emotions as if they'd never existed. Any hope I'd had of an answer fell away into dust.

"It doesn't matter. It was a long time ago and it's in the past."

Disappointment bleeds through me, tainting everything and making me feel tired to my bones. It might be in the past for him but it had defined my life, my relationships, and everything I had today is because of the path he'd put me on, both good and bad. I want to scream at him and yell, demand answers, and ask him why me. Why was I so disposable to him? But I couldn't allow him that kind of power. I had too much to do, and too many people relying on me to fall apart.

"Forget it, Jake. It doesn't matter anymore. Let's just get through this for Lexi and Hunter's sake."

He looks like he might argue but then nods. "You got it."

"Good, now the entire showroom needs a dust, so get to it." I bend beneath the counter and pull out the dusters and polish we use to keep everything shining and shove them towards him. I thought he'd balk, that the billionaire would think this beneath him, but he takes them with a smile before removing his jacket and rolling up his sleeves, showcasing veiny, muscular forearms that make my mouth water. Ruthlessly, I push my attraction down and get on with my endless list of tasks.

All morning my concentration wavers between the man moving

about my shop like it's his natural habitat and the letter I'm composing to KLM, rejecting another offer for my mother's salon.

So far I've only had one visit from a representative of theirs and they'd been pushy but polite. I know they'll be back though, and I want this nipped in the bud before my mom gets wind of it. My lawyer, Harvey, who much to my dismay looks nothing like the hot guy from Suits, is about as useless as a snooze button on a smoke alarm.

"What ya doing?"

I gasp as I jump and slam my laptop shut. "You need a fucking bell around your neck."

"Not my fault you were daydreaming while I slave away."

I turn to him and a bubble of laughter slips out at the dust covering his once pristine white shirt. "Aww poor little billionaire, did you break a nail doing manual labor?"

Jake gives me a withering glare and tosses the rags on the counter. "Physical labor has never been a problem for me, and you know it."

"I know nothing."

Jake doesn't respond but grabs my laptop before I can stop him. He holds it above my head as I fight the desire to stomp my foot and demand it back.

"Don't be a dick. Just give it back."

"Tell me what has you so twisted up for half the morning and I will."

"I'm not twisted up. I'm just concentrating on what I'm doing."

Jake lifts his hand and skims his thumb over my bottom lip. "Bullshit, your lip is all pink and pouty from the abuse you've given it."

I swear I see heat in his gaze before he blinks and I'm faced with the hardass again. Shrugging off his touch, I turn away, not wanting him to see the lie. "I'm just trying to organize some stuff for Lexi's baby shower." That isn't a complete lie, the cake maker isn't answering my messages and I still have to pick up the bunting and talk to the caterers about the food.

"Can I help?"

"I've got it."

"Come on, Blossom, let me help. Hunter is my best friend and I have a lot to do to gain his and Lexi's forgiveness for the stunt I pulled."

The snort leaves me before I can stop it. "You don't deserve it from either of them."

"Maybe not, but I did what I did to protect Hunter. He was hurting and I thought she'd fucked him over. You can't say you wouldn't have done the same thing."

I want to. I want to tell him that I'm a bigger person than he is, but I would've done that and worse. My blood boils at the thought of all the terrible things I want to do to Dean. Never in my life have I wanted blood more than his. So yes, I can relate to Jake in that but that doesn't mean I owe him my help.

"Please, Cherry. It guts me to know I made her pain worse. I might be the worst man on the planet in your eyes after what happened, but you know deep down I'd never hurt a woman for no reason."

A part of me wanted to argue with him, to tell him he'd do exactly that, he'd done it to me, after all, but I heard through Lexi how much it gutted Hunter to be at odds with his best friend and I want them to find peace and happiness through all this even if I have to suck it up and help Jake do it.

"Fine, you can help but I'm doing this for Lexi and Hunter, not you."

"Absolutely."

"Now give me my laptop back."

I thought I'd need to argue more but he hands it over just as my belly rumbles.

"You want me to go grab lunch?"

"Yes, that sounds good. Let me grab my purse." Anything to get him out of the shop for half an hour and give me some space to get my hormones wrangled back under control.

"I got it, Blossom."

"No, Jake, I pay for my own lunch. And stop calling me Blossom."

Jake bends close to me and my heart beats faster. "Nope and nope. Seems like you've forgotten how things are between us, Blossom. We eat, I pay. We travel, I drive or ride. And you'll always be Blossom."

My mind skitters to being on the back of his bike and I close my eyes. It's been an age since I'd ridden. His bike was the last because I just couldn't face being with anyone else after him.

"There isn't anything between us, Jake, and I don't ride."

Jake frowns. "Why not? You love bikes."

I don't want to tell him that all the joy had been stolen from me because of him, that because of him every time I so much as looked at a bike now it just reminds me of what it feels like to be cuddled up to his back with the wind in my hair and his warm, hard body protecting me.

"Grew up, I guess."

"Hmm."

"What does that mean?"

"Nothing. I'll grab lunch and be back."

Turning, he strides for the door, just as a client walking in distracts me from the tension that always seems to be in the air when he's close.

Everything between us feels unfinished, like we're hurtling toward something that could blow up our lives and I want so much to put the brakes on, but Jake is like a runaway train.

He isn't the boy I'd loved so hard I'd lost all sense of danger and perspective. He's a man who wields power now, who controls everything and everyone around him like they're all carefully maneuvered chess pieces. A part of me mourns the boy I'd loved, the boy I thought loved me. He'd made me feel safe, adored, like I could be myself, that I could let my true self shine, but it was all a lie.

A bigger part of me is glad that Jake has hardened, that he's different because I can never forget what he's done. Not even for Lexi.

17. Jake

AFTER THAT FIRST DAY, CHERRY AND I FIND A BALANCE working together. I took on most of the manual jobs like moving furniture, hanging pictures, and changing displays, and she spends hours designing and talking with clients so she understands their every need. She also lets me help her out with the things she was delegated for the baby shower. Her work ethic is damn impressive, but it doesn't surprise me. Cherry has always worked her ass off for what she wanted.

She'd created something impressive here, something she can be proud of, but I can never forget that I was the one who took her original dream away and I'm sure she'll never be able to either. I'd almost told her everything on that first day in her shop when she'd demanded answers, but a part of me wasn't ready, wasn't willing to risk her hatred when the truth of what happened came out. I need more time for her to see me as the man who adores her as much as the boy she'd loved did.

Gathering up the box of cupcakes iced in white and pale blue and decorated with tiny booties and pacifiers, I head into Hank and Vivian's home. This place hasn't been my home in a long time but every time I step inside I feel the love and comfort of family surround me.

"Hey, Jake." Vivian kisses my cheek, as she takes the top box.

"Hey, Viv. Where do you want these?"

"Take them through to the back. Hank is sorting out the drinks and the caterers with Cherry. Frank and Darla left to go home and change but should be back any minute."

Cherry. Just her name is enough to make my dick harden. I thought I could handle being around her and not touching her. I'd done it before when we were younger, when she'd had me firmly in the friend zone. But that was before I'd tasted her and before I'd felt what it was like to sink my cock into her. To have her consume me in every way.

The second I step outside, my eyes find her. I look around the patio, which is decorated with baby blue streamers and cream and blue flower bouquets that, on closer inspection, are made from tiny socks rolled into roses. White balloons are tied to the end of a table that's filled with baby-themed canapes, with a huge white cake covered in pale blue and lemon ribbons and a tiny fondant elephant in the middle, but I only have eyes for my Blossom.

Fuck me, she's beautiful, more beautiful than ever, and less attainable too. She thinks she hides it from me, but I see the hurt in her eyes, the betrayal in the bright smiles she fakes my way, and the careful control she uses to keep me at a distance.

She's dressed like a fifties pin-up, with a wave in her pink hair and a full, pink, polka dot dress with some kind of netting beneath the skirt. She looks hot as fuck, but it's her smile that she turns on Hank so easily, that makes me lose my breath.

"She's a knockout."

I twist to see Vivian has stepped up beside me. "Yeah, she is."

"I hear she slapped you in the elevator at the Lungo office."

My surprise must have shown because Vivian laughs. "You don't honestly think anything happens in that building that my husband doesn't know about, do you?"

"I guess not. Does Hunter know?"

Vivian shakes her head. "No, but I see the way you look at her. Whatever is going on between you could be good for you if you let it."

I have a reputation as a womanizer, as a man who never wants to settle down. They all think I'm just commitment-shy, but nobody knows it's because the only woman I'd ever wanted to lock down had ended up broken because of me, and now hates my guts. "It's not me that won't let it this time, Viv. I took something beautiful and broke it, and she won't forgive me."

"Then fix it."

I huff a laugh. "If only it were that easy."

"Nothing worth having is easy, Jake. Love isn't easy, but if you think she's worth the fight, then fight for her. Or with her, whatever you need to do."

I don't respond because at that moment she must sense me watching her and captures me in her heated gaze that's like a poison barb beneath my skin reminding me of what I've lost.

Walking up to her it takes everything in me not to take her in my arms and kiss the pink gloss from her lips.

"Thanks for bringing these."

Cherry takes the cakes and begins loading them onto the display as I watch her. She flits around the patio like a deranged fairy giving orders and making people laugh or smile. She's a force of nature and I want her back in my life. Not as Lexi's friend but as what she should always have been, mine. Yet, how do I do that without telling her the truth and breaking her heart?

There's only one way and that means causing chaos on a scale that would impact everyone I love. Everyone who's supported me could suffer if I do this and yet watching her I know I'm about to burn down the world for her and the chance of her forgiveness. Other guests begin to arrive, dragging my mind away from my plans, including Lexi's parents, who Hunter had flown in to surprise her.

Cherry greeted them like long-lost loved ones. I saw her mom, who was like an older version of Cherry, walk in with Frank who tipped his head in greeting at me. I nodded not wanting to engage in small talk right now. I had fences to mend but the first had to be Lexi. I'd wronged her shamefully and it was time to be the bigger person.

"They're here. Everyone be quiet."

We all huddle in the lounge as we wait for Hunter to lead Lexi in from the foyer, then as one, we all shout.

"Surprise."

Lexi blinks, looking completely shocked as she takes in all the faces of those she cares about in front of her. Then I see her lip wobble, her eyes grow wet as she spots her parents and turns to Hunter who looks at her like she hung the moon every night.

"You did this? You brought my parents over?"

Like a voyeur, I watch as he swipes her tears from her cheeks and kisses her, whispering softly before he pushes her toward her parents.

Standing back, I give Lexi time to do the rounds before I approach her. This is the first time I've seen her since the showdown at Lungo and she looks a million times better. The bruises have healed, her sunken eyes have lost their shadows, and her smile is radiant instead of defeated.

"Lexi."

She turns at the sound of my voice. "It's Jake, right?"

She asks, but I know she knows who I am. She's cautious and once again shame fills me. "Yes. I just want to apologize for my behavior at the office that day. I was a complete asshole and behaved despicably." My words aren't flowery but they're heartfelt.

"Well, I'd love to disagree but..." she says with a disarming grin.

Right in that moment I know it's going to be okay because the woman in front of me has more grace than I could ever hope for and she clearly loves Mac as much as he adores her. I smile as the tightness in my chest that had been so persistent these last months eases.

"I was a dick but it wasn't personal. I thought I was protecting my friend, but I was just jealous. I see that now. For what it's worth, I really am happy he has someone who makes him so happy."

"Why jealous?" She asks with a tilt of her head and I regret that admission as she studies me waiting for an answer I don't want to give, but she deserves my honesty no matter how uncomfortable it makes me.

"He's my best friend, my wingman, and I didn't want that to change. It was selfish and childish. He has the right to be happy with the woman he loves."

"And what about you?"

"Me? I think my chance is lost," I say wistfully as my gaze finds Cherry laughing with Cassie, but maybe I have a second shot.

"You never know what the future holds, Jake," she says with a grin as I pull my focus from Cherry and back to Lexi.

"Friends?" I ask as I hold out my hand for her to shake.

"Friends."

As she grasps my hand and goes to shake, her face contorts in surprise, her hand tightening on mine as a gasp leaves her lips. Lexi looks down and gasps again. "Oh no."

Her hand tightens around mine as her eyes widen in pain and a groan leaves her lips.

"What is it?" I ask as she doubles over holding her stomach, a moan ripping from her lips and not the good kind I'm used to hearing from a woman's mouth.

"My water just broke."

I hold her hand as I look around for help, spotting Hunter talking to Lexi's dad. It's too early for the baby to come, and I'm so far out of my comfort zone that it isn't funny. Did I do this? Did I put her into labor with my sorry excuse for an apology?

Hunter seems to sense something is off as he looks up and takes one look at Lexi before he rushes over to us.

"Lexi."

He shoves me out of the way and wraps his arms around her and I stand back feeling helpless, as my Cherry Blossom steps up beside me and glares an accusation at me.

Lexi looks up at Hunter and gives him a wobbly smile. "We're having a baby,"

"I know that, Lex," he says as if she's telling him the obvious but my friend hasn't quite grasped what she's telling him.

"No, I mean my water just broke. We're having a baby now."

I see him gulp as his eyes go wide. "Fuck. We're having a baby," he shouts to the entire group, catching my eye and smiling with pride and not a little fear.

Lexi and Hunter are herded out of the house and I can't help but let my gaze search for Cherry. I want to share this with her, it feels right.

"Are you going to the hospital?" I ask as I find her rushing around looking for her bag.

"Yes, of course."

"I can take you."

Cherry stops and looks at me with wariness. "Did you make things right with Lexi? Because I won't have you fucking this up for them with your toxicity, Jake."

"Relax, me and Lexi are good."

"Fine. You can drive me, but don't think this means anything."

I hold my hands up in defense. "Okay, I promise not to mistake this as you forgiving me."

"Good, let's go."

As I grab my keys, I hear Cherry shout to her mom and Frankie. "I got us a lift, let's go."

I'd hoped to get a few minutes alone with Cherry but endearing myself to her mom and friend is a good second. Cherry pushes her mom into the front seat and climbs in the back with Frankie, who is almost bouncing with excitement.

"Oh my God, do you think they'll name him Frank?"

I snort but hide it with a cough when Cherry kicks the back of my seat.

"I think they'll be more likely to name him after her dad or his."

"I guess, so but it would be fun to have another Frankie around."

I watch in the rear-view mirror as Cherry rests her head on her friend's shoulder, and jealousy slams into my gut even though I know he'd never be interested in her or vice versa. It wasn't that, it was the intimacy of her leaning on him and sharing her joy and excitement with him when I want her to share it with me.

I know I have no right, but it doesn't stop the feeling twisting in my belly.

"The world doesn't have the energy for two of you, my boy."

I glance at Darla who gives me a soft smile. She has a grace about her and a silent strength that I wonder if others see as clearly as I do. Her eyes twinkle and in that moment, I hate myself for the part I'd played in her daughter losing her dream.

Now I sit in a car with the woman I'd hurt and the people who loved her, and I get the strongest suspicion that Darla knows who I am. That she can see straight through the mask of civility I wear to the damaged little boy beneath.

We arrive at the hospital, and I hang back a little, waiting for Hank and Vivian, wanting to give Cherry the space she deserves to enjoy this with the people who love her.

The waiting room outside Lexi and Hunter's private room is full of laughter and chatter as we wait for news. Nurses and doctors come and go, each giving us a reassuring smile as they go in and out of the room. Hours pass and people talk and bonds are formed in the room. Bonds that I know will encircle their child with so much love and support and I find I want to be a part of that more than I ever realized. Until now, Lexi and her pregnancy have been almost ephemeral, unreal, and the baby hadn't been real either but now I felt the strongest urge to protect him.

"Hey, I got you this."

Blinking, I look up at Cherry holding a cup of coffee in front of me. "Thank you." I take a sip and smile. "You remember how I take it."

Her shrug is accompanied by a delicate blush on her cheeks. "Can I sit?"

I scoot sideways to give her room and she sits beside me, her shoulder grazing my arm.

"I know this is hard, Jake, but I think we should try and put the past behind us so that we can be there for Hunter and Lexi. Whatever this is with Dean isn't finished yet, and I don't want this little boy growing up surrounded by people fighting."

"I agree."

"That doesn't mean I forgive you, or we're friends. I just don't want us to be enemies either, at least not in front of them."

"Thank you, Blossom. I know I hurt you, and I know any apology I give you won't make up for what happened."

Cherry sighs. "It's done. Let's just get through this and then we don't have to see each other again until his christening or birthday party."

"I want more than that."

Cherry looks at me then, a sad tired look on her pretty face, that makes my gut clench.

"I can't give you more, Jake. I can't be your friend so let's just be civil for them."

Before I can respond, the door to the delivery suite opens and we all stand as Hunter walks out with the biggest smile on his face.

"Is he here?" Cherry asks as she moves to stand beside Cassie. I miss her instantly, but my attention is on my best friend who is struggling to hide his emotions.

"Yes, he's absolutely beautiful. Lexi did so well, and they're both perfect." Everyone surges forward to hug him and I see tears streaming down Cherry's cheeks as she turns to look at me. We share a moment of complete understanding before Hunter wraps her in his arms.

"Thank you for making my friend so happy."

Hunter hugs her tight and I shake his hand as he lets her go, a grin on his face that I've never seen before. I know in that moment that everything is changing, that our friendship will evolve because they'll always be his priority. It's how I know he'll be an amazing father to his son.

"Can we see them?" Elena asks.

"Yes, of course. She wants to see you all." Hunter opens the door and precedes us in taking a place next to Lexi. Oohs and aahs are exclaimed over the baby. Tears of joy are cried—and more hugs are passed out.

"What are you calling him?" Cosmo asks.

Lexi looks at Hunter with a nod and a grin. "Theo Henry Cosmo McKenzie," he announces as they watch their father's reactions.

Gasps of delight are heard around the room and I watch the man, who is more of a father to me than I deserve, tear up. He embraces his son hard, and I know that I'll cherish this moment for a long time to come.

"Would you like to hold him?"

"Yes, please." Hank sits in the chair beside Lexi, and Hunter lays his son in his father's arms. The look of love I see in his eyes touches me deeply.

"How much does he weigh?" Cherry asks as she leans over Hank and touches Theo's tiny fingers. I get the strongest image of her looking at our child that way and a well of grief opens inside my chest at all we lost.

"He was a whopping nine pounds, four ounces," Lexi replies.

"Wow, my ocean comment wasn't far off." She laughs but it's an inside joke that only the two friends understand. I see their bond and know how loyal she is to those she loves. It's why my betrayal cut so deep.

I stiffen as Hunter approaches me. "Got a second?" He nods to the door and I take one last look before he ejects me from the cozy scene before me.

We walk down the corridor a little before we sit in the chairs that we occupied for hours as we waited for Theo to enter the world.

Knowing he should be with Lexi, not out here handling me, I begin. "I know what you're going to say, Mac. I just wanted to see that the baby and Lexi are okay. I'll leave you in peace now." I turn to leave and Hunter calls me back.

"Jake, just wait a sec."

I stop and turn, I know the dejection I'm feeling is clear on my face. "Why? So, you can tell me what an asshole I've been? I know that, okay? I've apologized to Lexi. It was a douchebag move and I have no excuse."

"You were a dick, but I could've handled things better, too. The thing is, Lexi comes first. You cross her, then you cross me. That said, this whole year has been fucked up with one thing or another. Yes, you messed up but I'm ready to put it behind us if you are."

I process his words like the second chance they are before I let a grin split my face and I offer him my hand. "So, you're a dad now. Does that mean you're going to get boring and start drinking wheatgrass smoothies instead of coming out with me?"

"Fuck off, Jake. I've never touched a wheatgrass smoothie in my life and I don't intend to start now."

We move toward the door as if Hunter has an imaginary line that keeps him tethered close to the woman he loves and his son.

"Why don't we talk about the way you keep looking at Cherry."

I swallow past the pain and shake my head. I can't tell him what happened between us, not yet, and maybe not ever. "Yeah, okay, point taken. Can we just go coo over your son instead?"

"Sure, let's do that."

I catch Cherry's eyes as I walk in, my own drawn to her like the moon to the sun. She looks away first and I know what I should do next, I'm just not sure if I can.

18. Cherry

"Why are you here?"

Folding my arms in front of me, I glare at Jake who is working on his laptop at the end of the counter. My shop seems to have become his new base of operations and I don't like it, because I'm getting far too used to having him around and that's a dangerous thing. Not that we talk much, or do anything really, we kind of tiptoe around each other in a forced politeness.

Jake looks up from his screen and lifts his eyebrow in question as if I'm stupid. "You know why, Blossom."

"I don't need your help." I throw up my hands determined to talk to Lexi about this now that Theo is here and she's under slightly less stress. She and Hunter are in the Hamptons this weekend but when she comes back, she needs to call Jake off. Eight weeks of seeing him almost every day is too much for my poor heart.

"Maybe not but you have it anyway."

Not willing to deal with him anymore, I studiously ignore him, or at least I try to. Jake is too much of a presence to be ignored though. Even silent, he's loud. I'm aware of every move he makes. My phone ringing makes me jump, but that turns into a groan of frustration when I see Harvey's name on the screen.

Grabbing it up, I head to the back for some privacy. This call isn't going to be any less frustrating than the others, I'm sure. "Hey, Harvey, tell me you have some good news."

I hear a beleaguered sigh down the phone and roll my eyes to the heavens as he begins his litany of excuses. "Cherry, you should take the offer from KLM. You don't have the finances to fight them and win. At this point, you have the upper hand but once they've bled you dry they'll lower the offer for the property."

My blood almost boils with anger at the injustice of what these people are trying to do. "So that's it? I just have to let my mom lose the one thing in her life that brings her joy?"

"I wish I could say no, but a corporation this size has almost limitless funding. You can't win, Cherry. Not unless you have a fairy godmother tucked away somewhere."

I know I could ask Hunter. He'd help me in a minute, but I'd never abuse my friendships like that, and he and Lexi have enough on their plate.

Blowing out a breath, I feel nauseous anxiety build in my belly. A sick feeling that I'm going to have to sell my mom's salon to some rich developer who won't take no for an answer. "Okay, Harvey. Don't say anything to KLM yet. Just give me a week to think about it."

"It's the right thing to do, Cherry."

"I'll call you."

Hanging up, I close my eyes and lean my forehead against the wall of the storeroom as defeat washes over me.

"Why are you dealing with KLM?"

I push off the wall and move past Jake into the larger space of the showroom, busying myself shifting pieces around so I don't have to answer.

"Cherry, answer me, damn it!"

"No." I whirl on him in frustration. "My life is none of your business so keep out of it."

Jake stalks toward me, his muscles almost vibrating with tension and I feel my body respond to his anger. He has no right to poke his nose into my private life. Yet underneath my anger, I can feel the heat of desire curl inside me. He's a stunning specimen of a man and I know from personal experience that he has all the attributes and skill to back it up.

Seizing my arms, he gives me a gentle shake. "Do not fuck with me about this, Blossom. Tell me who that was or, so help me God, I'll turn you over my knee."

My skin prickles at his threat, my breaths coming quicker as I stare at him. What would it feel like to give in just this once and let my guard down enough to take what I need from him? To let his touch soothe away the worries and just let me feel for a while. Fighting with Jake has become my favorite thing to do. The banter we share is a distraction from the life that feels like it's too much.

"You wouldn't dare."

His hand moves swiftly, clamping around my throat in a grip that is just tight enough to remind me of his power over me but not tight enough to leave a mark. His eyes darken, his other hand sliding from my arm to my hip, as pulls me closer to his hard body.

A shiver runs through me as I fight the urge to let go and let him control me, like I know nobody else ever can.

"Wouldn't I, Cherry Blossom? You don't think I'll slide that sinful piece of fabric you call a skirt up and over that sexy ass. That I wouldn't tear those silk panties I know you wear from your body and lay you over my knee right here, right now."

His words are like a caress over my heated skin. Conjuring images in my mind that make my body pant. Yet still I poke and push, wanting him to lose control. "I'd fight you."

My nipples peak against my blouse desperate for his touch, and I feel him harden against my belly. The thick length of him so close makes my mouth flood with saliva.

"You think that puts me off, Blossom? You think the thought of having to fight you, having to tame you, turns me off? Feel me, feel how hard you make me, every fucking day."

I can hear the possessive hunger in his voice and my panties are soaked from it. His thumb caresses my pulse as it beats faster and his slow smirk shows how aware he is of what he does to me.

"You want it, don't you, Cherry Blossom? You want me to take you, to show you who owns this body."

His head dips and his lips feather against my throat as I tilt my head a little, my eyes falling closed. My denial is swift and automatic, even as the evidence of my lie, beats against his thumb. "I want nothing from you. You disgust me."

Jake chuckles but it's dark and husky, full of danger. "How about a wager?"

"You want to gamble with me, Jake?"

God, this banter is hotter than all the sex I've had in the last ten years.

"Yes, let's gamble. If I can make you come in under a minute, you tell me what your involvement is with KLM."

"And if you can't, what do I get?"

I feel fairly confident he'll lose this one because climaxing isn't something I find easy these days. Even my toys need some finesse to get the job done.

"What do you want?"

"You tell me why you set me up."

His eyes fall closed as if looking at me is too painful, but as I go to pull away he tightens his grip, his eyes springing open. "Deal."

With that he lifts me by my waist and carries me to the back storeroom, pushing the door almost closed so we're hidden from sight.

"I need to close up if we're going to do this."

Jake smirks as he shrugs his jacket from his shoulders and begins to fold his shirt sleeves up.

"What, worried someone might hear you scream my name, Blossom?"

"As if, I'm worried a customer will hear you cry when you lose."

"I never lose, Blossom."

His confidence gives me pause, but I know this is one time he *will* lose.

As I go to move, he catches my hand and pulls me against him, pinning me against the wall with his body. "Leave it."

I'd forgotten what it felt like to have Jake command me and instantly my body acquiesces to his demand. "Set your timer, Jake."

He smirks as he presses a button on his fifty-thousand-dollar watch, then drops to his knees. His hands smooth up my calves, pushing my skirt up as he exposes my panty-covered pussy. A growl escapes him as he looks at me and rips the lace away like it is nothing. His head dips and his tongue slides over my slit, forcing a moan from my lips. I grip his shoulders for support as he throws my leg over his shoulder and sucks my clit between his lips.

My head bangs against the wall as pleasure shoots up my body. Every nerve in my body is tingling as he works me over. His tongue flicks my clit as he spears two fingers inside me and curls them toward my G-spot. I move my hips, riding his face as I begin to lose control. My pussy clenches and he hums against my skin as if he's getting off on this as much as me.

The sound is all I need to push me over the edge into that bright abyss of bursting color. My fingers pull at his hair, my breathing is a pant and I scream his name as a climax so powerful it almost takes my legs from me slams through me.

Jake holds me steady, his lips placing tender kisses against my pussy as my orgasm recedes. I become aware of a faint beeping sound and look down to find Jake watching me.

"You win, Jake."

Taking my shredded panties from the floor, he pockets them and smooths my skirt down over my hips before standing in front of me. Now the intimacy is over I feel exposed, raw, the need to put space between us almost makes me desperate but I won't run, not again.

"Tell me."

Ducking my head, I move past him to the mirror so I can fix my hair. As I examine my flushed cheeks, I see him looming behind me, watching me closely. "KLM is trying to buy my mother's hair salon. They want to develop the land it's on, but it's the one place that saved her after my dad died. I don't want her to lose it."

"What did your lawyer say?"

"That KLM has too much money and will bleed me dry and get the land anyway."

"What does your mother say?"

"She doesn't know and she won't know. The building is in my name because that's how my father set up his will. It's why I'm dealing with them."

"Your lawyer's right. They're ruthless and have deep pockets."

"I'm not giving in, Jake. I won't be bullied by them."

"Then let me help you. I've dealt with a lot of companies like this and I know how the game is played."

I'm already shaking my head before he can finish. "No."

His hand rubs the back of his neck as he looks at me with frustration. "Why not?"

I have no choice but to give him the truth no matter how ugly it feels after what just happened. "I don't trust you."

His head snaps back slightly, a wince making him seem younger. Part of me wants to call my words back, but I can't. He did this and he's the one forcing his presence on me, not the other way around.

He gives me a nod, his lips pursed, and turns to leave the room, taking a chunk out of my heart with his wounded expression. He stops and turns and I wonder what threat he'll make, what coercion he'll use to force my hand, but he doesn't do any of those things.

"For the record, I didn't steal those exam papers. I was being blackmailed and did what I thought was the best thing to protect the woman I loved."

Before I can respond he is gone. My hand shakes as I straighten my blouse and skirt, I try to process his words, but none of it makes sense. Why has he told me this now? Why lie and is he lying now or then? One answered question leaves me with so many more unanswered ones.

19. Cherry

I'm just going through some inventory for the shop, trying to concentrate on work instead of the frustrating man who's been MIA since he dropped his last bombshell. The call from Lexi late Sunday night saying that Dean had sent her threatening texts had put everyone on edge too. That man needs to be taken down hard, and I have no doubt if he comes after Lexi and Theo, Hunter will have no hesitation in doing just that.

When Hunter calls me frantic not thirty minutes later, I hope it's with an update to say Dean is in jail, but it's my worst nightmare come to life.

"Cherry, he took her. That bastard has Lexi and my son."

Jumping up, I feel all my limbs begin to shake with fear. My heart races at the thought of that lunatic having Lexi and Theo. "How? When?"

"She took Theo to the doctor because he felt warm. Dean killed her protection officers and took her from the side of the road."

"I'm coming to you. Hunter, we will get them back, I promise you."

I know I'm making promises I can't possibly have any control over, but the need to reassure him is so strong I don't think.

"No, stay there and lock the door. Jake is coming to collect you and bring you here."

"Okay."

Hunter hangs up and I look around me at the wonderful business I've built with my best friend, and wonder if it's all going to end because of one sick man. The thought of losing Lexi makes me sink to my knees on a sob so guttural it's almost animal.

Anguish and terror have me folding in on myself, as I imagine the fear she must be feeling. I know Lexi and I know she'd die protecting her son if it comes to it. I pull my knees to my chest and try to breathe but it feels like everything is stuck. The air in my lungs is thick and suffocating.

I want to scream and wail, but I can't get air in. I feel like I'm dying as everything feels far away, and muted. My vision blurs as I see a figure walk towards me and begin to scramble away as he crouches closer.

"Cherry, baby, it's me."

"Jake?"

He folds around me and lifts me, his arm under my knees, and carries me into the back office, before sitting us both on the couch, with me on his lap. His arms feel tight and secure as he holds me to him and rocks me like I'm fragile.

"Breathe with me, Blossom." Placing my hand over his heart he lays his over mine and begins to breathe slowly in and out. Surrounded by his familiar scent and the warm security of his body, I begin to breathe with him, my body relaxing, the shakes that had wracked my body subsiding.

"He took her, Jake."

"I know, Blossom, but we're gonna get her back."

Lifting my head, I look into the handsome face that has been at the center of some of my happiest memories and some of my worst and see his belief in what he said.

"Okay." I don't know why I choose to believe him, but I do.

"Come on, let's take you to Hunter's. He needs us right now and we should all be together."

Silently we drive to Hunter's and Lexi's home, which is set up like mission control with huge trained mercenaries moving around like this is their show. I sit with Jake, Vivian, and Hank, as Hunter paces like a caged lion. After my mental breakdown at the shop, Jake has hardly left my side, but I'm feeling stronger and more focused now that I have others to concentrate on.

Yet sitting here doing nothing feels wrong, the heavy weight of helplessness making me want to claw my eyes out. Jumping up, I stride over to the scary hot guy who seems to be in charge and tap him on the shoulder. He turns, pinning me with a cool gaze that holds no warmth, only cold intelligence and control.

I force a shiver away and lift my chin. "I want an update."

"There is no update. You know what we know, so let us do our jobs."

Any other time, I would've swooned at his gorgeous British accent, but not now. Not when my best friend is at the mercy of a monster. "This is bullshit. We should know something by now."

"The best thing you can do is keep calm and remain with your friends."

Folding my arms, I lift a brow as Jake comes to stand behind me. "Oh, really? Is that the best thing to do, you condescending asshole?"

"Blossom, he's doing his best."

"Well, it's not enough and I can't sit here and do nothing."

"How well do you know Lexi?"

I glared at Mr. Tall, dark, and dangerous, knowing my anger is misplaced but not caring. "She's been my best friend since school. She's my business partner, my ride or die."

"Do you have a key to her home?"

"Of course."

"Okay, go there and look for anything that might be out of place. You know her best so look through paperwork for anything that might tell us where he's taken her."

"On it."

Spinning with a sense of purpose, I stride toward the door.

"Hey, wait up."

"What are you doing, Jake?" I ask as he steps into the elevator behind me. He gives me a look that indicates I'm stupid for even asking. "You don't need to come with me."

"I'm not letting you go alone so just shut up and tell me where to go."

I could argue but I know it won't do any good, so I just give him directions to Lexi's old home and let him drive.

It feels weird being here without her. Most of her things are gone, and the house has a sad air of ghosts from another life in it. It's hard to explain because I've spent so much time here with her, with her and Dean, and now it's like remembering a movie I once watched.

We spend hours looking for clues, some things we pass on to Hunter and his team in the hopes it helps but most of it is as useless as I feel.

Around nine we get the call. Lexi has been found but she's in a bad way. Theo is still missing. As we race to the hospital, Jake grips my hand tight, as if to quiet my racing thoughts.

When we reach the department, we're ushered in by Hunter's security team and find Vivian and Hank with Cassie. I rush toward them and Vivian hugs me close, as Jake hugs Hank. In this, we're an unbreakable unit. Nothing else matters right now, not the past, not the future, just getting Theo back and making sure Lexi is okay.

"What have they said?" Jake takes charge, asking the question that seems stuck in my throat.

"It's bad. They brought her in via life-flight. She has multiple injuries, including a head injury."

"Oh God." My hand covers my mouth and I sway towards Jake who wraps his arm around my shoulders, holding me up.

"Hunter is speaking to the doctor now."

Nodding, I let Jake lead me toward a chair and ease me down. Sitting next to me, he pulls me close and I rest my head on his shoulder. He's my strength right now, when deep down I know he's my weakness.

We wait for hours, getting updates on Lexi that do nothing to ease my fears. At some point, we get word that they've found Theo and Hunter heads out with the team to rescue his son. My best friend is still fighting for her life. That animal beat her head in and left her in the river to die, but she fought. She fought for her son and for the man she loves.

I know that kind of love. I felt it for the man who hasn't left my side. The difference is Hunter is right there fighting with Lexi, and when it came down to it, Jake didn't do the same for me.

I mull over his words as the clock ticks and the hours pass. He'd said he didn't steal the papers and part of me believes that, but it doesn't matter because he let me take the fall either way, and nothing can excuse that.

Sitting up, I move away from his warmth, knowing that I can't rely on it. I'd thought I could but it was a lie.

"You doing okay?"

I nod and stand, pretending to stretch, but really it's because I can't bear to be near him and not touch him. He's behaving like the man I fell in love with and it's confusing me too much when I can't afford to let myself be sucked in again. "Just stretching my legs."

I can feel him watching me as I walk to the window and look out over the city. People are going about their lives without any idea of the trauma and drama happening in this room. A phone rings behind me and I twist to see Hank answer. The relief that falls across his face, followed by the smile, tells me all I need to know.

Theo is safe. I wait in silence as Hank speaks and nods, my heart lighter than it has been in a very long time, especially when he announces that Dean is dead. My best friend's nightmare is over.

Glancing across at Jake, I see him watching me and know that mine is far from over. How can it be when I'm still in love with the devil that broke me?

20. Jake

For the past three weeks, Cherry has ignored every attempt I've made to speak with her and it's grinding my last nerve. Watching Hunter and Lexi recover from the trauma of her kidnapping and injuries has taught me a very valuable lesson and that is that life is short. It's short and it's precious and I'm too far gone for Cherry to waste another minute denying how I feel about her. I love her and I'm going to do whatever it takes to get her back. Starting with handling KLM.

"Joe, it's Jake Marshall. I have a job for you."

"Jake, long time no hear."

Joe is a shady character who I met on a case during my first year as a lawyer for Lungo. He's a fantastic private investigator but even better, he has a rather grey approach to how he gets things done. He's the man I call when I want something done off the books with no questions asked.

"Yeah, it's been a while. You still got a contact with the Mancini family? I need a sit-down."

Silence greets me and I hear Joe sucking on his cigarette before he blows out a breath. "You sure you want that, Jake? Getting in bed with the Mancini family is a big risk because they always make you pay up, and there's no getting out."

"Yes. It's worth it to me."

"Alright, let me make some calls."

Joe hangs up without another word and I sit back in my seat. My office at Lungo has always been my happy place. I look out over the city and know that I've made it. I'm at the height of my career. I have more money than I'll ever spend and I've earned it. I've turned my life around. I'm respected because of my own name now, not just because of my association with the McKenzie family.

Now, though, I found myself missing my setup on the end of Cherry's counter at the shop. With no need to worry about Dean hurting anyone, she and Lexi have hired help until Lexi goes back to work.

Taking out the worn file on my desk, I look at it and wonder how my life would've been if I'd just had access to this ten years ago. Would Cherry and I be married with a couple of kids? Would she still look at me as she had that day I told her I loved her, like I was the moon and she was the sun.

So many what-ifs and none of them matter because I'd let my fear and cowardice win. I should've told her when I found out. I should've gone to her and explained everything and let the chips fall. But I hadn't, I'd caved thinking I was protecting her but in truth, I was protecting myself.

Fingering the file, I placed it back in the drawer and locked it away. The time will come when I'll let her read every wrong deed I've done that has led us here, but not until I've fixed her future in stone. But first, I need to talk to Hunter.

Walking down to his office, I smile at Ruth, his secretary. "He free?"

"He is if you call harassing his girlfriend every ten minutes free."

I knock and wait for him to call enter before pushing inside.

Looking up, he gives me a half nod in greeting before frowning at his laptop screen. "What's up?"

"I need to tell you something."

I'm not sure if it's my tone or just that he knows me so well, but Hunter pushes away from his desk and walks towards me, ushering me towards the couches where he has a fridge and decanter of whiskey.

"Drink?"

I shake my head. "Nah, I gonna take the bike out after this."

"What's on your mind?"

"Do you remember me telling you about that girl from college? The one that got away?"

"I'm not senile, Jake, it was only a few weeks ago and, by the way, I'm still pissed you didn't tell me before."

"Yeah, well, you're gonna be more pissed when I tell you who it is."

Hunter groans. "Please don't say Lorelei."

"God, no."

"Then who?"

"Cherry."

"Cherry who?" Hunter frowns looking confused until I see the realization on his face. "No way."

"Yep. We met when you were out with your leg. I fell so hard, man. She was a whirlwind, beautiful, smart. Shit, you've met her."

Hunter dips his head silently. "What happened?"

"She friend-zoned me. She wasn't interested in getting involved. She'd worked so hard to get into Harvard. She was doing her degree in Architectural History, so I agreed to be friends. I knew she was it from day one, man. We became friends and eventually more. Honestly, I would've married that girl on the spot, but I knew we needed our degrees first and she needed to trust me. Losing her father had a huge impact on her."

"Lexi mentioned that. It must have been tough. How did it go wrong? You cheat?"

I shake my head, kinda pissed that he'd assume that, but

compared with the truth, it was better. "Never. I loved her. She was my entire world just like Lexi is yours."

Hunter holds his hands up. "Yet here we are."

"Nick Kendrick called me one night and told me he wanted me to steal the exam papers for the course Cherry was doing."

I see his lip curl at the mention of Kendrick. Hunter hates him almost as much as I do. "Oh fuck. Please tell me you didn't."

I stand and begin to pace angrily. "Of course not. I'll never do that to her. I told him no. He said I'll regret it and I called his bluff. The next day I got a call saying he'd had someone else steal the papers, but that he'd framed Cherry."

"How?"

"I'd taken Cherry to look at a rare book in the Dean's office. I'd broken us in but we didn't steal a thing. I swear I just wanted to do something nice for her."

Hunter scrubs his hands down his face. "Ah fuck, I don't like the sound of this."

"It was a shit show. Her face was all over the CCTV. Nick had edited it somehow to make it look like she took the papers but she never went near his desk. He'd also wiped my image from the video. He said I had to implicate Cherry and not give her an alibi. I told him to fuck off, but he told me if I didn't, he'd send her information I wouldn't want her to have."

"Which was? She would've forgiven you your past, Jake. Cherry is a hard ass but she's loyal to those she loves and it sounds like you two fell hard."

My chest feels like it's caving in as I relive those few days, the way she'd made me feel. "I know but would she forgive the boy who stole her father's car? Would she have forgiven me when I told her it was my fault he was walking on the road that night and got hit by that car?"

"Oh, shit. No!"

"Exactly. Nick sent me the file on the man whose car we stole.

Hank had always protected me before that, but when I realized, I felt trapped. I either told her I'd had a part in her dad's death and destroy her, or I let her get kicked out of Harvard for stealing and destroy her. It was an impossible situation. Either way, I broke her heart. She loved me, she trusted me, and I let her down." Sinking into the couch, I put my head in my hands, letting the despair I still felt for that choice bleed out.

The couch dips and I feel a hand on my shoulder. "I'm sorry, Jake. You should have told me."

"It gets worse. I found out after the fact that it was all a lie. Nick had made it up. The man who died wasn't her dad. He died two days before. I destroyed her life because I was a coward and, not just that, I was incompetent."

"Mother fucker."

"Right. I hate him, Mac. I fucking hate him, but I hate myself more. I should have just told her."

"It was an impossible situation, Jake."

"I stole her dream."

"No, Nick Kendrick did that just to fuck with you."

"But being with me cost her. She paid the price for being with me."

We sit in silence as Hunter processes the news and I feel like a weight has lifted just a little, but I'm not done with the revelations. "KLM is going after her mother's hair salon. The building is in Cherry's name and they want the land."

"What?"

"She hired a lawyer but he's useless. Taking kickbacks from KLM to persuade her to sell."

"Why didn't she come to me? I would have helped her."

"Pride. Cherry doesn't like to ask for help."

"So what's the plan? I assume you have one." Hunter smiles and it's like watching a shark grin. He's hungry for blood, but not as hungry as me.

"I'm taking him down. I've asked for a sit-down with the Mancini family. He's in bed with them but I'm going to owe them a favor if it means I get to end him."

Hunter whistles and I know this is big. The Mancini family isn't just a powerful family, they were *Mi Famiglia*. The Italian mob who ran the underbelly of this great country.

"You sure about this?"

I nod. "I'll give you my resignation so you and Hank don't get tangled up in this."

Hunter is already shaking his head. "No way. You're in, I'm in, and Dad will feel the same."

"I can't ask you to do that, Mac. This could get messy, and you have a family now."

"You're my family too, Jake."

"I appreciate that, but no."

"It wasn't a question. I'm gonna talk to Dad and we're gonna figure this out as a family. We may not need to talk to Mancini. Nick Kendrick is as dirty as fuck. There's bound to be a way we can find something on him."

"I've already asked for the meet."

"Then call it off."

"It's too late."

"Please, Jake, let me speak to Dad about this before you make any moves you can't come back from."

"Fine but either way, Nick is done."

"I agree. Now, the important question is, what are you going to do about Cherry?"

"I love her, Mac. I never stopped, and I want her back. I just need to figure out how the hell I can fix this before I tell her the truth."

"You should tell her now."

I shook my head. "No, I have to win her over first, remind her of the good times, of the chemistry between us."

"Well, this sure does explain the fireworks when you two are in the same room together."

I smile for the first time since finding out KLM had a bead on Cherry's mom's place.

"So what's the plan?"

"I'm gonna be where she is. Every time she turns around, I'm gonna be there."

"It won't be easy. I don't know her well but I do know she's stubborn and getting kicked out of Harvard will have left a bruise."

I punch his arm. "You're not helping, Mac."

He grins. "But I know a woman who might help."

I tip my head and give it a short shake. "No, don't involve Lexi. I need Cherry to know she has her best friend on her side."

"Alright, Jake."

I stand, needing to get out on my bike, and just forget about everything but the open road for a while.

"Jake?"

I swing back to look at my friend, who is still sitting on the couch, looking pensive. "You should have told me. I'd have been there."

"I know."

He would have, they all would have but I'd put enough pressure on his family, and adding to it or being a burden to them wasn't something I wanted to do. Not now and not ever.

21. Cherry

THE FRONT DOOR TO THE SHOP OPENS AND I LOOK UP WITH A smile, ready to greet my customer, but it freezes on my face when I see Jake walk in instead. He isn't dressed for work, the suit has been replaced by worn jeans that hang off his hips. A V-neck white tee molds to his muscular chest and I fight the urge to wet my lips. His feet are encased in tattered biker boots, and he still wears the jacket he'd had back then.

He looks like my Jake, the one who broke my heart but also the one who made it beat faster, who'd text me 'good morning, beautiful' or some other sweet greeting each day, just like the one I'd received this morning. My heart beat harder in my chest as he grins and walks closer.

"Good morning, Blossom."

God, why did he have to be so hot? Folding my arms over my chest, I cock my hip and glare. "What do you want?"

"Is it too cliché to say you?" He scrubs his chin and tries giving me a hopeful look.

"Don't be cute."

As he leans his elbows on my counter, his scent surrounds me, but this time I detect the subtle hint of motor oil too. Nostalgia invades my senses and I can't help but think of him on his bike. How it had felt to hold on to him and feel like every turn we made, no matter how fast or dangerous, knowing he'd always protect me.

"I want to show you something."

I narrowed my eyes in suspicion. "What?"

"I can't tell you. This is something you need to see in the flesh."

I'm intrigued, and a big part of me wants to spend time with him, wants to see whatever he wants to show me, but a bigger part knows it's too risky. Jake has hurt me more than anyone ever has, and I can't just forgive what he'd done. "I'm busy."

"The shop closes in ten minutes. I know you're only open for half a day on Saturday."

It was true. We didn't get enough footfall on a Saturday to warrant remaining open, so I usually used the afternoon to work on a room design. "That doesn't mean I'm not busy. I might have a date or client coming to see me."

The scowl on his handsome face is worth the white lie I'm about to tell and I hope like hell my next client will go along with it when he arrives.

"Who? I didn't know you were seeing someone?"

His indignation almost makes me laugh and I have to roll my lips between my teeth to hide my mirth. "Why would you? We aren't friends."

It is fleeting, but I see the wound I inflict land before he brushes it off with a smile. I wish I could say I don't care, that hurting him gives me some kind of satisfaction, but it doesn't.

"No, but that doesn't mean I don't care, Blossom. I know I hurt you but I never stopped caring."

"Don't, Jake. I don't want to talk about the past. You keep giving me small nuggets of information but never a true picture. So until you can do that, I don't want to hear it."

"Fair enough. I can agree to that. So, what time will you be free and where is he taking you? You better not have met on a dating website. Those things are full of creeps."

"Oh, are you on there too?"

"Haha, very funny. I'm serious, Blossom. I don't want you putting yourself in risky situations."

"Well, what you want is no concern of mine, but for the record, I know this man well and we met in a bar."

A frown mars his handsome brow, his lips thinning in annoyance. "I don't like it."

I gave him a big fake smile. "I don't care."

Before he can say more, the door opens again and my smile is genuine as I rush around the counter and run to the man who just walked in. He catches me in his arms and spins me around as I laugh.

"How's my favorite girl in the world?"

Eddie Crowe holds me off the ground in his big arms and gives me the grin that makes millions of his fans swoon. As the most famous country music star of the moment, he sings to packed arenas about love and heartbreak. We'd met on a night out with Lexi when he played an impromptu acoustic set, just before his star began to rise.

We'd hooked up once, but it never went as far as sex, just some hot making out, then decided we were better off as friends. Both of us had had our hearts broken, and so a friendship had developed. His blue eyes twinkle and his thick, dark hair falls to his shoulders, making him the pin-up choice of every woman from fifteen to fifty, but for me, it was his voice that melted butter. Deep and full of gravel, but with that lazy southern twang that makes you think of whispered secrets and sultry nights.

"I'm good, Eddie. I missed you."

"Missed you too, sugar."

"So I have a situation I could use some help with." My voice is low enough that only Eddie will hear.

"It involve the man glaring at me like he wants to kill me?"

"Yeah, that's Jake."

Eddie's brows shoot up a little before he rocks his head slowly. "Okay. I got you, baby girl. Lead the way."

A wave of warmth falls over me at how lucky I am to have this man as my friend.

Grabbing his hand, I tow him toward the counter where Jake is watching us with a measured expression. I can practically feel the tension dripping off him. It serves him right, thinking he could march back into my life like what he'd done was nothing.

"Eddie, this is Jake, a friend of Hunter's."

I still hold Eddie's hand and he gives mine a little squeeze before he offers his hand to Jake. "Nice to meet you."

"Nice to meet you, too, and I'm a very old friend of Cherry's. We go way back."

Eddie chuckles as he pulls me closer, wrapping an arm around my back and pasting me to his hard body. I play along, placing my hand on his chest and gazing up at him.

"Good to know." Eddie looked around the store before giving his attention back to Jake. "You here for some furniture?"

"No, I'm here for Cherry." Jake pins me with a gaze that says 'game on'. "Aren't I, Blossom?"

"Honestly, I'm not sure why you're here, Jake."

"I wanted to show you something, remember?"

"Well, make an appointment and I'll look then."

"Yeah, I'll do that."

Jake's slow, steady breaths and the tick in his jaw show how annoyed he is by not getting his own way. Good. It will do him good to know the world doesn't revolve around him.

"That your bike outside?"

Jake brought his bike? How had I missed that?

"Yeah. You ride?"

"Not as much as I used to, but yeah I do. That's a sweet ride."

"Yeah, it's a custom Arch KRGT-1."

"Nice. I wish I had the time to get out more."

"Yeah, I know the feeling. Nothing like your bike, your girl, and the open road. Hey, Blossom?"

What is happening here? These two idiots are bonding over a bike, even if said bike was a thing of absolute beauty.

"I'll take your word for it."

I give Eddie a sly pinch and he jumps a little before seeming to get the memo that he wasn't here to bond with Jake but to be my buffer.

Giving me a look of absolute adoration, he focuses back on me. "We should get going, baby girl."

"Of course." I turn to Jake with a sugary smile. "Sorry, Jake, I need to close up. Eddie and I have plans this afternoon."

I pull out of Eddie's arms and he lets his hand run down my arm as if he can't possibly let me go longer than a second. "Yeah, we've got plans all afternoon, sugar."

You'd need to be an idiot to miss the implication in Eddie's words and Jake was no idiot. His head tips back, his legs spread and he looks dangerous all of a sudden. Like he wants to rip Eddie apart.

"I'll let you go, but can I just get one word in private, first?"

That's the last thing I need after poking the bear for the last five minutes. "I don't—"

"It's about Lexi."

I narrow my eyes at him knowing he's up to something, but not willing to take the risk that he did want to talk about Lexi and ignoring him. "Oh, okay. Do you mind, Eddie?"

Eddie cups my cheek with a wink, playing his part to perfection. "Course not, sugar."

I lead the way to the back room and see Jake close the door and give Eddie a smug smile. Before I can start he's stepped into my personal space and has me pinned between his hands on either side of my desk. A whoosh of air leaves me as I lay my fingers on his chest with the idea of pushing him back, but he covers my fingers with his hand, pressing my hands against his pecs.

"Are you really seeing that playboy?"

His question is almost a snarl and I feel a grave sense of satisfaction that my plan has worked. "Eddie isn't a playboy."

"Oh, please. He has a different woman on his arm every week."

"Eddie and I are different." Not a lie. We were different in that I had no intention of being anything more than his friend and he feels the same way.

"He tell you that?"

Tilting my chin, I give him a haughty smile, but the warmth of his body beneath my fingertips takes the bite out of my words. "Yes, he did, and I believe him because he isn't a lying jerk like some people I know."

"He's not right for you," he says again through gritted teeth, a vein pulsing in his temple so hard I think he might have a stroke.

"Disagree."

"Have you fucked him?"

"My sex life is none of your business."

His body relaxes just a fraction. "You haven't."

"Well, even if I haven't today, hopefully by tomorrow I will have. More than once."

A growl comes from deep inside his throat as he crowds me back, his head dipping to my neck and skimming his lips over my pounding pulse. My eyes fall closed as desire makes me light-headed.

"I can still taste you on my tongue, Blossom. Every time I jerk off, it's with the memory of your pussy wrapped around my cock, the sweet salt of your climax on my lips. He doesn't get that."

My breaths become choppy as I picture his words, and feel his lips on my skin. "He gets whatever I decide to give him."

Jake lifts his head, his hooded eyes heavy with hunger. "If he touches you, he dies."

I start to roll my eyes, but he lifts his finger to my neck, a dangerous look of determination on his face.

"I mean it, Blossom. He touches you, I'll kill him."

With that he pushes off me, dropping my hand from his chest, and walks out the door.

My body sags against the desk as I hear the door to the shop open and close and then the roar of a powerful motorbike. My hand trembles as I push off the desk and blow out a breath.

I thought I'd seen every side of Jake, but that right then had been different. He'd meant every word of that threat and I should be afraid. I should be freaking out, but I wasn't. I was turned on.

"So, that's the infamous Jake."

I nod at Eddie who stands in the doorway, his shoulder braced against the jam, hands in his pockets.

He looks calm, almost amused. "Yep, that's him."

"Not what I imagined if I'm honest, sugar."

On wobbly legs, I push past Eddie, not sure how to respond to his comment. I feel him at my back as I lock up the shop and set the alarm. The sun is shining as we leave and I tip my face up and close my eyes, letting the warmth breathe joy back into me.

The last few months have been a slog, and it's taken everything in me to remain strong and keep my mask in place. I am the strong one, the one who fights for her friends and family, who smiles despite feeling hollow inside some days.

"You good, sugar? We can do this another day."

Pasting a smile on my face, I open my eyes and grin at Eddie. "Don't be silly. I said I'd look at your plans and I will. I'm excited to see them."

"Appreciate that, but I'm not sure your man does." Eddie nods his head toward the end of the road, where I see a sleek black bike with a scary ominous rider watching me from beneath his helmet, visor raised.

I clench my thighs as heat floods my body. Even from this distance, our connection is tenable. Like a live wire that pulls between us and sends pulses of electricity bouncing along the line.

"He's not my man."

"Yeah, I think he is, sugar."

I can't tear my gaze away as I continue my conversation with Eddie who stands at my back. "He hurt me."

"We all make mistakes, Cherry."

"I know, but I'm not sure I can forgive him."

"I'm not sure you have a choice. That man isn't giving up and the chemistry between you is atomic bomb level."

"If you mean destructive, then I agree."

A chuckle is all I get in response as he opens the door to the black Range Rover waiting at the curb. I watch as Jake snaps his visor closed, revs his engine, and rides away with a sense of inevitability that makes a thrill run through me.

22. Jake

I don't know how a penthouse worth millions can feel like a jail cell, but that's exactly how it feels as I pace the halls of my home. I can't stop thinking about Cherry in that fucker's arms. How she looked at him with such adoration and love.

For some reason, it had never occurred to me that she might be dating someone. Probably because, for me, the second I saw her again, she was all I could think about. Maybe that's why I'm so uptight, I haven't gotten laid in months. No other woman holds any interest for me. No other woman even begins to compare with my Cherry Blossom.

I check my watch for what feels like the thousandth time and wonder what she's doing. Is she writhing beneath him, is she screaming his name? Bile rushes up my throat at the thought, a pain so savage in my gut that I can hardly breathe.

I stride to my home gym and try to work off some of the anger and pain. I run until my legs feel like Jello. I lift weights until my arms shake and still this leashed energy inside me fills my brain with images that make me want to put my head in the blender. I shower and make myself a protein smoothy, not really caring for the taste but knowing my body needs the fuel.

Checking the time again, I see it's past ten. I wonder if she's home or if her stunning, pliant body is laid out on his sheets like a gift. Despite my fury, my dick hardens at the thought of her like that. Cherry is a goddess and was always meant to be worshipped, not by other men, but by me and I have to find some way to convince her that what we had was real and that it's still real.

Grabbing my keys, I head out on the bike, not really sure where I'm going, but needing to be out where I feel free. Ever since the night my sister died, I've had this almost uncontrollable urge for fresh air on my face. It's why I hate to fly long haul, too much time without access to fresh air.

My therapist says it's because of the fire that killed my baby sister and she's probably right. It's also why I never attend bonfire celebrations. The smell of smoke turns my stomach and makes me want to run.

Rounding the corner, I realize I've driven to Cherry's place. Glancing up, I see her bedroom light on and wonder if he's there. If Eddie Crowe has stolen her away, and my chance of anything with her is gone for good.

No!

My brain rejects that idea, instantly. I didn't get where I am today by backing down when things get hard and giving up when I want something, and I've never wanted anything more than I want Blossom.

Swinging my leg off my bike, I stride toward her door. I wrap my knuckles hard and wait, praying he doesn't answer the door. I don't want to fight the biggest star in the music industry right now, but if he's laid a finger on my girl, I'm gonna break every bone in his hand.

A shadow passes the glass and disappears. I knock again, taking out my frustration on the door. "Blossom, open the damn door before I kick it in."

"Go away, Jake, I'm busy."

Gritting my teeth, I suck in breath through my nose. "You better not have that fucker in your bed. I warned you what would happen." I know for a fact one of two things will happen next. She'll either call the cops on me, or she'll answer the door and give me a taste of her anger. I'm banking on the second, but my girl is just wild enough to get me locked up.

Leaning my arm against the top frame, I smile when I hear the lock disengage. I'm smiling when she pulls the door open and gives me a glare that would freeze the flames in hell. I let my gaze travel over her hungrily. Short pink pajamas with red lips and teddy bears all over them. Cute but not what you wear to bed when you have someone with you. At least not unless it's an established relationship, and she and Eddie didn't have that vibe.

"Cute pj's."

"What do you want, Jake?"

She's standing in the doorway like some bouncer ready to throw down with me. It's hot as fuck, but I still need to get inside and see if she took my warning seriously. Pushing past her, I walk into her home for the first time and take it in.

"Hey, asshole, I didn't invite you into my home."

I turn to give her a smirk. "Lucky I'm not a vampire then."

"No, just a jerk."

I feel her at my back as I walk through the hallway that leads to an open-plan kitchen diner at the back. It's all whites and greys, with touches of her signature pink in the details. Double doors lead out onto a small garden that has a deck, with pots of flowers and cute string lights hung over the pergola above.

"Nice place, Blossom. It suits you."

"Gee, I can die happy now I've had the seal of approval from the design police."

I give her a smirk. "You didn't sleep with him, did you?"

Hands on her hips, she doesn't realize how enticing she looks. All fire and fury, but her nipples are peaked and her skin is flushed a delicious pink that wasn't there when I arrived.

"That is none of your business."

I ignore that because it doesn't warrant a response. She'll always be my business. "You don't have to answer, I already know."

She steps closer and angles her chin up to me, and all I want to do is take those pouty lips in mine.

"How could you possibly know that?"

"Two reasons. The first is that if he was here, he wouldn't let you talk to the man who wants to fuck you with his come still inside you. The second is you're still snarky, and I distinctly remember that when I fucked you, Blossom, you never had the energy to move afterward."

"Arrogant prick."

I shrug but I know I'm right. "Truth."

"So is that why you're here? You want to stamp your authority on me or do you just like annoying me?"

I snatch her around her waist and haul her forward so fast her hands fall on my chest to brace herself. Her touch sears my skin like a brand and I want to wear it all over my body. Being touched by her is addictive.

"I'm here because no matter how much you deny it, or hate it, there's still something between us."

"That's just chemistry, Jake."

I was expecting her to fight me and deny it, but she isn't, and it gives me a tiny bit of hope. "So you admit you want me?"

"It doesn't matter. How can we come back from what you did? You betrayed me. You stole my dream."

I hang my head as shame washes over me. I did do that, and she has every right to feel the way she does. I'm not sure I'd forgive someone for doing that to me, even knowing the circumstances but I have to try.

"I know. Give me some time, and I'll explain all of that. I'll tell you everything but in the meantime, what will it take for you to spend some time getting to know me now?"

"Jake, we didn't break up because what we had wasn't good for me. You were perfect. I just didn't know it was all an act." Her head drops as she says the words.

I grip her chin, forcing her eyes back up to mine, letting my fingertips stroke her throat. "None of what I felt for you, or the way I was with you, was a lie. Let me show you, please?"

"To what end, Jake? I won't let you hurt me again."

"Closure? Friendship? Whatever reason you need. Just name your price."

Her lips twitch as she shakes her head and pulls out of my arms. I let her go, hating how empty my arms feel without her in them.

"Jake, if you gave me a thousand dollars for every beat of my heart to spend time with you, I'd get on a treadmill and run until I dropped."

God, I love this woman. "Deal." Bending, I drop a hard, swift kiss on her upturned lips, and head for the door.

"Wait, what?" Cherry trails me to the door, confusion on her pretty face.

"We made a deal. I'll be back tomorrow to show you that thing I told you about earlier. We can take the bike."

Cherry waves her hands no. "Stop, that wasn't real."

"A thousand dollars for every one of your heartbeats is a bargain, Blossom. I would've paid ten times that amount."

"You're insane."

"Nah, just willing to do whatever it takes to make you forgive me."

"You have a time machine?"

I cup her face and wish like hell I did. So many things I'd change, so many bad choices I'd fix. But then, maybe changing the past would mean I never met her. "If I did, hurting you would be the only thing I changed, baby." Leaning in, I press a kiss to her temple and close my eyes, inhaling her sweetness.

"See you in the morning, Blossom."

With that, I wait for her to close and lock up and then head home, feeling the tension in my chest ease for the first time in weeks.

Love Lies Bleeding

Step one in winning back my Cherry Blossom is happening. Now, onto step two, make her fall in love with me again. That I can do. I did it before, and I can do it again. Getting her to forgive me though might be harder, and for that, I might need to open some old wounds of my own and let them bleed.

23. Cherry

I HAVE NO IDEA WHAT JAKE HAS PLANNED FOR TODAY, SO I DON'T have a clue what to wear or think. I feel unsettled, out of control, and it isn't a feeling I like. I woke to a text from him this morning and it was so reminiscent of how he was before, butterflies take flight in my belly.

> Jake: Morning beautiful. What book are you reading right now?

> Cherry: Morning, Jake. I'm reading one called How to Kill Your Ex.

Apparently, he found that amusing because he'd sent me a laughing emoji. I wasn't sure this was a good idea, but he'd railroaded me and I'm not backing down like a frightened child. If he needs me to spend time with him to prove that I'm over him, then so be it.

The fact that I'm not over him and probably never will be, is immaterial. So I pull on a cute pair of denim shorts, and a sleeveless pink and white gingham shirt, and tie it under my boobs. I'm not giving him the satisfaction of dressing up for him, but neither am I taking my standards down too far.

A knock at my door reminds me I need to charge my doorbell as I go to answer it. "Who is it?"

"The man from your dreams."

I roll my eyes but can't help the grin at Jake's outlandish comeback. Although it isn't entirely wrong, he'd been in my dreams last night, and I'd had to get up extra early to spend some time with my bullet vibrator this morning because of it.

I pull open the door and school my expression to one of mild boredom. Those pesky butterflies swarm again at the sight of him in dark jeans, a black tee, and his worn leather jacket. "Good morning."

His eyes skim over me in approval which only makes my body respond more. Jake has never hidden his attraction to me before and he doesn't now either, and I like that.

"You look beautiful."

"This is old, but as you didn't tell me where or what we were doing, I just threw it on."

"It's almost perfect."

"Almost?"

"You gonna let me through the door, Blossom?"

Stepping back, I give him plenty of room, so that his body doesn't touch mine as he walks past. The smirk on his face tells me he knows exactly what I'm doing.

"Almost?"

I follow him into my kitchen where he sets a bag on my counter and pulls out a pair of black leather trousers and a leather jacket. "I got you these. I don't want you getting road rash on that gorgeous body if we come off for any reason."

"You plan on wrecking your bike, Jake?"

"No, but I'm not taking risks with your safety."

"It never bothered you before."

A frown mars his face. "Yes, well, we've established I was a jerk back then who took things for granted, most especially you and that isn't happening again."

His words make a crack form in the shell of anger I wear around my heart. I point to a package on the side. "Fine. What's that?"

"This is the new Lungo smartwatch." Jake removes the pale pink watch with a rose gold face from the package and reaches for my wrist.

"Why are you giving me this?"

Jake bends closer and his woodsy, sexy scent makes me feel weak with lust.

"Because it can monitor your heartbeats, and this way I know how much I owe you for your time."

"Oh."

It had been a joke, a way to express how much I didn't want to spend time with him, but now that it's happening, the fact he's followed up on what I said is touching.

"Put these on and we'll head out."

"You gonna give me any hint about where we're going?"

"Nope."

"It had better not be cliff diving or some other dumb, meathead activity."

"Cliff diving isn't a meathead activity, it's fun, but you can relax because this doesn't involve water." He rubs his chin. "Although the thought of you in a bikini does give me an idea for our next date."

"This isn't a date."

"It's a date."

"Urgh, you are so annoying."

"Blossom, that's not how you pronounce irresistible."

I shake my head and begin to drag on the leather trousers over my shorts. They fit perfectly and even have two pink lines running up the side of the legs. The jacket matches perfectly and fits like a glove.

Outside, Jake takes my bag and secures it in the back storage under the seat, then slides the helmet over my head. His hands are gentle as he secures the strap and then lifts me onto the bike before sliding his leg over the front.

The rumble of the engine between my legs is an instant turn-on, but when Jake leans back and strokes my thigh, I almost jump him right there and then.

"You ready, Blossom?"

I nod and he pulls my hands around his waist, flattening my breasts against his back. With one hand on the handlebars, the other covering my linked hands on his abdomen, we speed off.

God, I'd forgotten what a rush it is being on a bike, the freedom, the air on my skin. A smile spreads across my face despite the fact I'm trying to control every emotion possible when it comes to Jake.

We're about twenty minutes from my shop heading into the countryside, with sidewalks becoming fields and buildings giving way to trees and cattle. We pass several beautiful properties, including a few farmhouses and a barn conversion.

I know this area well. I've always wanted to renovate one of the properties here because that is as close as I'll ever get to living in one. I do well. I'm more than comfortable but I'll never have money like Jake.

We stop at the end of a long driveway with a dirt track, and Jake turns the bike. Navigating the gravel slowly, I take in the trees on either side of the drive. It's picturesque and from another era, when life must have been slower, and the problems faced by those living them now came with rose-tinted glasses.

My breath catches when the house comes into view and I wonder who he knows that owns such a stunning period property. White with a blue trim, the wrap-around porch is to die for and then when I look up and see the same on the second floor I almost swoon.

"Wow." I pull the helmet off and shake my hair out but my gaze never leaves the stunning home in front of me.

Jake helps me off the bike and keeps hold of my hand as we walk forward. To the left of the magnificent home is a huge pond with a white fence around the edge and huge, established climbing roses in pink and white cover the entrance.

"It's pretty special, huh?"

I drag my gaze from the house to Jake and find him watching me. A blush colors my cheeks but I drop his gaze and focus on the house. "Who does it belong to?"

"Me."

"What?" I spin towards him, my mouth hanging open in surprise.

Jake chuckles and closes my mouth with his knuckle, mumbling something I probably don't want to hear.

"You bought this place? Why? When?"

"I bought it a few weeks ago. I wanted somewhere closer to where Mac and Lexi will be with Theo and I know they bought somewhere a few miles from here. Plus, Hank and Vivian are close and I want to be where my family is. I want something different from what I have."

"Well, this place is absolutely gorgeous."

"Want to see inside?"

"Try and stop me."

Jake leads me inside and I ooh and ahh over every single detail. The rooms are huge, with hardwood flooring. The back of the property houses the huge kitchen and dining room, that leads to a den on the left and a formal living room on the right. Out the back, the previous owners had added a pool and lush green lawns.

"How many bedrooms?"

"Why? You want to try them out, Blossom?"

Jake waggles his eyebrows and I fight not to find it endearing. "In your dreams."

"Every night, baby."

My gut clenches at the familiar words he'd said to me in college. The lines between the Jake of then and now are blurring until I have to squint to see the difference.

"Ha-ha. Show me the rest."

Jake leads me upstairs, his hand on the base of my spine, as we ascend the double-wide staircase that curves around to the second-floor landing.

"It has six bedrooms and eight bathrooms, but as you've probably noticed, it needs a fair bit of updating."

"It has great bones though and a lot of the original features are in really good condition."

"Yeah, I liked that about it."

As we tour each room, I hate the stab of jealousy that knots in my stomach at the thought that one day, some lucky woman would get to share this with him. That eventually, he'll give up on me like every other man before him, and in a lot of ways, including him, and he'll move on. Meet some lucky bitch and have a horde of gorgeous kids running around this house.

"Who do you have in mind? I can recommend a few great contractors who can handle something of this scale with the finesse it deserves. Just make sure your designer works with them."

Jake shoves his hands in his pockets and tilts his head to look at me. "Actually, I was hoping you'd be my designer."

"Me?" I pointed at myself like an imbecile, my eyes going wide.

Jake chuckles and nods. "Yes. You have an amazing talent for this stuff and I trust you to do right by this property."

I hadn't expected this and don't how I feel about his proposition. I'm not dumb enough to think this was because he thinks I'm the best, although I'm damn good. This is likely a ruse to spend time with me, but as I look around the property, I know I won't turn down this chance either. "What if I turn it into a bright pink Barbie dream house just to fuck with you?"

Jake shrugs. "As I said, I trust you. I know despite how you may feel about me, you'll do right by this property. You love architecture too much to do anything else."

He's right. I'll never let my personal feelings affect how I approach a project like this. "What's the budget and time frame? I'm just finishing up a few projects and, with Lexi out, it might take a little longer than usual."

"Unlimited budget and no set time frame. I have my place in the city, so it's not like I need it finished in any great rush."

"I wish I'd bought my notepad and sketchbook."

"Hang on."

Jake bounds away and I take the moment to really admire the master suite. I have so many ideas. My brain is alive with them, a few of the pieces in the shop would work too. Excitement bubbles in my veins like champagne bubbles, and I do a little dance on the spot.

"Here you go."

I spin to see Jake holding out a notepad and sketchbook. "Where did you get these?"

"I remembered you always liked to sketch your designs."

Taking the book and pencils, I try not to let him see how touched I am by the gesture. We spend the next few hours walking around the property while I question him on every style choice he might like. Some are obvious but others he shows a great insight as I lead him through.

"I have lunch set up by the pond if you're hungry?"

"Starved."

Somehow through this visit, we've established a tentative truce, and I'm glad of it. I'm exhausted from constantly being angry with him and this feels nice. Have I forgiven him? No. Do I trust him? Also no. But I'm seeing maybe there might be a way forward for us in some way, even if that's only as friends of friends.

We go out to the pond, which is the size of a small lake, to find food set up on a blanket under the shade of one of the trees. The sun shines down on us in the late summer afternoon and a tranquil sense of peace falls over me as I sigh and lay back, closing my eyes.

"It's so peaceful here."

"It's one of the reasons I bought it."

"Tired of the city?" I open my eyes and gaze at Jake as he looks off into the distance. "I never liked the city but it's where work is, and where my family was."

"You never talk about them. Not in college, either."

"No point. It's in the past."

"Do you ever see them?"

He's never talked about his family at all, so I never pushed in college for fear of upsetting what we had, but now that's a shipwreck at the bottom of the ocean, I have no qualms about bringing it up.

Jake turns to look at me, and I sit up at the haunted look on his face. An ice-cold finger slides down my spine.

"They're dead. Or at least most of them are. I never knew what happened to my father after he left us. He might be dead. I have no idea."

"Oh, Jake, I'm so sorry."

"Don't feel sorry for me, Blossom. It was my fault they died."

Reaching out, I lay my hand on his shoulder. "I don't believe that, Jake."

"Really? Even after what I did, you still think I'm incapable of that?"

"Yes."

He's silent for a few moments and I let him have his space, he clearly wants to get this off his chest, and I'm worried that if I say more he'll shut down, and this is the first real insight I'm getting into the man I'd once loved.

"I was twelve, my sister Tiffany was five. I was babysitting while my mom went out to work. I knew even at that age that her work wasn't right. That the strange men she sometimes brought home weren't really friends but I was too young to realize that she was hooked on drugs."

My breath freezes in my lungs as dread weighs me down. I hate the direction this is taking for him, but I need to hear it and he needs me to listen.

"Mom was out scoring drugs and I was meant to be watching Tiff. I thought she was watching cartoons. I went to play soccer in the alley with my friends. She found some matches and before I knew it, the apartment was on fire. I rushed back inside and she was unconscious by the window. I got her out and the fire department cleared the building but it was too late. Tiff died of smoke inhalation."

"Oh, Jake."

Tears run down my cheeks as I think of the little boy who blamed himself for an accident that wasn't his fault. He was just a kid being given responsibility by a lazy, neglectful mother.

"Hey, no. Don't cry for me, Blossom."

Jake wraps me in his arms and holds me tight as the tears fall. I rarely cry and, after my father died, I thought I was broken because I couldn't cry. Jake's betrayal had fixed that problem. Although, even now, I'm not a weepy person. My therapist says it's because I was forced to grow up and not crying had been my way of shielding my mom. I'm not sure if that's right, but it doesn't matter.

"I can't help it. You were a child, Jake. That must have been so awful for you."

"I was numb. My mom blamed me. Fuck, I blamed me. She wouldn't even look at me and said it should've been me, not Tiff, and I agreed."

I can feel the coiled tension in his body as he continues. "She was so beautiful, so full of life, and I killed her."

"No." I pull back to look him in the eyes. "You did *not* kill her. It was an awful accident and you were not responsible."

"You sound like Hunter."

I snort. "I knew I liked that man."

A small, sad twitch of his lips makes me want to erase his pain, but guilt and grief don't work that way.

"Indirectly, I was to blame for their deaths. My mom took an overdose six months later and died."

My heart breaks for that young boy, who'd had to grow up too young, who was led to believe he was bad and ugly inside by the person who should have protected him.

"Jake, No. However hard it is to hear it, your mother was responsible for both you and your sister, and ultimately herself, too."

"I was the man of the house. I should have done better but I got worse."

"What does that mean? You got worse?"

"After mom died, I went into the system. I was a little asshole, Blossom. I stole, I got into fights. I hated everyone and everything, but I was smart and I landed in a program that got me a scholarship to the same school as Mac. If it wasn't for him and his family, I'd be dead or in jail, because I was headed down that road. I was running with some absolute bastards and I liked it."

His arms loosen around me and I look up to see disgust and self-loathing on his handsome face. Pain gathers in my heart for that boy and this man who still blames himself and thinks himself so undeserving.

"Why didn't you tell me this when we were together?"

Jake blows out a breath and shakes his head. "I was young, confident, playing the part I wanted to land. I loved you so much. I thought if you knew the old me, the vile kid with a record, you would've run a mile."

"I would've loved you regardless."

"Maybe, but I couldn't take the risk."

"Is this why you did what you did?"

He shakes his head, frustration etched into every pore on his face. "Yes and no. My past came back to haunt me, but it's no excuse. I should never have done it."

"No, you shouldn't have but we all make mistakes."

"Yeah, except mine cost me the girl I loved."

I can't argue or absolve him of those sins because he'd had a choice and made the wrong one. Maybe one day he'll divulge the details but I can already feel him pulling away and I let him go. Today has been a lot, but I have hope that the festering wounds of the past, once out in the open, will be able to heal and maybe this is the start for both of us.

"We should go. I have plans later."

Now it's my turn to wrestle with the green-eyed monster.

Jumping up, I dust myself off and give a nonchalant shrug. "Oh yeah, of course. You probably have a date. Wouldn't want to deprive all those ladies of Jake the playboy."

His lips twitch, before he breaks into a belly laugh, his hand holding his belly and he throws his head back. "Fuck me. You're beautiful when you're jealous."

"I'm not jealous. Why would I be? You're not mine and I'm not yours."

A growl slips past his lips as he snags my waist and hauls me into his arms. His lips find mine in a kiss that bleeds any thought from my brain. His hands are firm, his lips soft and familiar, and the scruff on his jaw scratches enough to evoke the memory of what he felt like between my legs.

Pulling back, he cups my face in his hands as I try to wrangle my heart back into a normal rhythm.

"You *are* mine, and I *am* yours. I have been since the day we met in that coffee shop, so get used to it."

He doesn't give me a chance to respond, just places the helmet back on my head and helps me onto the bike. We ride home in silence but with a new understanding between us that, while unspoken and tentative, feels like the seed from which beauty might grow.

He walks me to my door and hands me my sketchbook and notepad.

"I'll see you soon, Blossom."

I watch as he gets on his bike, pulls his helmet on, and turns, giving me a wink that makes my knees wobble, before he pulls the visor down and rides away, taking my equilibrium with him.

24. Jake

PULLING INTO THE UNDERGROUND PARKING OF THE BUILDING where Mac and Lexi currently live, I feel lighter than I have in a long while. Today had gone better than expected, even though it had taken a turn I hadn't imagined when I decided to show Cherry my future home. One I hope I'll share with her one day, but I'm getting ahead of myself.

Today had been about forging new connections and, instead, I'd spilled my guts about my biggest shame, or at least one of them. Seeing her cry tears for me gutted me, twisting me up inside. When we were younger she confided she couldn't cry. Not that she didn't feel, just that losing her dad somehow had choked that act of releasing grief through crying.

Now, though, she seems to be able to, and I wonder what had triggered it, but suspect it's something to do with the way I'd hurt her. Rubbing my chest, I try to erase the heaviness of regret. I've made so many mistakes in my life, but maybe losing Blossom is one I can fix, even if I can't go back and undo what I did, maybe I can heal her and perhaps myself in the process.

"Jake, I'm so glad you're here."

Lexi greets me at the door, looking relaxed and happier than I've ever seen her. The woman is a warrior.

"Thanks for the invite." I handed over the flowers I'd bought for her and the brandy for after dinner, which I know is a favorite of Mac's, and drop a kiss on her cheek. Lexi is gracious and welcoming, which is more than I deserve.

"These are beautiful. Thank you."

Mac walks toward me as we move into the lounge, Theo strapped to a carrier around his chest. I grin at him as we share an awkward man hug, careful not to wake the sleeping baby.

"You buy my wife flowers?"

"Yes, but I bought you brandy, so don't get all jealous. I still love you, too, Mac, but she's way prettier than you are."

Mac punches my arm. "Agreed."

I subtly look around, seeing if I can spot Cherry, but I know she hasn't arrived yet.

"She's running late."

"I didn't say anything," I snap as Mac hands me a beer.

His smirk says it all and I shake my head.

"You and Cherry."

He chuckles and I give him a dead stare. "What about us?"

"I just can't believe I didn't see it before."

"Yeah, well, you had a lot going on."

Mac tips his beer back and then bobs his head in agreement. "It's been one hell of a year. But if changing it meant I didn't get them for the rest of my life, I wouldn't change a damn thing."

I watch my best friend stroke his son's downy soft hair and gaze at Lexi, who is fussing over something in the kitchen.

"So you think every decision we take leads us to where we are now and even the slightest deviation can change everything?"

"I do believe that."

"Hmm."

"I spoke to Dad about what we discussed."

My body stiffens, my hand gripping the beer bottle tighter. "And?"

"He's going to make some calls. Turns out he and the elder Mancini are somewhat friends. If you can call it that."

"Really? I didn't see that coming."

"Me either. Apparently, they met when they were both young and starting their careers."

Hank is such an enigma sometimes. He's the ultimate family man, and his love and devotion to them is evident for anyone to witness. Yet he's also the hardnosed businessman who puts the fear of God into his competitors. A more ferocious and calculating businessman I've never met. Yet he's kind. The way he'd treated Lexi is further proof of that. Not that I, of all people, need it. Without Hank and Vivian, I don't know what would have become of me.

"I should call him. I'm sure he's disappointed in me."

"He said you'd say that. He also said you should go to the house tomorrow for Sunday lunch, but he isn't disappointed, just worried about you. Truth is, so am I, Jake."

"Why?"

Mac turns to me and places a hand on my shoulder. "You're so worried about letting people down that you make horrible decisions to try and protect them, and you always become the collateral damage."

"Not true."

"Yes, my friend, it is."

Before I can retort, the buzzer announces a guest and I focus on the door where Lexi is ushering Cherry inside. She looks delicious in a pale pink playsuit, with a deep V-neckline and a lace see-through waistline that I know is going to torture me all night. Her hair is up in a messy ponytail, giving me a glimpse of her long elegant neck, which fits perfectly in my hand.

She must sense me watching because she glances up. I see surprise then pleasure wash over her face, which gives me a warm feeling in my chest. I stay silent as she greets Hunter with a hug and

L. Knight

kiss, and leans in to drop a kiss on Theo's head which is way too close to my best friend's chest in my opinion. A growl of possession slips past my lips and I see Hunter try and smother a laugh.

As if lured by an invisible force, we met in the middle of the lounge as Hunter goes off to help his fiancée. Cherry nibbles on the gloss on her bottom lip and I fist my hands to keep from reaching for her.

"So, these were your big plans."

"You didn't really think I'd spend the day with you and then go out with another woman, did you?"

She does this cute little shoulder shimmy. "Maybe. It's not like we're dating or anything."

"No," I agreed, "but why would I go out with another woman when I'd spend the entire time thinking about you?"

A blush creeps over her cheeks and I want to stroke it with my finger, follow it as it travels over her skin and disappears into the V of her neckline. I bend my head closer to her, noting the pulse in her neck speeds up as I do.

"You consume me, Blossom. You always have and I have a feeling you always will."

Before she can respond, Lexi calls us in for dinner. The table is a round, nook affair where they'd usually eat breakfast, but as it was only the four of us, Lexi had suggested this. There's no artifice about Lexi and I like that. It suits my friend and the way he looks at her as the night wears on, almost makes me feel voyeuristic. Not in a creepy way, but like I'm a witness to a love that not many people got to enjoy.

Seated beside Cherry, I can smell her scent and make it my mission to revel in the accidental touches of our arms as we eat.

"So, the gala for Funding the Future is next week."

I chew a piece of the perfectly cooked pork loin and nod at Lexi's statement.

"What's that?"

I glance at Cherry, who's watching me thoughtfully and with much less malice than she has for the last month or so. "It's a charity

186

to raise funding for scholarships for children who show academic promise but don't have the funds or the opportunity." It was something I'd taken over from Hank and I truly believed in it. It changed my life and gave me a future I could never have imagined. Having Hank and Vivian practically adopt me hadn't hurt either.

"Wow, that's amazing."

Her praise makes me sit up straighter, makes me proud of what we'd done and how many kids we'd helped in the last nine years since I took over.

"We have another one that's similar but geared towards kids with less academic success. It focuses on trades, like construction, plumbing, electrics, etcetera, but that's a different event."

"I think it's great that you're helping kids that need a hand up. Nobody chooses the life they are born into, and money shouldn't be the reason kids fail."

Cherry is stunning when she's passionate about something. I'd witnessed it in the past when she talked about architecture, and again today when she was touring the house.

"Oh my God, I have the best idea. You should take Cherry as your date for the gala. She could see firsthand how it works. We could even offer an internship with us at the shop if that's allowed."

I could lean over and kiss Lexi for handing me this opportunity but knew I'd get a punch in the teeth from Mac.

"No, no. I'm sure Jake has a date already."

Twisting to face Blossom head on, I grin at her, loving the discomfort she's feeling, and watching her try and squirm her way out of this will be fun, especially as I have no intention of letting her off the hook. "No. No date and I'd love to show you what we do and see if it's something you'd be interested in for the future."

Cherry grinds her jaw and glares at her friend who just smiles.

"I think I might be busy that night."

Her sentence is said through clenched teeth and I feel my lips pull into a soft smile before hiding it. "I haven't told you the date yet, Blossom."

"I have plans to work every night next week. Especially as we just landed a huge new project today. I'd hate to have to turn that down."

"We did? You didn't tell me."

Cherry glances over at Lexi, who wears a slightly hurt expression.

"Honey, no." Cherry reaches for her friend and I see the bond these two women have up close and personal once more. Cherry would go to war for Lexi and I believed Lexi would do the same in her own way.

"Why didn't you tell me?"

"Honestly, it's been a day but seeing as the client is right here in the room, maybe he can tell you."

I felt a hand on my thigh and almost smile as my dick responds to her unexpected touch, until she pinches the inside of my leg, and makes me jump and almost knock my glass of wine over.

Little minx.

Entirely unaware of our position, Lexi looks at me with wide eyes and a huge smile. "You're the client, Jake?"

"I sure am."

Sliding my hand under the table, I grip Cherry's wrist as she tries to remove her hand and hold it against my thigh. As I explain in detail to Lexi about the house and what I want, I skate her hand up and over the erection she's caused. My dick pulses under her touch and I swear I hear her breathing change as her hand begins a slow exploration of my cock.

My ability to focus on two things at once is severely tested as I let my hand skim over her soft thigh, and up the pant leg of the play suit she's wearing. Her thighs tighten and she goes to close them, but I give her a squeeze and she relaxes.

She's still my good girl.

Sliding my fingers higher, I expect to find panties but instead find hot, wet flesh. My dick jumps and I glance sideways as Cherry coughs to cover the snort she'd made at my reaction to her bare form.

My index finger skims her slit, gathering her juices on the tip before I begin to rub firm, slow circles on her clit. Her breathing picks up as I work her until she's fighting to stay still under my touch. My cock is throbbing with the need to feel her hands on me, but this isn't about me. Pulling away, I inch my finger down, and push my middle finger inside her tight cunt. I almost groan at how good she feels. Her pussy is home to me, it's where my cock, my tongue, and my fingers belong. My mouth floods with saliva and the memory of her taste in the shop a few days ago.

Her hand wraps around my covered cock and inches toward my zip but I stop her with a firm hand on her wrist. If she touches me, I know I won't be able to hold back, and hauling her out of my best friend's home halfway through dinner so I can fuck her, won't go over well with Cherry.

My fingers curl as I use my thumb on the sensitive bundle of nerves that is so responsive to my touch. I feel her hips move and she fights the urge to ride my hand. I know I'll jack my cock to this scene later and cover my belly with cum meant for her pussy.

I feel her leg begin to shake as she grips my wrist, not sure if she wants me to finish her or stop, but I already know I'm not going to let her finish. Tonight I want her either riding my cock, or going to bed so desperate for the climax only I can give her that she dreams of me like I do her.

Just as Cherry gets close, her fist clenching around the wine-glass like it's her lifeline, I stop and withdraw my touch. I want to suck her juices from my fingers, to savor every drop but with Hunter watching me with a suspicious tilt of his head, I know I can't. I turn to my Blossom as I surreptitiously wipe my fingers on my napkin. Her glare is like liquid fire as she hits me with her flushed gaze.

God, she's something else when she's pissed. Alive, wild, untamable, and I fucking love every inch of her.

"So, Cherry, what do you say to going with Jake to the event?"

"Huh?"

My girl is completely discombobulated and, truth be told, the effect she has on me is just as strong. Only years of practice in the boardroom and inside a courtroom keep me from being a blithering idiot.

"The gala." Lexi frowns at her friend. "Are you okay, Cher? You look a little flushed."

"I'm fine. Just drank the wine too fast."

I smirk knowingly and she stomps on my foot under the table, making me chuckle into my napkin. "So, Cherry Blossom, are you going to be my date?"

"I don't have anything to wear to a function like that."

"No problem, I'll handle it."

Cherry wrinkles her nose. "I'm not letting you choose a dress for me."

"Even better, I'll take you shopping."

Lexi claps her hands. "Yes! This is perfect. I can cover the store for a few hours on Monday if that works, Jake."

"You're the best, Lex."

I see Mac grumble something under his breath, but don't hear what it is, but guess it's about her overdoing it.

"I guess you have it all worked out, then."

Arms crossed, Cherry glares at me but I'm pretty sure most of it is from sexual frustration. "I guess I do."

I didn't, far from it, but I seem to have a guardian angel working in my favor and I'm not going to be fool enough not to take advantage. I'm finally making headway with Cherry and I intend to push my advantage any way I can.

25. Cherry

"Lex, I really don't have time to go galivanting to get a dress or go to some stupid gala."

My best friend looked at me with a disapproving tilt of her head, she had this mom look down already.

"Please, Cher, do this for me. It's a great cause. I know you don't like Jake, but he's a good guy."

I still haven't told her about the history Jake and I share and, at this point, I'm not sure why. Tucking the pencils I'd used to sketch a few designs this morning away, I suppress a sigh. "It's not that I don't like him, Lex."

"Then what is it?" Lexi grips my hand tight and a lump forms in my throat. I should tell her, but what's the point in going over it again? It will only make her feel conflicted between her loyalty to me and her loyalty to Hunter, who's Jake's best friend. I can't do that to her.

"It's nothing. I'm just tired."

I see a fleeting look of disappointment flit over her face before she hides it with a smile and my gut twists that I've inadvertently hurt her.

"Even more reason, to cut loose and have some fun. Get drunk, flirt with some hot guys, and maybe fix that dry spell."

"Now that sounds like fun."

"What sounds like fun?"

My spine stiffens as his voice caresses my skin like warm caramel. What is it about this man that he can just ignite my body without trying? I'm still an aching mess after the stunt he pulled on Saturday night. It will serve him right if I go and find some guy to take home right under his nose.

"Hey, Jake."

Jake kisses Lexi's cheek and I can't help the rush of jealousy at his lips on another woman, even if that woman is my best friend and it's completely platonic.

"Hey, Lex." Jake looks at me with a raised brow and I give him what I hope is a bored look and glance back at my freshly painted nails, dismissing him.

"So what sounds like fun?"

"I was telling Cherry she should look for some hot guy to take home at the gala on Saturday."

The satisfaction I get from watching Jake's jaw tic in annoyance at my friend's statement is unreal. I'm doing a mental happy dance that his dark stare only gets harder when I grin.

"You know, Lex, you're right. I definitely need to get laid. I can't remember the last time a man left me satisfied. Maybe I can find someone who actually knows where to find the clit without me having to draw him a map."

Jake narrows his eyes at me in warning, but I don't heed it and keep going. "What do you say, Jake? You know anyone who might be able to help a girl out?"

"No." His curt, short, reply is filled with anger and I almost laugh but hold myself back. I do have a small dose of self-preservation left in my brain.

"Ah, well, I'll find someone."

Jake, seemingly having enough of this conversation, grips my upper arm and steers me towards the exit. "Time to go. We don't want to be late for your fitting."

Jake drags me past a smirking Lexi, who shoves my bag at me and waves me out the door.

"Take your hands off me."

"No."

My brain is clearly malfunctioning because it sounds like he said no. "What the hell, Jake?"

Opening the back door to the town car before his driver can, he gently pushes me inside and climbs in after me.

With a huff, I slide to the far side of the car and glare a hole in his head. "This is kidnapping."

"Don't test me, Blossom. I know exactly what you're doing and it won't work."

"Oh, and pray tell, what it is I'm doing?"

Jake pins me with a laser-like stare that feels like it's stripping the clothes from my skin. "You're trying to find another reason to hate me and I'm not going to give you one. I get that I hurt you, Cherry, but I'm trying to put things right."

The air leaves me in a whoosh as the fight he'd pinpointed so accurately leaves me.

"Good girl."

I glare at his sexy smirk, wanting to pick a fight and knowing he isn't going to bite. Jake has always been particularly good at seeing through my hard shell to the tender spot inside that bleeds.

Ignoring my outrage, he instructs the driver to take us to Bella Allure, the boutique where every socialite worthy of the name got their gowns, but that isn't me. I'm not in that league and never will be.

"I don't belong there, Jake. Just take me to the mall and I can grab something off the rack."

His scorching gaze slides over me as he closes the partition between us and his driver. My pulse jumps to my throat as the tension inside the confines of the car rises to almost impossible levels.

My breath freezes in my lungs as he leans forward and grips my chin gently but firmly between his thumb and forefinger.

"You belong anywhere you damn well choose, Blossom. If you want it, it's yours, you got that? Because queens don't ask permission and you're a fucking queen and don't ever forget it."

With that, he drops a chaste kiss on my lips and releases me. My heart beats a frantic tap dance against my ribs as I watch him in silence. His belief in me had always given me confidence when I was wavering on whether I could do something, so it had been a double blow when he'd been the one to destroy it.

With his elbow leaning against the window as he looks out broodingly, I would give everything I own to know what he's thinking about or what he'd meant by calling me a queen. I know once upon a time he'd said I was his princess, but that was all a lie, wasn't it?

Is it possible that what Jake had felt for me back then had been real? Am I cutting off my nose to spite my face by not giving him a real chance? It's so terrifying to think of ever feeling that kind of pain again, but the temptation to let myself sink into everything that is how Jake makes me feel is too much. Luckily, I'm saved from any decision as we pull to a stop outside a lavish-looking building.

Bella Allure is located on the outskirts of the city and is appointment only. I look up, feeling my bravado waver, but snap out of it as Jake exits the car, and comes around to open my door. Prickles of memory tingle across my skin as he smiles at me and takes my hand, tucking it into the crook of his arm and walking us inside, where we are met by the owner of the store.

"Mr. Marshall, what a pleasure it is to have you visit us."

Jake nods and turns to me as the woman practically drools over him, without a single glance my way.

"This is Cherry Baker. Isn't she the most exquisite beauty you've ever seen?"

Summarily put in her place, the owner glances at me with an assessing eye. I'm not a docile wallflower, far from it. In fact, most people would call me an extrovert, but under this woman's scrutiny, I feel every insecurity times a thousand. Shrewd blue eyes travel over me like I'm a prime piece of rib and I want to pass this imaginary test more than I should, especially with Jake watching.

"She's like the flower she was named for, delicate and yet powerful."

Jake nods his agreement. "Agreed. Do you have the dresses I requested?"

"I do, and I can't wait to see them on her."

Jake keeps his hand on my back as we are led through to the back, past white and gold accented walls with racks of designer garments. We pass through a black door where a dressing room is set up with Champagne and fruit in the shape of a flower, and long comfy couches and floor-to-ceiling mirrors along three walls. At the back is a velvet-curtained area, which I'm guessing is where I can change. It is opulent and classy and, as a designer, I can recognize what they are trying to achieve here; understated elegance, and it works.

"If you'd like to go in and slip off your clothes, I'll bring the first dress in for you to try."

"Okay."

This passive woman is so not me, but I want to get my bearings and I'm still reeling from what Jake said in the car. Our past is so complicated, and it intrudes on every interaction we have, but if I were to examine who he is now, would I find a person I liked, admired, wanted? Probably, but letting go of the past means taking a risk and I'm not sure if I'm brave enough.

"Are you ready?" Bella calls.

"Yes."

Slipping between the small gap, she enters the space and I stand in my underwear, thankfully having regained a little of my body confidence after her perusal.

"I have four options Mr. Marshall has picked out for you to try on. I thought we could try this one first and see how we go."

The first one is black with a high neckline, but the back is open in a large keyhole shape with cap sleeves that clasp at the top. Nude fabric underlay is accented with contrasting black lace detailing that covers the shoulders, and bodice, and accentuates the hemline of the trumpet skirt.

It is stunning.

The fabric molds over my body, as I'm zipped into it, and makes me feel invincible, powerful like I can take on anything and win. I slide my feet into black satin four-inch-high pumps and let Bella clip the hooks at the neckline. It is snug, but I guess that's the idea, and the length is perfect which makes me wonder if Jake had sent some of my measurements through because gowns like this are not made for women of five feet.

"Ravishing. Let's go in the other room and allow Mr. Marshall a glimpse."

I'm not the type of woman to allow a man to dress me or tell me what to wear, but Jake has hit this out of the park and I want to see his reaction to me in this dress. A bubble of excitement fizzes in my veins as I anticipate his reaction.

As the curtain swishes back, Jake looks up from his phone and my breath catches in my throat at the naked hunger I see in his gaze. He stands and comes towards me, hands tucked firmly in his pockets as if he doesn't trust himself not to touch me. He doesn't speak as he walks around me, his gaze like a whisper-soft caress over my fevered skin.

"She looks stunning, don't you think, Mr. Marshall?"

Jake gives a slow nod as he appraises me. "You look breathtaking, Blossom, but do you like it? I know that whatever you wear you'll bewitch every man and woman that lays eyes on you, but I want you to feel it."

"I love it, but I want to try the others to make sure." And also because I'm intrigued to see what else he'd chosen for me. Light dances in his eyes and I so want to feel his lips on mine. I want to revel in the way he makes me feel like I can conquer the world. Jake has always had that ability.

"Go, I'll wait with bated breath to see which one you try next."

While I was talking with Jake, Bella had hung the other three dresses in the room. One is a cornflower blue taffeta with a ruffle skirt. The next is a pale pink tulle A-line dress with a beaded bodice, spaghetti straps, and the last one is a blush pink sheath with a boned bodice, and beads covering the entire dress.

Deciding on the blue one, I put it on and again find myself holding my head higher, but not in the same way the black dress did. This one is lighter, I feel freer, and more myself in this one. Stepping out, I see Jake watching me, his features spreading into a smile that makes my toes curl.

"There she is."

I return his grin, as he reaches for my hand, and lifts my arm, twirling me beneath it like I'm a princess. "What do you think?"

"It's beautiful, fun, and sexy."

Bending, he kisses my collarbone. "You'd look sexy in a burlap sack, Blossom. Sexiness is from the inside. It's not worn, it's exuded."

"You been reading Cosmo again, Jake?"

His bark of laughter is like the soft stroke of a finger down my spine. He looks handsome and carefree and shows me the boy I'd adored is still there, inside the man who ties me in knots.

"My guilty secret is out."

"News flash, Jake, it was never a secret from me."

He looks at me then, a thousand feelings moving across his face and I want to know every one of them.

"Go try on the last two, Blossom, and then I'll take you to lunch."

"I have to get back to work."

His hand grazed my cheek. "Please?"

If he'd argued, I could've held my ground but that one little word is enough to shred any argument I have to dust. "Okay, but I'm choosing where we eat."

"You got it." His lips graze mine as if they belong there before he pulls back and gives me a slight push toward the dressing room. "Go."

"Bossy."

"Yeah, and you still love it."

I give him a flirty look over my shoulder. "Lies." But we both know I'm the one lying.

I try the last two dresses on but they don't speak to me like the first two did, and although Jake looks like a rabid beast every time I walk out, it's the first dress he asks me to try on again.

Standing in front of the mirror, Jake steps up behind me, his height dwarfing me even in these ridiculously high heels. His hands cup my upper arms, sending tingles down my skin as he rubs almost absentmindedly, but I feel every neuron respond to him.

"You look like Cleopatra in this dress, Blossom."

"I'm pretty sure Cleopatra wasn't a petite shop owner with pink hair."

His gaze catches mine in the mirror and what I see makes my pulse pound in my throat.

"No, she was a warrior, a leader, a ruler of men."

"That doesn't sound like me."

"Doesn't it? I'll follow you anywhere, Blossom. I'll destroy the world for you if you asked. I need you to see that power, to own that power, and then decide if you can forgive my sins."

I'm not sure if I understand his words or at least the meaning behind them, but they hold so much potency it's hard to ignore. He wants my forgiveness, but he won't give me the truth or the reason why he'd imploded the love we'd shared, the love that had been so real, so pivotal to who I am now. "I'll try."

It's all I can give him now. His eyes drop to my lips and the air crackles around us, all the sexual tension I'd been living with since Saturday slams into me.

"Jake." It's neither a question nor a statement, just a plea for something I don't know how to voice.

"What do you need, Blossom? I can't think, I can't focus on anything but the memory of how you feel and taste. I need to slate this hunger inside of me."

This is the moment, the one where I get to decide how our story evolves. I can keep running away from him or I can run towards whatever this will be and take ownership. I can be the woman he sees when he looks at me. I can control this or I can let it control me.

"I want to see you on your knees for me, Mr. Marshall."

A glint shines in his eyes before he goes down on his knees for me. Jake is a man who relishes control, and who needs it. Even back when we were younger, he'd dominated me, and I loved every second, I still do. I want his hands in my hair, his fingers at my throat but, for this single moment, I need him to show me that I hold the power, even if it isn't real.

Even now on his knees for me, he looks powerful, strong, indestructible. I reach out to skim my fingers over his cheek and his head turns, his lips finding my palm as he lays a kiss there. My skin flares with bright, hot desire as he looks up at me with all the adoration I've fought so hard to dismiss as his guilt.

His eyes remain on my face as I slide my foot up his chest, planting the stiletto heel over his heart. Strong fingers grip my bare ankle, before smoothing over the skin of my calf.

"Make me come, Jake."

My chest feels tight as he smirks up at me with all the confidence of a god. His free hand finds my hands. "Hold this pretty dress up, Blossom."

A small smile touches his lips as I do what he asks and then I feel his fingers skim over my panties before they are wrenched from me, the action causing the fabric to bite into my skin in the most delicious way.

Then there's nothing but pleasure as his mouth finds me. His lips close over my clit and pull every sensation from me. He doesn't stop as he takes, and takes, stealing every sensation from me until all I can do is hold on for the ride. My fingers thread through his hair, dropping the hem of the dress, so I can hold on. He moves his hands to grip my ass as he licks and sucks until my knees feel like they might give out.

My breathing is stuttered and my entire body shakes with little jolts of electricity. Jake pulls his mouth away and I want to scream as I hang on the precipice of the most powerful climax I've ever had.

"No."

His lips and chin are covered with evidence of my arousal, and I'd never seen anything more erotic. Even now on his knees, covered in my juices, he holds me captive.

"Say you're mine."

My breath chokes in my chest. Fear of him, of us, holding me hostage. "No."

A knowing smirk slips over his face. "There's my girl."

Then he buries his head against my pussy and bites down on my clit, forcing all the air from my lungs, as my body shakes, and pulses with the climax I'd known would change me and it does.

As I come down from my orgasm, Jake stands and holds me steady until my legs can do the job, then he wipes his chin with his fingers and holds my gaze while he licks them clean.

"I think I better buy this dress for you, Blossom. I want to do that again, and soon."

A dry laugh falls from my lips and as I give him my back. "We'll see."

I say it but we both know the lid is off whatever this is between us and for as long as it lasts, I won't let the past interfere. Or at least I'll try.

26. Jake

I CAN STILL TASTE HER ON MY TONGUE AS I SLIDE INTO THE BACK of the town car that will take me to collect Cherry for the gala. Her perfume lingers in the air and I close my eyes as every second of our time together choosing that dress flits through my mind.

When she'd asked me to get on my knees for her, I'd almost caved and told her how much I still loved her, how much I regretted caving to weakness and fear instead of being the man she deserved. Looking up at her, I know that if it took every cent I have and every minute for the rest of my life, I was going to win her back.

Our lunch was easy, surprisingly so after the heaviness of the scene in the dressing room. We'd talked about the house and she'd asked if I had any designs she'd like me to incorporate. It had been easy like a tentative truce was in place.

Pulling up outside her house, I smooth a hand over my shirt, nerves attacking my composure in a way no other woman will ever be able to achieve because nobody else matters but her.

Walking to the door, I knock and wait, hearing voices from inside. I'm slightly taken aback when an older version of the woman I love appears. Petite but still taller than her daughter, Darla Baker has a

201

timeless beauty and grace that will lead others to think she's weak, but I'm no fool. She assesses me before stepping outside and pulling the door closed.

A ball of dread fills my belly, not because I fear this woman but because if she hates me it will complicate any hope I have of a relationship with her daughter.

"May I have a word, Jake?" We'd met before at the baby shower for Lex and Hunter and again as we all waited for news of Lexi and Theo after her ex-husband's brutal attack, but we'd never really talked more than pleasantries. I have a feeling that's about to change.

"Yes of course. What can I do for you, Mrs. Baker?"

"Let's sit."

Like a schoolboy about to be reprimanded for being caught with the coach's daughter, I sit next to her on the porch swing my Cherry Blossom had set next to her front door.

"I didn't realize at first, but now I see it."

"See what?"

"You're the one who broke my daughter's heart."

My chest feels like it's filled with cement as she stares at me with all the unflinching determination of a Southern woman about to protect her child. She looks like butter wouldn't melt and her voice is soft-spoken and sweet but I know from my time with Vivian, that looks can be deceiving.

I have two choices here, I can lie or I can admit the truth and hope it will grant me some kind of credit. "Yes."

I can see I've caught her off guard with my honesty, and a huff of laughter falls from me. "No point lying, Mrs. Baker."

"You were the reason she gave up her dream."

"I was, and I've regretted my actions every single day since, and I will until I draw my last breath on this earth."

"Do you love her?"

"With all my heart."

Darla is silent for a beat before she speaks again. "Are you going to hurt her again?"

I shake my head, looking her straight in the eye with the respect she deserves. "No. I'll never do anything to hurt her again. I'll die first."

"Hmm, something tells me that would hurt my daughter very much. My sweet Cherry Pie comes across as strong and invincible but she's soft inside and when she loves, she does so with her whole heart. She protects, and she's loyal like nobody I've ever met, but she often does it at her own expense."

"I know."

Her shrewd gaze meets my own and I feel a sudden kinship with this woman. We both love Cherry and it gives us a common goal.

"Make things right with my daughter. She deserves to be loved for who she is, not who she thinks she should be for those around her."

"I agree. I just need to make amends first."

"Then make them, and then stop her from going head-to-head with that crooked KLM. My daughter is the biggest love of my life, and my greatest achievement, but sometimes she can be so stubborn I want to tan her hide for her."

My expression must have shown my surprise because she chuckles and it's deep and rich.

"Ah, she thinks I don't know, but people talk and I think Cherry forgets she gets that iron will from someone, and it isn't her father like she thinks."

"She just wants to protect you."

"Protecting me isn't her job. It's mine to protect her, so I'll say this once. Handle those crooks, before she gets hurt."

"It's in hand, Mrs. Baker."

She stands and places a hand on my shoulder, the touch firm and full of warmth. "Call me, Darla."

"Does this mean I have your blessing?"

"It means I won't get my gun and shoot you for hurting my baby, but do it again and there won't be any place you can hide. No matter who you are."

A smile weathers my face, as I realize that my Cherry Blossom has more support than she realizes. "Can I ask you something, Darla?"

"You can ask."

"Why haven't you told her you know about KLM?"

"Because Cherry needs to be useful, she needs that control. When we lost her dad, she changed. She thought that if she controlled every emotion and everything around her, she could save herself from pain. When you broke her heart, it hardened that behavior."

Guilt sours my stomach, cutting deep into the scars I wear on the inside. "How did you know it was me?"

"I saw the way you looked at her, and I saw the way she looked at you. No pain like that comes without an even greater love."

"Mom!"

I stand as I hear Cherry call from inside.

"Cherry pie, look who I found on the doorstep."

Darla steps inside and I follow suit, my gaze swinging to the bottom of the stairs where Cherry is waiting. My breath whooshes from my lungs, my stomach bottoming out as the world around me dims to nothing. She looks heart-stoppingly beautiful, her pink hair in a softly curled chignon at her nape, her makeup sinful with smokey eyes and gloss lips that make me desperate to taste them.

"You look stunning."

A delicate blush steals across her cheeks and her head dips, before her eyes find mine.

"You look nice too."

God I love her, I love this soft side that only a few get to see, and I love her feisty abrasive side too. "Shall we?"

I hold my hand out to her and she takes my arm, as her mom watches on from the doorway of the living room. I give her a nod as we pass and an understanding passes between us. A baton is being handed over to me and with a trust I'm not sure I deserve but will treasure and guard with my life.

"Mom, lock up when you leave, and don't forget to call Frankie about that leaky tap."

Her mom shakes her head. "Get on with you. Go enjoy this handsome man in that gorgeous dress and have fun."

"Fine. I'll call you later."

"No offense, my darling girl, but I hope you don't. I know for sure if I was out with a man that looked like that, and looked at me like he's looking at you, then I wouldn't be calling anyone until very late tomorrow morning."

"Mom!"

I chuckle at Cherry's scandalized expression and lead her out the door before she can start fussing again.

"We need to get going."

"Sorry about her," she says when we are safely in the car and headed to the hotel where the gala will be held.

"Whatever for? I happen to agree with everything she said."

Cherry snorts, and the sound is so natural, so imperfectly perfect, that I can't resist the soft kiss I place on her lips. I want more, but I won't rush tonight. Not when it's so important.

"So tell me a bit more about what's going to happen tonight?"

I go over what to expect, starting with drinks in the main hall where people can enter the silent auction, then dinner, speeches, and dancing.

"Are you giving a speech?"

"Yes, I'll give a speech to kick off the auction but then my official duties, apart from schmoozing, will be done."

"And what does schmoozing entail?"

"Lots of ass-kissing and generally making them feel like they're important so they open their wallets and donate to the charity."

"Will Hank and Vivian be there?"

"They will, and so will Cassie, Hunter's sister."

"Oh, I love Cassie. She's so sweet."

"Yeah, she's great. They all are but don't tell Hunter I said so. He has a big head. He needs me to keep him level-headed."

"And who keeps you level-headed when you get too big for your boots?"

"I have you for that."

"Maybe."

"Always. Even when you weren't around, I tried to live my life in a way that would make you proud. I didn't always succeed but I always tried. You were my North Star, Blossom. Always will be."

The slack, soft look on her face makes me want to turn the car around, forget about my responsibilities, and spend the night making love to her in a way that would imprint on her the truth of my words. The other part wants every man in the state, no, the country, to know she's mine and see her on my arm.

We enter the ballroom after walking the red carpet, which I hadn't warned her about, and her gasp is audible.

"Oh, Jake, this is stunning. It almost makes up for you not warning me there'd be paparazzi and a red carpet."

"How else was I going to make sure Eddie fucking Crowe knows you're off the market?"

Cherry stops and glances up at me with a furrow between her brows. "You did *not* set that up just for Eddie."

I bloody well had. That asshole needs to know that Cherry isn't his and never will be. "Maybe."

Her hand slides to her hip and I face down her wrath as my dick hardens in my tuxedo pants. Cherry in a snit is the hottest thing on the planet.

"You know we're just friends right? And who says I'm off the market?"

"I say so, but if I have to fight every man who looks at you to prove it, then so be it."

"Jake, you're being ridiculous."

"No, I'm protecting what's mine, and you're mine, Blossom. You always have been."

"Well, let's agree to disagree."

She makes to walk off, and I grab her hand and tuck her into my side. "If I'm fucking you, and I will be by the end of tonight, then I'm the only one fucking you."

"So confident, Jake."

My hand skims the exposed skin of her spine and dips beneath the lace, making her shiver, and making every cent of the twenty-five grand I spent on it worth it. I'll happily buy her an entire wardrobe full of these if it means I get to enjoy her in them.

"Jake, Cherry. Oh, don't you two look adorable together."

"Vivian, Hank." We greet my pseudo-adopted family with hugs and kisses and I listen as Vivian gushes over Cherry's dress, telling her how stunning she is and I wholeheartedly agree. She's the most beautiful woman in the room, in any room ever as far as I'm concerned.

"Have you got a second, Jake?"

Awareness runs down my spine at the tone Hank uses, but I nod.

"I'll grab us drinks," I whisper to Cherry as I drop a kiss on her shoulder, and she nods as if this interaction is perfectly normal for us, and it should be. If I hadn't allowed fear to control me, I have no doubt we'd be married and living a blissful life together.

I step away as Hank indicates but stay close enough that I can keep an eye on Cherry.

"I spoke with Hunter."

My spine stiffens at Hank's words, expecting him to fire me for putting the company at risk by contacting the Mancini family or at least tell me how disappointed he was in me. I don't regret it but I'll forever mourn the loss of these people if they choose to cut ties with me. "And?"

"I'm sorry, son."

I glance at him in shock as I grab two flutes of Champagne from a passing waiter and step back to hand one to Cherry who smiles in appreciation, before going back to her conversation with Vivian and Cassie and allowing me the space to speak with Hank.

"Sorry? Why would you be sorry?"

"I should have known. I should have protected you."

"How could you? I never told you about any of it."

Hank grips my shoulder tight. "As far as Viv and I are concerned, you're one of our kids and we failed you."

"Hank, no. You're the only people in my life who ever gave a shit about me. Without you and Vivian, I'd be dead or in prison. You didn't fail anyone."

Hank shakes his head sadly. "You deserved better than the start you had, Jake. I want you to know I've spoken to Mancini Senior, and he, as a favor to me, will be handling the situation with Nicholas Kendrick."

"At what cost, Hank? I didn't want you involved. This is my mess and I need to handle it."

"No cost. He owed me. Now the debt he owed is repaid, we're done."

"So Cherry is safe from Kendrick and KLM?"

"Yes."

A weight lifts so fast I feel dizzy with it. "The land?"

"I don't have control over the KLM board, and they may still go after it, even with Kendrick out of the picture, but my guess is they'll go after something more profitable and less of a headache."

"Thank you, Hank. Truly."

Hank slaps me on the shoulder. "No need, son. Now go enjoy yourself."

"I have a speech to make first." I roll my eyes because everyone knows I hate this part. I love this charity and feel passionate about it, so I'll do what's needed but I'm the back-room guy. Hunter and Hank are the face of Lungo, and rightly so. No matter how many shares I now own.

But now at least I can let myself breathe without the pressure of KLM and Kendrick, and a deal I almost made with the Mafia to secure the future of the woman I loved. Now all I need to do is tell her the whole truth about the past.

27. Cherry

WATCHING JAKE SPEAK ABOUT THE CHARITY HE'S CLEARLY SO passionate about makes me think about what he'd told me about his mom and sister. My heart breaks for the young boy who'd been forced to grow up so quickly, who'd taken on more than any adult should be expected to let alone a child.

His command of the room, the way he looks out at the people gathered tonight and bleeds every emotion he feels about this charity into them, is making me feel things I know I shouldn't.

It would be so easy to fall back into the easy love we'd shared, so simple to let my heart beat for him again. A part of me wants to just let go and see what happens, to see if we crash and burn or have what it takes to last the test of time, but I know if we crash again, I won't be getting up and walking away this time. It will crush me in a way I'll never recover from.

"Still have that childish pink hair, I see."

I glance sideways at the woman who's just insulted me and find myself staring at a second blast from the past.

"Lorelei. Still bitchy and insecure, I see."

Lorelei looks at me like she's chewed a wasp, her lip curling and I imagine if she could move any other part of her face, it would be the same.

"Still clinging onto people who don't really want you, I see."

I bark out a laugh, not in the least bit affected by her attempt to make me feel insecure. "You're gonna have to do better than that, Lorelei."

I turn to leave, not willing to spare another second of my time sparring with such an unworthy opponent, but she grabs my arm. I snatch my arm away and glare at her. "Touch me again and you won't be needing lip filler for a month."

Lorelei lets go, stepping back from my reach. Clearly aware I'll happily follow through on my threat.

"How can you have such low self-respect that you'd sleep with a man who was in my bed just last week? Really, I thought after he went to all the trouble of getting you kicked out of Harvard just to get rid of you, that you'd get the hint."

Her words sting, picking the scabs of old wounds that still haven't healed. Jake's past sexual exploits have no bearing on us now. We both have a past. And as much as I hate the idea of him with anyone else, I'm not an idiot. The other thing though, the thought he wanted out of our relationship and he set me up to get me out of the picture, sits uncomfortably in that spot in my brain where all my self-doubts have built a cozy little home.

I smell him before I feel his hand on my hip and see the fear morph over Lorelei's features before she recovers her composure.

"Still peddling your bullshit, Lorelei? We both know the last time my cock was anywhere near you, I was still growing out the baby fluff on my chin."

My snort is inelegant, but I don't care as Jake squeezes my side and looks down at me with a conspiratorial smile and a wink that makes my belly flutter like an army of butterflies just took flight.

"Why are you with her, Jake? She's not even in the same league as you."

My skin bristles at her swipe, reminding me of the deep void of wealth between Jake and me.

"You're right, she isn't."

I stiffen at his words and watch as a smug smile spreads across my enemy's face. Jake better pull something out of the bag with this or he'll be having a painful meeting with the pointy end of my shoe.

"Cherry is so far out of my league we're not even in the same stratosphere. I'm the luckiest bastard in the world that she chose to come here with me tonight and grace me with her time." His body moves closer to mine and I lean in as he continues, his words like a balm over my skin, chasing away the doubts this woman has torn open and exposed.

"That I failed her by allowing someone such as you to speak to her with such disrespect is unacceptable, and I only hope she can forgive me."

With that, Jake turns and lifts his chin at two muscular guards, who have been watching from a respectful distance.

"Please escort this woman out and ensure she doesn't return to any future events held by, or for, Lungo."

"Jake, what are you doing? This is a silly mistake. I didn't know she was with you."

Jake holds his finger up and Lorelei goes silent at the deadly coldness emanating from him towards her.

"Stop. You're boring me. This isn't a mistake, this was another attempt by you to try and assert power over someone for your own enjoyment. I am telling you and anyone else that even wants to think about it, Cherry Baker is off fucking limits. She's mine, she's the woman I love, and if you fuck with her, then you fuck with me and you do *not* want that."

As the two men escort a pissed off Lorelei from the room, I'm left reeling from all the confessions of the last few minutes. The fact he says I'm out of his league is nice and flattering but can be put down to showmanship, no matter how much I enjoyed it. But him declaring

I'm the woman he loves is a lot, and I don't know how to feel about it, or even if it is real.

"I've left you speechless. Not quite the way I expected it to happen, but we adapt. How about a dance?"

Jake whisks me off my feet onto the dance floor before I can process his words, and maybe that was his intention.

As the upbeat song plays, I shove the encounter to the back of my head as I let the music thrum through my body. Jake catches my hand and spins me out, before pulling back in as I laugh and let myself just feel. His hands skim over my body as we dance, and the release of the music flowing through my veins becomes something heavier, something headier.

My gaze falls to his lips, the memory of how soft they are, how much pleasure they give me, how his words hold such power over me floods through my brain. Warmth spreads through me, making my nipples pucker and my pussy ache for his touch.

The band slows things down, and I feel Jake's heated stare on me as he snags me around the waist and hauls me against his chest. His scent is so familiar and intoxicating that it makes my head fuzzy as oxygen is stolen by his hands on me.

"You're so fucking beautiful, Blossom."

"Thank you. I am a ten, after all."

It's the first time I've referenced our past in any way but bitterness, and I see pleasure stain his cheeks as one hand smooths over the skin of my spine, and the other moves slowly over my hip and up.

"No, baby, you're a twelve and I'm still your humble servant."

"You remembered!" Surprise makes me stop moving and Jake looks down at me as he holds me like I'm something precious, his eyes revealing every emotion he's feeling.

"I remember everything about you, Blossom. I remember that you hate olives because you think they look too much like grapes, and then you're disappointed when you eat them. I remember how it feels to have your legs wrapped around me as I fuck you. I remember you love dark romance and your belief that all men should be made to read them so we can understand what a woman really wants."

I place a finger over his lips, and he stops speaking to nip my skin and press a kiss to the pad. My skin is feverish, my body tingles, and I know I'm about to take a huge risk. What is life without risk though but a rolling monotony of days until you die?

"Come with me." Taking his hand, I wonder if he'll follow and look back to see a bemused smile on his face as he lets me drag him from the room. I'm not thinking right now, I'm acting on instinct and my instinct is telling me to show Jake what his gesture with Lorelei means to me.

Spying the door to the restroom I know is cleaner and posher than any bathroom I've ever been inside, I head towards it. Once Jake is inside, I close and lock the door before turning to him and finding him watching me with a dark look of a man starved. His gaze trips over me from head to toe, and I let him.

I don't know if it's the dress or the way he looks at me, but I feel powerful. Like I could own this man if I choose to, but I also recognize he owns a big piece of me, too. With my eyes still on his hungry gaze, I lift the hem of my dress and sink to my knees.

His tongue comes out to lick his bottom lip and the action makes my body squirm with desire as a flood of wetness hits my panties. Reaching up, I palm the steel of his erection through the fabric of his tuxedo pants, and his hiss of appreciation makes my head spin.

This is power. Not the dress, but the way he looks at me, the way he lets me see how much I affect him. His cock flexes beneath my hand as I slide the zipper down inch by inch, our breathing growing louder as anticipation fills the room with oxygen.

I free his hard cock and saliva floods my mouth as the musky scent of him hits my nose. I know how it feels to choke on his cock. I know how it tastes, how soft the skin is, and how good it feels when he takes control, which I can see he's on the brink of doing. There he is, the dominant man who makes me want to weep with how much pleasure he gives me. No man has ever been able to please me like

Jake, and that's because he was, and still is, the only one I trust to have this control.

"Are you sure about this, Blossom?"

"Yes."

"Good girl."

My body practically purrs at his praise and I feel myself relax for the first time in so long. Jake holds my gaze as he reaches out and presses my bottom lip open, forcing his thumb between my lips. His skin is salty as he drags it over my tongue and I moan. Not from the taste but from the action.

"Suck. Show me how much you need my cock."

I do as he asks, forgetting everything else except his command and the feel of him taking control. When he slides his thumb out, he hums as I look up at him.

"Stand up."

He gives me his hand as I stand, his gentle touch at odds with the dominance radiating from his body. It should be a contradiction, but Jake was always gentle with me, even when his hand was around my throat.

"Lift your dress and show me my pretty pussy."

Walking my fingers down my thighs, I drag the hem of the dress higher until it's above my hips. I squeeze my thighs together to ease the throb of arousal sliding through me. Jake watches me and his body tenses, his cock proud and erect as it bobs between us from his open zipper. Pre-cum slides down his length and I lick my lips, desperate to taste him.

A dark chuckle falls from him. "Such a little slut for my cock, Blossom."

I'd argue but what is the point when it's true? His words force an overwhelming sensation of lust to skitter through my bloodstream and though he's hardly touched me, I can feel the first flickers of climax edging my vision.

His fingertips toy with the edge of my panties, making my head feel too heavy for my neck. Then with a flick of his wrist, he tears the silk from my skin. Bringing it to his face, he inhales like my scent is a drug and he's starved for his next fix, his eyes falling closed as his cock throbs, bumping against my swollen clit. A whimper slips from my lips and Jake smirks as he shoves the sodden, destroyed silk in his pocket.

God, this is turning into so much more than the quick blow job I planned to give him in the cloakroom, but then I should have known it would. Jake isn't a man to let anyone, even me, control his sexual encounters.

Without warning, his hand comes up and grips my throat as the other slides between my thighs, his fingers sliding over my sensitive flesh that is soaked for him.

"Fuck."

Gathering the moisture from my aching pussy, he rubs the pads of his fingers over my clit, before pushing his thumb inside my needy cunt. Just like that, sensation slams into me, and I have to grip his arm as my climax hits me like an out-of-control tornado. My legs shake, my whole body spasms and Jake holds my gaze through it all. A connection that has always been between us springs to life in a way I can't deny anymore. This is us, this indescribable understanding of each other is what I've missed for the last ten years.

Removing his fingers from my pussy, he slides them between his lips and sucks every drop of my climax from them, his growl of appreciation making my body eager for round two.

"You're still my favorite dessert, Blossom."

Familiar words, once uttered between two kids in love, now fill me with something else. Hope, fear, lust, all swimming around in a pool of confusion in my brain.

"On your knees."

His words snap me out of my spiral and I sink to the floor of the restroom, the lace of my dress pooling around me, and look up at the man who owns me, body and soul. Even when I hated him, he was the one who could make me feel more than any other man ever has or will.

His strong fingers grip his cock as he guides the blunt end of his dick to my lips.

"Open and take what I give you, little slut."

I should hate that he calls me that, but knowing that he also calls me his queen makes it hot in a way that I control.

I open my mouth and he paints his cock across my lips, coating my skin with his pre-cum like lip gloss.

"So pretty."

My eyes flutter closed at his words, savoring every sensation.

"Open your eyes, Blossom."

My eyes pop open as he gives me a look of approval that makes my shoulders lift back. Jake guides his cock between my lips, his hands gripping my cheeks.

"You gonna be a good girl and take what I give you?"

My mouth is full of his thick, veiny cock, so I nod my assent instead. Jake hums and pulls back before sliding between my lips again, his head thrown back in pleasure as he begins to fuck my mouth.

I suck and lick as best I can, but this isn't in my control, he has it all, and I love it. He uses my mouth as tears run down my cheeks, his cock head making me gag as saliva drools down my chin.

This isn't romantic, nor is it polite. It's raw, base fucking and I own it. I revel in the power I've willingly handed over to him. His cock blocks my airway as my nose tickles against the hair of his groin. My vision flitters black at the edges and my hand slides between my legs but firm fingers stop me as he pulls back, allowing air to rush into my burning lungs.

"Did I say you could touch my pussy?"

A moan of frustration has me digging my fingers into his hard thighs as he increases his pace. His body is rigid, his movements jerky as he stills for a split second and then a roar of pleasure leaves him and thick ropes of his come hit my throat. It's salty as I swallow every drop until he slides out from between my lips with a pop.

I sag back on my heels as he leans against the counter. Jake bends, hooking me under the arms with his hands and lifting me so my feet dangle off the ground and his nose rubs against my neck. I wrap my arms around his shoulders and we stay wrapped in our bubble until someone bangs on the door.

"Get a fucking room. Some people need to pee."

A burst of laughter falls from me and soon we're both laughing like loons. As we sober, reality intrudes and Jake holds my cheek in one hand, his free arm holding up against his body.

"I meant it, Blossom, what I said tonight. Not the way I wanted to tell you, but it doesn't make it less true. I do love you. I've always loved you and I always will."

"Then tell me the truth."

"Let me take you home and I'll tell you everything."

I stare into his eyes and see nothing but honesty waiting for me. I nod once, hoping I don't end this night with my heart in tatters.

28. Cherry

My beautiful little home, which once felt perfectly proportioned, feels small as I close and lock the door behind Jake and I. Sudden nerves flutter over my skin as I walk into the living room, and dump my purse on the small credenza that splits the living area from the dining table.

"Can I get you a drink?" My hands feel lost like they don't know where they should be as I rub wet palms against my dress.

"Blossom, come here."

My feet are moving before I can stop them and I find myself in front of Jake who's standing in front of the couch. His hands reach for me, his palms on my ass as he pulls me close. I can feel the hardness of his cock against me and a frisson of desire sparks along my spine, making me wriggle.

A sharp slap has me stilling.

"Behave, or I'll forget every good intention in my head and fuck you right here."

My hips shimmy and I give him a coy look meant to entice, but all I get is a bewildered frown, followed by a soft look that makes me want to weep.

"What are you afraid of? You wanted this, you deserve these answers but now you're trying to distract me from telling you."

He's right. I've wanted these answers for so long. Conjured up different scenarios in my head where he begs for my forgiveness, but now it's happening, I'm afraid that maybe there is some truth in what Lorelei said. Perhaps he was looking for a way out.

"Nothing. Just... the unknown, I guess."

Things with Jake and I feel so tentative right now, like the slightest wrong move and this house of cards we've built will tumble to the ground.

Jake falls backward on the couch, taking me with him, so I'm sprawled out across his lap, his arms cradling me close. I go to push off him and he tightens his hold.

"Stay."

I see the vulnerability on his face, as he makes that one request, and realize that I'm not the only one afraid of what might happen when the truth is finally out in the open. I nod and settle against him.

"Tell me why?"

"I was being blackmailed."

Shock prickles my skin, a sudden feeling of cold, heaviness expanding from my belly, as I try to pull away from his hold only to have him tighten his arms around me. I glare at him as I try to shove away and he closes his eyes and drops his head.

"Please, Blossom, I need to say this and I need you close when I do or I won't get it all out, and I need to."

"Fine, but only because I need answers."

"Thank you."

I'm caught between my natural reaction to fly off the handle and my need to soothe this man who has always managed to get the soft side of me to come out so easily.

"Who blackmailed you, Jake?"

Jake's fingers tap out a distracted dance on my leg, the muscles in his neck corded so tight he looks like the slightest movement will cause him to snap. "An old acquaintance."

He looks like he's been thrown back in time, but these one-word answers are fraying my nerves.

"Who? Stop making me work for this, Jake. You owe me this and if you can't give it to me you need to get out and leave me the hell alone."

Jake gives a curt nod. "A man named Nick Kendrick. He and I got into some trouble when we were younger and I almost went to jail. He threatened to tell you everything if I didn't steal the paper."

"No." My voice is barely a whisper as nausea swirls in my belly. Something stirs in my brain at the name, but I can't quite place it.

Jake grips me tighter, his hand smoothing slow circles over the skin of my thigh.

"I said no, I would never have done that and risk you, Blossom. You were my whole world, you still are, but he set you up anyway. When I tried to intervene, he threatened to tell you about my past."

My hand flutters to my throat as a heavy sense of dread sinks to the pit of my stomach. I know he never killed anyone or hurt someone because he already told me that and, despite everything, I believed him and still do.

"What did you do?"

"I stole a car with him."

I rear back, confusion pulling at my brow. "A car? Is that it? You destroyed my life over a stolen car?"

"Well. There's a little more, but that was the only crime I committed."

I turned to him then, laying my hand on his chest. "And you didn't think I would love you knowing that? You thought so little of me?" Hurt and anger color my words and I push off his lap to give myself some room to think and process his words. Jake sighs and hangs his hand between his knees in defeat unlike anything I've seen on him before, and I hate it. His head lifts and he holds my gaze with his own, anger, despair, fear, and regret swimming in those pools of green.

"I wasn't the man I am now, Blossom. I owed the McKenzies

everything and they did, and still do, treat me like family, but I never believed I deserved it or you, so I was terrified you'd hate me. I was a coward."

"You're lying. There's more to this story."

Jake hangs his head and blows out a breath. "Yes. After the Dean found the tape of you stealing the papers, I was going to go to him and tell him what really happened, but I got an email from Nick with a file attached."

"He threatened you?"

Shame is a funny thing to see on such a proud man, and despite spending the majority of the last ten years wanting to see it, now I hate it more than anything.

"Tell me." I move toward him and sink to my knees, my palm on his bristled cheek making him look up and I see so much love there that I don't know what to do with it. I'm so angry still, and I know letting go of years of hatred won't be easy.

"The file contained the name of the man whose car we stole. I never knew it and Hank said it was better not to know the details. I always went along with it, because by that point, I didn't trust a single decision I made not to land me back in the shit."

"Who was it?"

I know, even before he says the words, I know the only reason he would've hidden it from me is because the truth is just too awful. I shuffle back, dropping my hand from his touch as he reaches out to try and stop me, but I can feel my body shutting down, my emotions going cold before he even utters the words.

"It was your father."

"No!"

I scramble back, almost tripping on my dress as I stand before he reaches for me. I step out of his reach as he falls to his knees in front of me, the bowtie he's worn all night hanging loose around his neck, his hair disheveled from my fingers.

"Blossom, listen, it's not true. The file was fake. It was all bullshit. The man we stole the car from did die, but two days earlier and it was nothing to do with us stealing his car. His wife shot him after years of abuse. I was nowhere near your father's car when it was stolen."

"You promise?"

Relief hits me so hard that my legs give way and Jake catches me as we go down. His strong arms hold me as I shake, my emotions so scrambled that I don't know what to feel. He cradles me against him as we sit like that on my living room floor for what feels like forever, both of us silent as we process the revelation.

Eventually, I slide out from under his arms and he lets me go as I step back, putting the coffee table I painstakingly restored between us. Jake watches me, his expression guarded and I don't know how to let go of this anger.

"I don't know where we go from here, Jake. You've told me what happened but it doesn't change the outcome. I left Harvard, the place my father dreamed of going, under an ugly cloud. It colored every decision I made going forward. I gave up on my dream career. But what was so much worse was that I stopped believing in love. I fought not to fall for you. Then when I did, I fell so hard that when the rug was pulled away, I smashed into the rocks and I was left putting fragments of myself back together."

Tears sting my eyes and, for once, I let them fall. If we're to have any hope of making this right, he needs to see how his actions impacted my life.

"I know, baby."

I shake my head. "No, you don't know. I was destroyed. I couldn't eat, I barely slept. I was a shell, and I was so ashamed for being a fool and falling for someone out of my league that I never shared a word of our time together with anyone for months. It was only when my mom dragged me to the doctor, thinking I was sick, that I got my shit together and realized that I didn't even have the luxury of falling apart because I had people who needed me. Your actions did that."

I hold my hand up as he goes to speak. "I know you didn't mean it, I know you were in an awful spot, but if you had only trusted me, and believed me then this wouldn't have happened."

My chest is heaving as I feel the last of the anger drain from me having allowed myself to voice aloud the pain I had felt. His scent surrounds me and all I want is to feel his arms around me, but I need him to understand. Forgiveness isn't like flipping a switch, at least not for me. Yes, a burden has lifted tonight but it will take time for me to trust him again, if that is even what he wants. "You were a coward." My voice is softer as I move to sit beside him.

Jake winces but he doesn't shy away from my angry words or reach for me.

"I was. I chose my fear of losing your love over your future and lost anyway. I think in my head, I couldn't stand the thought of you thinking I killed your dad. I hoped one day you'd forgive me for stealing your future. It was selfish and wrong and my biggest regret. I am truly, truly sorry, Blossom. If I live to be a thousand, I'll never be able to make up for the pain I caused you, but I want to try."

And just like that, my anger at him dies, turning to dust in the face of his truth and honesty. I crawl into his open arms and bury my head in his neck, as he holds me like I'm the most precious thing in the world. Had he denied my accusation or tried to defend himself, I might have fought harder to forgive him. But the truth is, he made a mistake from fear and as I sit in his arms on my living room floor, I'm not sure I would've done things any differently. Jake didn't engineer what happened to hurt me, he didn't knowingly put me in that position. He just made an impossible choice from two options that both had tragically heartbreaking outcomes.

"You picked the choice that would hurt me the least."

His nod brushes his lips against my temple. "I knew if you thought you'd fallen in love with your father's killer, it would destroy you. This way you lost but you got to hate me without hating yourself."

It's a bitter pill to swallow, but I know in my heart he's right. I would've hated myself, and though his actions were to protect himself, I can see he was thinking of me too.

"I'm sorry. I shouldn't have called you a coward."

Jake's arms flex around my waist. "You were right, I was a coward. I should have checked the facts but I panicked and when I did find out, I was too ashamed to come after you."

"I'm not sure I would've listened back then. I can be a bit stubborn when I'm mad."

Jake's eyebrow rose and a smirk twitches on his lips. "A bit?"

"Oh, shut up." I swat his chest and he catches my hand and brings my fingertips to his lips.

"What happens now?" I ask as butterflies flutter in my belly from his touch. "I do forgive you, Jake, but trusting you is going to take longer."

He nods as he twines our fingers together, seeming to need the contact. "I know, Blossom. I have a lot of work to do to put right the wrongs I caused you, but if you give me the chance, I won't ever let you down again."

"You'd better not, I have friends that would happily help me hide your body if you fuck up again, Jake, and that includes Hunter."

Jake chuckles, his eyes bright and full of love.

"You have my word."

I nod, taking his word being my first act of trusting him. "So what now?"

"I need to handle Nick Kendrick. I won't give him the chance to hurt us again. Hank has handled most of it, but I need to make sure the message is crystal clear."

"Kendrick," I say as the name once again tickles something at the back of my mind. "Why do I know that name?"

"He's the CEO of KLM. At least for now."

Recognition clouds my brain for a second before clearing. "Is that why he's coming after the land?"

"Actually, he shouldn't be an issue now."

"Why won't he be an issue?"

Jake smirks. "Well, it turns out Hank has some friends in very high, or maybe that's low places."

"Oh?"

"Yeah, he's friends with the Mancini family and has called in a favor as Kendrick is linked back to them."

Something in his voice makes me take a second look at his face, and I realize right now how open he's being with me. His expression hides nothing.

"Ask me, Blossom."

His smirk makes me poke out my tongue. "Don't act like you can read my mind."

His hand skims up my calf and over the delicate flesh at the back of my knee, making me shiver.

"Oh, I can read that beautiful mind of yours better than you think."

The air thickens with the heat of our arousal as my body leans closer, erasing the space between us as I straddle him. Jake's hands go to my hips as the skirt of my dress pools around my thighs. Part of me wants to know how the Mancini family, a well-known mafia family, will deal with Kendrick, but right now I don't care enough to pursue it. Not when Jake is here and we have a whole lot of time to make up for.

"Oh, yeah, and what's on my mind right now?"

Jake's deep chuckle sends a spark of heat straight to my clit.

"You need to make this harder, Blossom."

I wriggled in his lap, my pussy grazing over his thick, hard cock. "It feels plenty hard enough to me."

"Umm, she wants to play." Jake grips my hips in his firm hold and directs my movements over his cock, my bare pussy soaking the fabric over his cock with my desire.

"Maybe."

Palming the back of my head he brings my lips closer until we're sharing the same breath. My heart races beneath his touch, excitement and the anticipation of being with him again, skin to skin, heightening every feeling.

"I know you want me. I know you're terrified this will end badly, and I know that right now you don't care because this is us. You and

225

me, Blossom, the girl with the pink hair who pretends to give zero fucks, when all she does is care too much, and the boy who loves every single version of her."

Then he slams his lips against mine and kisses me as if I'm the only oxygen he'll ever need to breathe again. My skin prickles from the fire in his kiss, every sweep of his tongue like a brand. His fingers fist in my hair, the pinch of pain making me moan into his mouth as he tilts my head exactly how he wants it.

I'd forgotten what it's like to kiss Jake. It was never an act just to get to the main event for him. He applied himself with as much passion to kissing me senseless as he did to fucking me until I screamed.

"Fuck, I missed this mouth."

His words are a deep rasp against my skin, and I claw at his jacket, needing to feel his skin under my fingertips.

"Rip it, Blossom."

His lips ghost down my neck as I tear at his shirt until the buttons pop and I finally get to feel all that warm, golden muscle under my fingertips.

"You taste so good and your scent. Fuck, I could get high on the smell of you."

My hands feel frantic as I touch everywhere, never stopping in my haste to consume this feeling between us. My hands curl into his thick, silky soft hair and groan as he ups the rhythm of his hands on my hips so that I'm humping his cock like a wanton whore.

I'm shameless in my pursuit of my climax as he lifts his head to watch me.

"Come all over my cock, baby. Soak me with that pussy until it drips all over me."

"Such a dirty mouth," I gasp as my toes curl and my orgasm slams into me like a freight train.

Jake claims my lips and kisses me hard and deep, only slowing and turning his kiss into a lazy assault when my climax leaves me spent.

"I missed you, Jake."

The admission is a lot for me and Jake knows it. He kisses me softly and stands with me in his arms. I wish I could say his act of strength wasn't a turn-on but it would be a lie.

"Not done with you yet, Blossom. I never will be."

"Then take me to bed and convince me to stay."

I giggle as he slaps my ass. "Woman, behave or maybe I'll punish you."

"Hmm, maybe you should."

A growl is the last thing he says before he's carrying up my stairs, where the night is just beginning.

29. Jake

"Fuck, I missed you, Blossom."

"Hurry."

Her desperation is like an aphrodisiac and I feel the tight leash of my control begin to fray. As my feet hit the landing of her small house, I glance at the three closed doors and hate the time it's costing me to be inside her. "Which door, Blossom? And hurry or I'm fucking you in the hallway."

"Left."

Her hands are tearing at my shirt as I kick open the door and her scent hits me in the balls. This room is the essence of her. I stride to the bed and toss her in the middle of it, rolling her to her front with more haste than finesse, but I need her out of this dress. Undoing the tiny devil hooks isn't easy but I know she'll kill me if I damage this dress, even though I'd buy her an entire wardrobe just to have the pleasure of tearing them from her body. I expose the perfection of her body as I kiss down her spine, and her hands clench the sheets beneath her. Lifting her hips, I drag the fabric off and drape it over the pink chair.

Cherry looks at me over her shoulder, her gaze a sultry tease as she wiggles her hips. With a growl, I shed my clothes in record time, not giving a fuck if they tear, just desperate to get to her.

I fist my cock as she lifts up to watch me over her shoulder.

"Turn over, Blossom."

She does as I ask, and my eyes sweep over her perfect, creamy skin. Her gorgeous tits are just begging for my mouth, and I know, no matter how desperate we are, I need to taste her first. Bracing my hands against the bed, I pull one taut nipple into my mouth, laving and sucking the tight bud as she moans my name. I give the same attention to the other breast before I let her nipple pop free from my lips with a growl. "Fuck, I missed these tits."

Her eyes are almost navy blue as she stares at me with hunger in her eyes.

I drop to my knees in front of her, hauling her to the end of the bed by her hips so her feet hang off the edge, putting her pussy right where I need it, and bend my head to kiss along her hip bones before I look up and see a look of utter trust, mixed with naked desire, and I almost come right then and there.

A growl leaves my throat as I bend my head and hook her legs over my shoulders. Her desire coats her thighs, and I kiss my way to her perfect pussy, finding her wet and ready for me. I tease her entrance before thrusting two fingers inside her as my tongue teases her clit. Her back arches as I stroke my fingers over her inner walls and flick her clit until she's writhing beneath me.

"Jake, oh God."

"Not God, baby."

I work her body until she's begging me, as my own desire sits on the edge, my cock aching to the point of pain to be inside her again, but I need her to come first. I'm not sure I'll last once I'm inside her.

"That's it, Blossom, ride my fingers with that hot cunt." I feel her body clench, her breath coming in short, sharp gasps.

"Oh, God. Oh fuccckkk. I'm gonna come."

"Come all over my face, Blossom. Give me all of you."

My words send her over the edge and I feel her body grow taut as a bow before she's riding my face, hopeless, incoherent words falling from her lips as she drenches my chin with her come and I drink down every drop. My wild, fucking perfect Blossom.

Her legs go slack and fall to the bed as I pull away, the taste and scent of her all over my skin. I stand and fist my cock as she looks up at me through hooded eyes. Her gaze makes me feel marked, claimed, and I've never seen her more beautiful.

"Come here."

I should deny her. I wish I could, but I want this as much as she does, if not more. It's not about who's in charge in this moment, it's about me not being able to go another second without being inside her. Putting my knee on the bed, I stretch out over her body, careful not to crush her into the bed. My body nestles between her soft thighs, her wet pussy cushioning my hard cock.

"I can't believe I survived so long without you. Don't ever make me have to endure it again, Blossom."

Lifting up on my elbows, my arms cradle either side of her face. I need to see her eyes when I claim her so that I know we're on the same page.

"I love you, Cherry Baker."

I watch her eyes go liquid, like the ocean on a perfect summer day, and she reaches up to skim her fingertips over my lips.

"I know."

Her words force a bark of laughter from my lips but when she pulls my head to hers and kisses me, I taste the salt of her tears.

"No tears, Blossom."

"They're happy tears, and you should feel blessed I'd shed them for you."

Rubbing my cock through the folds of her pussy lips, I watch her sharp intake of breath and give her the truth.

"I feel blessed by every emotion you give me, Blossom. Anger, hate, love, lust. All of it. I'll take it all because to have even a fraction of your attention is more than I deserve."

I've worked so hard these last few months to win her over, to earn her forgiveness, but I'm fully aware I don't deserve it. If she chooses to be angry with me for the rest of my life, I'll understand. It will kill me, but I'll understand. Now she has forgiven me though, I'm going to make sure she never suffers a single day of pain again. And if ending Nick Kendrick is the price, then so be it.

Her soft warm body wriggles against mine and I bend, taking a nipple between my lips and sucking until she arches into me and moans.

Fuck, I love her tits, her pussy, her ass. Everything about this woman was made for me.

My cock nudges inside her, and she sighs, her back arching in pleasure as I groan from the feel of her tight heat surrounding me. She's better than perfection, my Blossom has been molded in heaven just for me. Her legs come up and lock around my waist as I slide deeper inside, my cock rubbing against her G-spot as I slowly thrust into her. Being inside her is like being home. I never want to fucking leave this place. I make love to her as we keep eye contact, the connection re-forming from what we had years ago into something new, something unbreakable.

My thrusts become deeper, and I feel a flood of wet heat coat my dick when I tease the pucker of her asshole with my finger.

"Hmm, you like the thought of me fucking your sweet ass, Blossom?"

"I want you everywhere, Jake. Make me yours."

Some would see her words as surrender, and in this room, she does surrender to me, but outside of this room, she's the one who owns every piece of me. I'll die for this woman. I would kill for her.

Gripping my fingers around her throat, I squeeze gently as her eyes dilate and she soaks my cock with her pleasure.

"You gonna come for me, Blossom?"

Her body responds to my dark command as I squeeze her pretty throat, my cock punishing her pussy just how she likes. Then her fingers grip my wrist and her legs shake as she writhes beneath me. I release my hold on her neck and she screams my name in ecstasy.

Seeing her fall over the edge so beautifully is enough to send my cock wild and I drive into her, railing into her like a beast, and my vision blanks and I see heaven.

30. Cherry

THINGS WITH JAKE AND I ARE PERFECT. I'VE NEVER BEEN happier and that in itself is a little scary. Since the gala three weeks ago, we've been wrapped in a perfect bubble. We spend every night either at my place or his, and every weekend has been at the new house I'm helping him renovate. In the week he works, doing whatever it is corporate lawyers for huge companies do, but he never fails to let me know he's thinking of me.

I get regular text messages from him, like the one from ten minutes ago.

> Jake: You make my heart beat fast.

or,

> Jake: Every thought I have these days, always circles back to you.

It makes me feel happy in a way I haven't felt since we were together before. Being loved isn't something new to me. I have people who love me, I have people who need me, but Jake worships me. He shows me what it is to be loved and have someone to lean on. He lets me be me without the mask of strength.

No promises have been made and I'm okay with that. He's told me how he feels, and I know this thing between us has some kind of future, but I still haven't told him I love him yet. I know he feels that, even though he says he'll wait forever if that's what it takes.

Now, though, I have a different conversation to have and that's the one I've been avoiding with my best friend. Lexi hasn't pushed me, but I know she has questions about me and Jake and the past we clearly share.

I step out of my car and onto the drive of the home she and Hunter have just closed on, which is two minutes away from the one Jake bought. The only real difference is that this one is new and built to her and Hunter's design plan.

"Hey, you!"

Lexi greets me with a hug as I tap the door and enter. "Hey, I brought strawberry tarts from that bakery you love."

Lexi takes them and I follow her into the perfect chef's kitchen that opens up into the family room behind and an informal dining table to the left. Beyond that is the huge garden that sweeps into an orchard with a gated pool and patio area for entertaining.

"You trying to butter me up, Cher?"

"Me? No, of course not." We both know I'm lying. This conversation is going to be tough but it's long overdue. "Where is my gorgeous godson?"

"Out doing some errands with his gorgeous father."

I wrinkle my nose and she squints at me in warning. "I mean he's okay looking, but I wouldn't say gorgeous."

"Oh, yeah, I forgot. You like your men with green eyes, and thick brown hair, and a jaw line that would make an artist weep."

Her eyebrows rise and I swallow. "I guess we're doing this now. Going straight in without any lube or anything?"

Lexi stomps, yes stomps, her foot at me as we face off across the kitchen of her dream home.

"Why didn't you tell me?"

"Tell you what?"

Lexi throws up her hands. "How the hell should I know? You won't fucking tell me."

Lexi isn't known for her potty mouth, she's the good one of our little duet, so her breaking out the F-bomb is a testament to how pissed she is with me.

"Okay, let's grab a drink and go outside and I'll tell you everything."

"Fine, but I'm holding these strawberry tarts hostage until you tell me every detail."

"Gee, Lex, I didn't realize you had such a kinky side," I tease.

She pokes her tongue out at me and that's when I know it's going to be okay. Whatever I tell her today will have no bearing on our friendship. It never would have, I was just too insecure to see it.

The sun is warm on my skin as I take a seat beside my oldest friend on the lawn chairs that look out over the orchard. The birds chirp, the fluffy white clouds floating in the sky giving the blue a much brighter color. Something about this place is so peaceful and I envy her living here. Soon Jake will move here too, and I want to think one day so might I, but first I need to get over my own fears and get out of my own way.

Lexi reaches out and takes my hand. "Talk to me, Cher." Her voice is soft and comforting but with a hidden strength now after what she's been through this last year. I see my friend in an entirely new light and have gained such admiration for her.

"Jake and I met at Harvard." I pause, waiting for her to speak, but she just squeezes my hand. "We literally bumped into each other my first day. I knew even then, Lexi. I knew he'd be my ruin in some way, and I was determined to stay away from him but he was so persistent. We became friends. He'd take me out on his bike, we'd watch movies together and eat pizza, and then it evolved slowly over time. He'd send me a good morning text every day before I woke and I fell so hard for him."

I choke down the emotion as the memories of the past are so clear in my mind. I see the way he looked at me, the gentle touches, the protective way he held me in his arms.

"What went wrong?"

I glance across at my friend who is patiently waiting to hear my story. "We became us. We went from friends to so much more. I loved him like I've never loved anyone and he felt the same way. We'd whisper about our plans for the future, the places we'd go, the things we'd see and then one day, just the day after I finally told him I loved, him he broke my heart."

"I swear, Cher, if he cheated on you, I'm taking a baseball bat to his balls."

I laugh at the thought of my beautiful friend going all crazy on Jake but shake my head. "He didn't cheat. At least not with a girl."

I go on to tell her exactly what happened, giving her every detail of the break-up that shaped my life. Her hand stays in mine as I give her everything and she never falters.

"Wow, that's a lot to process."

"Yeah, I know."

We sit in silence for a bit, sipping our iced tea and letting the beauty of the garden wash over us.

"Can I ask you something?"

I turn to Lexi and see sadness swimming in her eyes as I nod. "Of course."

"Why didn't you tell me? Was it because I was a horrible friend, too wrapped up in her own bullshit with Dean to notice?"

"No. God, no. I just... I guess I was ashamed that I'd fallen for his charm and been made into a fool. I just wanted to forget about it and move on."

"But you didn't, did you?"

Prickles of discomfort move over my skin, and I hate how much being vulnerable makes me want to run away. Lowering my walls isn't easy, it never has been. Each event in my life that caused me pain has only reinforced those walls, building them higher and thicker until I became a prisoner behind them, and that's a lonely place to live.

"No, I didn't. I can't explain it, Lex. Me and Jake were so fucking perfect together. He got me. He loved every crazy part of me. No, he loved me because of them and he saw past the bullshit no one else did. He's the first I cried over after my dad. I was so locked up over his death and after that initial shock, where I cried my heart out in front of my heartbroken mother, I never shed another tear."

"Why?"

"Because it was my job to make sure my mom was okay and seeing me cry hurt her, so I stopped. Then it was like I'd locked it up too tight and I couldn't cry."

"Until Jake."

"Until Jake," I agreed.

"You know we all love you, Cher. You don't need to be strong for us all the time. Friendship and loving someone is about knowing when to lean and when to be strong and you've taken on far too much of the strong. I need you to know that shit won't fly anymore, okay?"

A sob tears past Lexi's throat and I reach my arms out as tears wet my own eyes, blinking furiously. "Bitch, you made me cry," I whisper in her ear.

"Good. You deserve it for keeping secrets."

A watery laugh spills past my throat and I snort. "I deserve a strawberry tart is what I deserve."

Lexi wipes her eyes and rolls them at me. "Fine, but we aren't done."

"Fine. What else do you need to know?"

I get up and follow her to the kitchen where she begins to place the individual desserts on a plate.

"Well, what happens now? Are you and Jake together? Have you forgiven him?"

I laugh, feeling lighter than I have in a long time, the regret for not telling Lexi any of this sooner far outweighed by the relief that I can now talk to her about it.

"I honestly don't know. We haven't talked about the future, but he says he loves me."

"Duh, you'd have to be blind and deaf not to know that. He can't take his eyes off you whenever you walk in the room."

A blush steals over my cheeks. "That doesn't mean we have a future."

"So, you can't forgive him?"

Lexi hands me a plate with extra clotted cream on the side and I smile at her. She knows I have a weakness for any sweet thing, and clotted cream is my favorite.

"I think I actually do. I didn't think I could. What he did hurt me and, worse, it made me doubt myself, but looking back and knowing what I know now, what else could he do? If he'd told me what that prick had on him, I would've hated myself as much as him, so he took the only path he could in the situation."

"Nick Kendrick sounds like an absolute asshole."

"Yeah, and if I ever come face to face with him, he's getting more than a baseball bat to the balls."

"He'd be stupid to mess with Jake and Hunter now."

"I agree, and from what I understand, he's been taken care of. I don't know details but apparently Hank has friends."

"I love Hank."

"He's the coolest father-in-law, and I know Jake loves him like a father."

"So, last question. Do you love him?"

Pursing my lips I nod. "I don't think I ever stopped. Even when I hated him, I loved him."

"Have you told him?"

I shake my head, "No, the last time I told him I loved him, my life imploded. It's made me nervous to say it again."

Lexi places her hand over mine in a comforting gesture. "You will when you're ready."

"I hope so."

I dig into the strawberry tart, a moan ripping from my throat just as a commotion at the front door makes me turn to see Hunter walking through with two bags, and Jake behind him carrying Theo. My ovaries almost explode at the site of my handsome Jake and my favorite boy.

"Why are there sex noises coming from my new kitchen and I'm not even in it?" Hunter demands as he drops a kiss on Lexi that makes steam cover the windows.

Jake comes up behind me, wrapping a strong arm around me as his delicious scent surrounds me.

"Missed you, Blossom."

His lips land on mine and I sigh into him, my body a complete whore for this man.

"Can we not scar my baby son?"

Hunter takes his son from Jake with a smirk, and I allow Jake to pull me into his arms as I sit at the kitchen island on one of those stupidly uncomfortable bar chairs. They do have the advantage of putting me at the perfect height for his lips.

"What you got there?"

His eyes hold mischief that makes me want to do very bad things to him as he looks at me and then my dessert.

"Strawberry tart. Wanna try?"

I forked a small bite between his lips, and he hums his approval and chews. God, the sounds he makes should be illegal. I want to jump him right there and then. Moisture slicks between my thighs at the dark look he's giving me, the air suddenly charged with desire.

Placing his hands either side of me, so I'm pinned against the island, he dips his head, his lips grazing my ear and making me shiver.

"You're still my favorite dessert, Cherry Blossom."

I grip the collar of his shirt. "Why don't you take me home and show me?"

A glint of the hunger that simmers between us makes the dark look in his eyes so much more potent. Then before I can react, I find myself thrown over his shoulder as he marches toward the door.

"Bye, Lex, bye, Hunter."

I lift my head to find my friends laughing at us, and it feels good. I feel happy and I push aside the fear that feeling usually comes with.

31. Jake

My life is almost perfect right now. I have the love of my life in my arms, my friends are safe and happy, and I have a job I love. The only fly in the ointment is Nick Kendrick. The bastard has gone off the grid after he'd been voted out as CEO of KLM by his board. I know it was forced by the Mancini family, but the result is the same.

I'd hoped he'd slink off into the dirt with the rest of the scum, or try and confront me because I'd made sure to let him know it was me behind it. I need that asshole to heed the warning that I wasn't to be fucked with this time.

Instead, I'd heard rumblings about him being drunk in the exclusive clubs we both belonged to and spouting off his mouth about getting even. His threats wouldn't bother me despite our past, but if he comes near Cherry, he's a dead man, and I mean that as literally as I can.

Talking to Hunter this afternoon has helped and he's assured me that the man he'd recommended for surveillance on Kendrick was good, and so far he's sent me regular updates about Kendrick's whereabouts, and no move has been made towards either me or Cherry.

Still, I know a confrontation and a more personal warning is warranted and I have every intention of making that happen next week. I might be part of the Lungo empire now, and Hank might see me as one of his own, but I grew up in the slums and know how to fight dirty when needed. I have no qualms about getting my hands dirty, and, in fact, might relish it.

Perhaps I should tell Cherry all this, but I don't want her to worry. We are happy and things are perfect between us. The last thing I want is to bring that prick's name up and watch the light in her eyes dim for even a second, so I keep quiet and tell her it's over, because as far as she's concerned, it is. KLM have even given up pursuing the land her mom's salon is on after Hunter and I made some calls to the planning offices and had the permits they'd need revoked.

"Jake?" I blink out of my deep, dark thoughts to focus on the woman I love.

"Yeah, Blossom?"

We'd fallen into bed the second we got through the door of her little home, and by bed, I mean couch. I hadn't been able to wait a single second longer to taste her sweet pussy, and now we're lying in her bed with an empty pizza box on the floor. Rolling, I pull her closer as she snuggles her body into mine, draping her leg over my thighs so her pussy is resting against my hip.

"Thank you."

I glance down at her as she looks up, and I know it's corny but every second I spend with her I fall deeper in love with her. "For what?"

Cherry shrugs, forcing her tits to rub against my ribs and my arms, and my cock comes alive.

"For not giving up on me. I know I can be a lot."

Rolling up on my elbow so I can look at her in the dusk light of the evening sun, I feel a wave of love almost clog my throat. Her hair is the palest shade of pink now and shines against her perfect, pale skin. Sweeping a lock of hair from her face, I run my knuckles down her cheek and over her delicate throat, watching the goosebumps appear, and loving the way she responds to my touch.

"You never have to thank me for that. I'll never give up on you or on us because that would be like giving up on breathing. You'll never be too much for me, Blossom. Not when you were made for me."

Dipping my head, I kiss her slowly, deeply, showing her how I feel about her. Cherry hasn't said she loves me back yet, and I'm trying to be patient because she shows me with her actions how she feels. But I can't lie to myself and say I don't crave those words from her lips. She clings to me, her fingernails leaving tiny divots in my shoulders as our kiss becomes more desperate. I kiss my way down her neck, nipping at the thundering pulse in her neck. My hand smooths over the silken skin of her ribs and up. My thumb rubs over the peak of her sensitive nipple. Lifting my head, I watch it harden into a tight peak as Cherry squirms beneath my touch.

"Tell me what you need, Blossom."

"Everything."

A chuckle leaves my mouth at her demand. "Be specific, use your words or I stop."

Her huff of displeasure makes my aching cock twitch as she glares at me. I love when she gives me attitude, her sass gets me so fucking hard I could come like a teenage boy with his first porn movie.

"Your mouth. I want your mouth on me, please," she moans almost desperately.

The sound of her so hungry for my touch almost undoes me, but I rein it in and give her what she needs, seeing as she asked so sweetly.

"Good girl."

My lips close over the hard pink nipple, and I suck hard, her back bowing as her fingers thread through my hair, holding me where she wants me. I lap at her skin, nip, kiss, and suck first one and then the other nipple, until she's rubbing her pussy against my thigh to get herself off. Her reaction has pre-come leaking from my aching cock. I love seeing her getting herself off using my body.

Lifting up, I look down at her swollen lips, her eyes dilated with desire, hair spread all over the pillow, and I know there was never any chance of me getting over her, not then and certainly not now.

"I love you so fucking much, Blossom."

I don't give her a chance to reply, stealing her breath and kissing her hard, my fingers slipping through the soaking wet folds of her pussy. Cherry gasps into my mouth as I stroke her pussy and then push a finger inside her tight cunt, my thumb grazing her clit and making her ass rise off the bed.

"Jake, please."

Her words sounded breathy as if my hand is already around her delicate throat, cutting off her air as I drive her toward her climax. I add a second finger, curling them as I finger fuck her tight pussy, my thumb continuing its assault on her clit as she gets wetter, the smell of her desire for me permeating the room with her heady scent.

"Let go, gorgeous. I've got you."

At my words, her body clamps down on my hand with her pussy and thighs, her fingers digging into my scalp as I pull a nipple between my lips, and she comes hard, her body detonating on a long moan.

"Oh, fuck. Oh, God."

Her words are a jumbled list of exclamations as her orgasm washes over her until she's boneless beneath me. I release her nipple with a pop and lift my head to see her looking at me with hooded eyes full of trust.

"Fuck, you're beautiful."

Cherry palms my cheek and I turn my head, placing a kiss on her palm before I kiss my way down her body, idolizing every inch of her with my mouth and hands until I'm lying between her silky thighs.

"Hold onto the headboard."

Cherry does as I ask without question, and I stroke my hand down her body in pleasure.

Her bare pussy glistens, and I'd be lying if I said it didn't get me off to see every inch of her pink pussy wet for me. I blow on her lips and she arches her back, trying to get closer to my mouth, her arms thrown above her head like a goddess, waiting to be served by her servant, and fuck, I'm a slave for this woman.

Spreading her folds apart with my thumb, I lick her from the tight bud of her asshole to the swell of her clit, loving the taste of her on my tongue. Her body jolts as I gently suck on her clit and lay a palm on her lower belly to keep her still.

"Easy, gorgeous."

I continue my attack on her pussy until she's writhing beneath me, her legs shaking, breath heaving as she chants my name. It's powerful and my cock feels like it will explode if I don't hurry this up, but I want to savor every second I get to spend with this woman because I know what it's like to try and exist without her.

Knowing she's on the peak of another climax, I work two fingers inside her and feel her muscles clamp down like a vice. The wet sound of my fingers in her cunt fill the room like a song, and I could spend every day for the rest of my life listening to the sounds in this room.

Curling my fingers I massage her G-spot and she comes suddenly and violently, her legs shaking, body arching, her hands pulling at the metal headboard but not disobeying my command, even in her euphoric orgasm. Until the day I die, I'll never see a more beautiful sight than my Cherry Blossom coming from my touch.

Cherry lifts her heavy head and I withdraw my fingers, sliding them into my mouth and sucking her flavor off them. Cherry's eyes dilate even further as I fist my cock, her starved gaze on me as she licks her lips. She reaches for my cock, her tiny fist circling my length and stroking. Throwing my head back, I groan at the feel of her grip ping my cock. This is what heaven feels like. I lift my head and watch her for a few moments before I pull away as her mouth descends.

"Not this time, Blossom. I want to end tonight inside this pretty pussy."

Her little pout of displeasure dissipates at my words.

"You have a filthy mouth for a suit, Jake."

I watch her lazily as I stroke my cock, squeezing the base as she looks at me like I'm an oasis in the desert. "Not a suit to you, Blossom."

Cherry cocks her head. "Then who are you?"

"I'm the man who's gonna love you until the day I die."

"God, Jake, you're gonna make me cry."

"No tears, baby. I just never want you to suffer a single second of doubt about how I feel."

I get on my knees between her thighs and push them apart to give me more space. Holding my cock, I swipe the head through her wet heat before locking eyes with her one last time to make sure she's with me on this.

"Fuck me like you hate me, Jake."

"Jesus Christ, Blossom."

Her words are like gasoline on a fire. My cock pulses with the need to be inside her. I want to consume her, claim her, mark her as mine in every way. I wanted to take it slow but her words push me over the edge and I slam into her, my whole body rippling with pleasure as her cunt hugs my cock. I stop for a second to let her adjust as her moan precedes a flood of wetness from her pussy, soaking my cock in her juices, and giving me a minute to get my body back under control.

"You good, baby?"

"Perfect."

I grin at the way she purrs the word and begin to fuck her, sliding in and out of her tight sheath, loving the way she grips my cock, how I can feel her desire for me drip down my balls. Dipping my head, I take her mouth in a wild kiss, her legs wrap around me and hook at the base of my spine, holding me close as I rail into her hard and then slow, before sliding my hand up her middle between her breasts and grasping her throat.

Flexing my hand, her pulse beats against my fingers and I feel the force of her life beat beneath my fingertips. Does it make me fucked up that the thought of controlling her oxygen gets me off? Maybe, but as her eyes sparkle and her chin lifts, I know she wants this as much as me.

"Tap my arm if it's too much and I'll stop."

"I trust you, Jake."

Nothing else she could have said would have meant so much to me.

"Deep breath."

Cherry does as I say and I tighten my grip on her neck, cutting off her oxygen. My other hand slips between our bodies, and I stroke her swollen clit as she flails beneath me. My cock is so hard as I slam into her. As her body shakes, her pussy squeezing me like a vice, I release my hold on her neck. Air rushes into her body and a scream tears from her as she comes so hard, she almost breaks my dick off. I can't hold back and I come on a roar that feels torn from my body like a beast. My vision turns black as intense pleasure sweeps through me. With a sigh, I sag over her, both of us breathing hard, our sweat-slicked skin pressed together as she holds me to her. Cherry strokes my shoulders and back with gentle fingers, causing a ripple of pleasure to shoot through me.

"You okay, Blossom?"

She hums a response and I smile against her sweaty skin before kissing her temple and easing from the bed.

"Where are you going?"

"To get a cloth to clean you up. You have my cum all over you."

"Come back. I want you all over me."

Fuck me!

If I die right this second, I'll be the happiest man in the world. Unable and unwilling to deny her request, I slide back into bed and pull her into my arms, the mess we made drying on her skin and mine, giving me a rush.

"Love you, Jake."

I smile at her sleepy mumbled words and wonder if she knows she just said them.

Within minutes, I feel her body go slack against me, her slight weight sinking into me in a way I want to feel every night for the rest of my life.

32. Cherry

RUNNING THE MEASURING TAPE OVER THE ENTRY FROM THE master bath to the dressing room, I make some more notes on my notepad. Jake had an emergency meeting in the city today, so I said I'd be happy to come out here and get started on some more designs and he could join me later.

The truth is, I love this house, and would happily spend every second here. I glance around for my bag as I hear my phone ringing and find it wedged between two cans of paint. Taking it out I expect to see Jake's name but it's not him, it's my mom.

I smile as I answer. "Hey, mom."

"So you are alive."

Her words hold censure, but her tone is full of mirth and I love that. She's been so in favor of me and Jake, even after I confessed to her about our past. She told me that everyone made mistakes and nobody was perfect. It led to a long discussion about me fighting her battles, and how she was fully aware of who he was and thought I should forgive him.

By that point I already had, but I let her think she was the reason. Old habits die hard, and I'll always want to see my mom happy and shelter her as much as I can. It's a part of me now, and that is okay because now I have Jake, who can take the strain when it becomes too much.

"Sorry. We've been busy with the house and work."

"That's okay, Cherry Pie. I just wanted to check in about our girls' night next week. Frankie is bringing the main course and Lexi the desserts. Do you want to do starters or cocktails?"

It has become a tradition in the last six months for us to have a girls' night once a month. Each of us brings a course or board with the theme we'd chosen. This week we're doing Bridgerton-themed boards. Frankie had crashed the first and sulked so hard for not getting an invite that we caved, and he's become the sole male member of our girls' nights.

"Hmm, I think maybe cocktails."

Glancing out of the window to the drive, I see a truck parked at an odd angle across the front drive. It looks like a tradesman, but I haven't booked anyone in yet.

"Okay, my darling. I might do those little soul breads you like to start then. It'll help soak up the alcohol. You do tend to go a little heavy."

An eerie feeling makes the hairs on the back of my neck stand on end, and I turn to see a man in what was once an expensive suit but now looks like a dishrag, standing in the doorway of the master bedroom. His pupils are dilated, and he looks like he's slept in a hedge but there is no mistaking who it is; Nicholas Kendrick. The man who'd ruined my life and almost destroyed the man I loved, and who was behind the proposed buyout of my mom's salon. I recognised him from the photos of him I'd found online after KLM had contacted me.

"What the fuck are you doing here?"

I dropped my phone from my ear but make sure to keep the line open to my mom's call. If what Lexi went through with Dean taught me anything, it's that silence only ever protects the aggressor.

"Hello, Cherry. I've been hoping to catch you alone."

A shiver snakes down my spine at the emotionless way he says the words. His eyes rake over my body in a way that makes nausea slither up my throat. I can hear my mom calling my name, asking what is going on, and I pray she realizes something is off because I can't tell her, not when I have to keep my focus on the threat in front of me.

"The feeling isn't mutual, Kendick," I say, deliberately mispronouncing his name, my desire to live clearly not outweighed by my smart mouth.

His eyes narrow, his lips thinning spitefully, as he dives for me, knocking the phone from my hand. It's the opening I need. I run, screaming for help in the hopes my mom will hear me and he hadn't cut the connection.

My feet skid on the stairs, and I almost lose my footing and take a header down the grand staircase, but I catch myself on the handrail. I can hear the thunder of his footsteps behind me, gaining on me, but I have some advantage in that I know this house like the back of my hand after exploring it for days.

I run for the front door and try to wrench it open, but it won't budge. I waste precious seconds fighting with the lock before I abandon it.

"You can't escape me, Cherry."

I glanced behind me to see Kendrick standing between me and the back door. He's holding a gun, but I know I'd rather die of a bullet in my back trying to escape him, rather than buckling to the fear clawing its way up my throat.

"Fuck you."

I run left towards the kitchen, hoping that the back French doors are unlocked. As I near the entrance, a soft billow of smoke hazes the room and I cough. Fire. The house is on fire. With Kendrick behind me, I have no choice but to go forward, knowing I'd foolishly allowed him to herd me exactly where he wanted me. I run in the direction of the doors, unable to see a foot in front of me, and falling over samples of wood I'd ordered for the flooring in this room. Suddenly disorientated, I begin to cough as my lungs struggle to draw in oxygen.

The sound of a loud bang behind me makes me scream as I race toward the direction I think the doors lay. Finally, I feel the glass and sobs of relief tear through my burning throat. I feel around for the key and find the handle but not the key. I press down, but it's no use, the bastard has locked it. I'm trapped.

"Why are you doing this?"

A laugh echoes through the smoke, and I sink to the floor, remembering it's what you're told to do, or maybe that's wrong. My head is foggy, my thoughts muddled.

"Because he was mine first."

That makes zero sense. What is he talking about? Who was his first?

"What the hell are you talking about, crazy man."

"Jake. He was mine then Hunter stole him from me."

"Boohoo, you lost your BFF. Get over it." My last word is cut off as a cough wracks my body. I'm going to die here with this fucking maniac and I haven't told Jake I love him, at least not properly. A sleepy half-attempt doesn't count and he deserves more. He deserves to know how much I adore him.

"You don't get it. He was the only one who saw me. I love him."

Holy shit balls, he's in love with Jake? I'd say the man has great taste but he's a fucking nut job.

An explosion cuts through the right side of the house, rattling the windows as dust and debris rain down on me. Heat. I can feel the heat in the room and finally see fire lick the walls and up the ceiling. Kendrick is silent and I hope some big piece of timber has fallen on that fucker's head.

I try to suck in air but there is none and my vision begins to falter as I hear sirens in the distance. Black spots pool my vision and I wonder if Jake will stay here after I'm gone. If he'll find love with someone else and bring them to live in this home. A sob makes my chest convulse and then the world goes black.

33. Jake

I'M AT MY DESK, DEALING WITH A HICCUP WITH A CONTRACT FOR China that should have been dealt with weeks ago when the call comes through. My muscles tense as I see a call from the man watching Nick Kendrick. Unexpected calls never bring good news.

"Yes?" I answer briskly.

"I'm sorry to bother you, but I wanted to let you know that I lost eyes on Kendrick."

"What the fuck do you mean you lost eyes on him?"

I crack my knuckles as I stand, grabbing my jacket. Something telling me to get to Cherry.

"He went into his club but got thrown out. I followed him to a bar down the road and watched him go in, but he never came out. I went in and the barman said he'd left through the back with some woman."

"What did she look like?"

"I didn't ask."

Fuck me!

"Find the fuck out and call me immediately."

I hang up and dial Cherry, but only get the engaged tone. I keep trying as I go to get in my car and then decide to take the bike I some-times kept here for when I need to let off steam.

I link my phone through the helmet, wasting precious seconds, and then dial again. This time it rings and rings with no answer. No need to freak out, she's probably busy or has the music loud again. Yet I can't help the blind fear that is scratching at my insides like a rat trying to escape a hot steel drum.

My phone rings and I answer as I hit the freeway at breakneck speed. "Yes?"

"A blonde. Tall, slim, who was dressed like a socialite."

Fuck, that has to be Lorelei. I knew she'd been working with Kendrick and they hooked up a few times from the report and the gossip rags. It seems they've teamed up again and that can't be anything but bad news. "Call the police and have them sent to my property in Mariemont. Then find Kendrick before I do, or this will end badly for both of you."

I kill the call and dial Hunter.

"Please don't tell me they fucked this deal over a tiny detail, Jake."

"I can't get hold of Cherry and the fucking PI lost Kendrick."

I knew my best friend would pick up the abject terror in my voice.

"I'm heading that way now. Is she at the house?"

"Yes."

"It's probably fine."

"I'm five minutes out. Just get to her, Mac."

"I've got you, Jake."

I throttled the engine, taking curves way too fast, my knee skim-ming the tarmac as I race to get to her.

My phone goes again and I answer without looking.

"This better be good, asshole."

"Jake, it's Darla. I was on the phone with Cherry when some-thing happened. I think she's in trouble."

"Fuck. I'm already on my way and so are Hunter and the police, but tell me everything."

"We were talking and then went kind of distant like she wasn't listening. I heard her say what the fuck do you want or maybe it was who the fuck are you, I can't recall, and then the call went dead. I tried to call back but she isn't answering."

"I'm just a minute out, and as soon as we confirm it's all a misunderstanding, I'll have her call you."

The words die in my throat as I round the corner and see smoke billowing out of my property. Thick dark plumes of it roll out of the windows as my heart almost beats from my chest.

As I fly down the drive, I hear sirens behind me, but I don't stop. I don't think, all I care about is getting to Cherry. I let the bike fall to the ground and I race to the door. I try the handle but it's locked. I spend precious seconds putting my shoulder into it before I give up and race around the side. Flames lick at the windows as I try and see, calling her name like a prayer.

Memories assault me of the last time I was in this position and ended up carrying my dead sister out in my arms. I won't lose Cherry the same way, I can't. I'll never survive it. I skid on the gravel near the back French doors and try and peer inside. I squint, feeling hopelessness drag at my chest, trying to carve me in two.

That's when I see it, a shot of shocking pink near the door on the ground.

"Cherry! Fuck, I'm coming. You just keep breathing, Blossom."

I hunt around for something I can use to smash the windows. As I grab a rusty spade, Mac races around the corner.

"She's inside. Help me."

Never in my life have I felt such desperation. Not the night my sister died, not when my mother overdosed, not when I was arrested, and not even when I watched Cherry walk away from me, her heart broken ten years ago.

Between Mac and I, we smash the glass and are driven back for a

255

second as smoke pours out of the space and poisons the air. I push forward and Mac grabs my arm.

"The fire department is here."

"Fuck that, I'm not waiting."

I shake his hand off and push through the gap, hardly feeling the glass cut my arms. I gather her limp body in my arms and cradle her to my chest as I cough and splutter. Turning, I let Mac help me through the broken glass as heat singes my back.

Stepping through the broken door, I rush toward the ambulance as the firemen take over. A paramedic tries to take her from me, and I almost bite his head off, but then I feel Mac's hand.

"Let them take care of her, Jake."

My arms shake as I fight the urge to run away with her. The thought of letting her out of my arms is torture, but I know deep down I can't help, only they can. I sit on the bench as the EMTs, two female paramedics, check her over, listening to her lungs, checking her airway, and placing an oxygen mask over her face.

I reach for her hand, not willing to sit here and not let her know I'm here. Tears track down my cheek, and I choke on a sob. I can't lose her. I love her so much. It would be hell on earth without her. If she dies, I'll live for one reason and one only, and that will be to hunt down Kendrick and Lorelei and torture them to death.

"Jake."

My head snaps up at the weak, raspy sound that is the most beautiful thing I've ever heard.

"Blossom. Oh my God, I thought I'd lost you."

Her face is covered in soot and dust but her weak smile almost stops my heart as she reaches out to stroke my face. "You'll never lose me, Jake. I love you."

I never thought I'd be the type of man to lose it, but at her words, I put my head on her belly and hold on to her while I sob. Her hand stays in my hair as the paramedics give us some space for a minute.

When my mental breakdown is over, I lift my head, and she's looking at me with so much love.

"You really like me, huh?"

Her ridiculous statement has me laughing as I sit forward and kiss her beautiful lips, tasting the smoke she's inhaled.

"I really fucking love you, Blossom."

"I love you, too. I'm sorry I was so afraid to say it before."

"I'd wait a lifetime for you, Blossom."

"Sappy."

"You love my sappy."

"I do."

"I'm sorry, sir, but we really need to get her checked over at the hospital."

I glance at the blonde paramedic who addressed me and nod. "Fine but I'm coming with you."

"That's fine."

I know Mac will handle things here, and I don't give a fuck if the house burns to the ground, we can rebuild. The only thing that matters is my Cherry Blossom.

At the hospital, they check Cherry over and run some blood tests and lung function tests. I growl at the nurse who tries to clean her up and take the cloth from her so that I can wipe the dirt from her face. Her eyes are closed and I know she's exhausted and needs rest but I'm not leaving her alone.

"Jake."

"Hey, you."

"It was Kendrick."

My jaw practically snaps with the force of my anger when she confirms my fears. "I'm sorry. I should have known he'd find a way. That bastard is dead when I find him."

"He's jealous."

I frown, not understanding what she means. "Why? He has more money than God."

Cherry shakes her head, a hacking cough taking hold and I help her sit up and take a sip of water, fucking hating that he caused this and knowing for every second she suffers, he'll suffer ten times worse before I end his miserable life.

"He was jealous of Hunter and then me. He says he loves you."

What the fuck kind of twisted messed up bullshit is this? "We were never more than friends, and barely that."

"I know but he's clearly sick."

"Don't give a fuck. He's still going to pay with his life, so please don't ask me to spare him, Blossom. That's twice now he's tried to take you from me, and I'm not giving him the chance to have a third go."

"I'm not asking you to. I just want you to know what you're facing with him."

I stroke her hair back from her face and her eyes close. "Don't worry about me. You just get better so we can go house hunting."

"You have a house. You can rebuild."

"No fucking way. We rebuild, Blossom. From now on, I'm not wasting time. We're moving in together. We're starting our life together and that includes you in a white dress, saying I do, and a handful of obnoxiously gorgeous kids."

"Worst proposal ever."

I laugh at her sass, even as the weakness in her voice makes me want to rip out Kendrick's heart and feed it to him.

"That was a statement of fact, not a proposal, Blossom. When I propose, you'll know."

Her energy fades then and I sit by her side until her mother and Lexi come rushing in like the hounds of hell are chasing them. I lift my finger, indicating she's sleeping and the two women nod, and sit on either side of her in silence.

"How is she?"

"She's going to be okay. They want to keep her in overnight to be sure her lungs are clear. But other than a few bumps and some minor smoke inhalation, she's going to be fine."

"Thank God." Her mom sniffs and I wrap an arm around her while she gets herself together.

"Is Mac outside?"

Lexi nods and I ask if they're okay to stay with Cherry while I talk to my best friend and get an update. I'd rather never leave her ever again, but I need to end this threat to her for good.

Mac is waiting when I exit Cherry's room and this is too reminiscent of the time we spent waiting for news on Lexi. Lines of stress bracket his mouth and, for the first time, I can honestly say I understand how he felt and I wish with all my heart I didn't.

"How is she?"

"She's gonna be fine. Just an overnight stay for observation."

"Good."

I place my hands on my hips and try and control the rolling rage trying to break through my skin.

"Kendrick?"

"I have a team looking for him and my dad put a call into the Mancinis. They won't get involved but they're happy to clean up any mess for us as an apology for letting him slip through the net."

"Okay. Call me when you find him. He's mine, Mac."

"You got it. You just take care of Cherry and I'll handle this."

"Thank you."

"No need, it's what friends do."

That's more than I deserve. I certainly didn't have his back quick enough with Lexi, but I'll make sure that going forward, I don't let anything happen to the people I love and that starts with Cherry.

34. Jake

My phone rings and I blink away sleep as I grab it to stop it from waking Cherry. The hospital lights are dim, but my brain clears quickly as I head for the hallway to take the call from an unknown number.

"Mr. Marshall, this is Nico Mancini."

My spine straightens at the sound of his voice. Nico is the oldest son of the head of the Neapolitan Camorra, Enzo Mancini. Feared and revered in equal measure, he's known for slicing a man's throat for spitting his gum out in front of him and has allegedly killed his best friend's entire family. Although that's never been proven.

"What can I do for you, Mr. Mancini?"

"It's what I can do for you, Mr. Marshall. I have left a gift for you at the following address."

He rattles off an address in the meatpacking area of the city that has long been forgotten by industry. "This gift, is it a mutual acquaintance?"

"Indeed."

"Why are you helping me?"

"Because, Mr. Marshall, I do not believe in bringing women into a war between men."

The line goes dead and I look at my phone in shock, and with a hefty dose of apprehension. The Camorra doesn't get involved without a reason and, while I want to take his reason at face value, I have to weigh up whether this gift will cost me a favor in the future.

It takes me about half a second to decide that whatever he wanted, I'd pay to avenge the woman I love.

Deciding to drive instead of taking my bike, I leave Cherry knowing that the men I'd hired to protect her at the hospital would get the job done. I'd been lucky that Eidolon, the team who'd helped Hunter get Lexi and Theo back, were currently in the States and were willing to do me a solid.

Reid and Alex are mean-looking bastards who'd never let anyone get past them and hurt her and it's the only reason I feel happy leaving her. I text Alex and let him know I'm leaving, and he texts me back saying she'll be safe until my return. I don't doubt it, and only wish I could hire them full-time, but they work for someone even more powerful than even the McKenzies and are loyal as hell to her.

I arrive at the abandoned industrial estate and find the disused factory Nico had indicated. Stepping out, I hear the crunch of gravel and spin to see Eddie Crowe stepping out of the shadows.

My lips curl at his presence and the bastard has the nerve to grin as he puts his hands up.

"I come in peace. I hear you have some trash to take care of and I want in on it."

"Why?"

Cherry had told me that she and Eddie were just friends and her flirting with him had all been to get under my skin. Still, the thought that he'd had his hands anywhere near my girl makes me want to rip his arms off and beat him with them.

"We both love Cherry."

I bristle and step forward, ready to make good on my violent thoughts but he steps back.

"Not like that. Cherry is like a sister to me and that fucker almost killed her."

"This seems like a dark path for a country music star."

He shrugs, shoving his hands in his pockets and looking as relaxed as a pig at a vegetarian conference.

"I wasn't always a rock star, just like you weren't always a billionaire lawyer. People change, but for this, I'm happy to crack some skulls." He rocks his neck and crunches his knuckles and I can see that I've wildly misjudged this man.

"You have my back and you get one punch, so make it a good one. Then he's mine."

"Fair enough."

I lead the way toward the side fire exit door and enter the room. It smells like piss and rotting meat and my stomach rebels. Stepping over the used needles, and fast-food wrappers, I head into the center of the room, past the conveyor belt and toward the sounds of rattling.

In the middle, is a line of meat hooks for hanging the meat to age, and hanging from his shoulders on two rusty hooks, is Nicholas Kendrick. His shirt is missing and his feet are bloody and bare but other than the blood dripping from the two wounds in his shoulders, he's unharmed.

Glass crunches under my shoe and Kendrick looks up, fear and pain in his eyes, the glassy look of infection already setting in through his body.

"Jake." His voice holds misguided hope and I shake my head as I walk closer. "You need to help me, they're gonna kill me."

I stop in front of him as sweat and the stench of his piss hits my nose. "Help you! I'm the one here to kill you, Nick."

Snot bubbles from his nose as he begins to cry, his expression that of a man who has no idea of the repercussions of his actions. Too many years of having his family's money bail him out have left him with an entitlement that has made him weak.

"No, we're friends."

I snort, and kick out at his legs, making him swing on the bloody hooks. A scream of pain spills from his lips, but nobody can hear but me and Eddie, and neither of us are gonna save him.

"Friends don't blackmail each other. Friends don't try and ruin each other's lives and hurt the person they love."

"Jake, it was just a bit of fun. A prank that went too far."

Rage rushes through my veins, hatred for this person almost clouding my vision. I clench my fists and spin on my heel, moving two steps back to remove my jacket, casting a glance at Eddie who, in this setting, looks like a different man, a lethal killer who grins wide at the thought of hurting the man swinging from two hooks.

"Take your shot because I'm done listening to his bullshit."

Eddie walks slowly over to Kendrick, his smile holding nothing but malice. "You know who I am?"

Kendrick nods, snot dripping off his chin and I curl my lip in disgust. "You're the singer, Eddie Crowe."

Eddie rubs his chin and looks away with a laugh. "Yeah, but you know what else I am?"

I'm intrigued as Eddie works this man's fear like a fucking pro. I'm no hardened killer but I've done things I needed to, to protect the company but this man, he's a maestro.

"No."

"Your worst nightmare. You see I'm friends with Cherry Baker. She's like a sister to me and I'm gonna watch while her man dishes out the vengeance she deserves, and then clean up the mess, but first...."

Eddie hauls back and punches Kendrick in the balls so hard that his howl of animalistic pain makes even me inwardly wince. A punch to the balls is brutal and Kendrick pukes all over himself as piss darkens the area around his groin.

Eddie steps back and holds out his hand for me to go forward. I step closer and Kendrick is openly weeping.

"Please, Jake. It was a joke."

"A joke? You made her lose her place at Harvard. You lost me the love of my life, and made me believe I'd killed her father."

263

"I'm sorry. I have money. I can pay you."

I look at Eddie and he smirks before I grip Kendrick's jaw in a brutal hold that has him fighting to pull away. "Do we look like men who need your money, Kendrick?"

"Nooo."

"No, we do not. So tell me, why would I spare you your sorry life when all you've done is cause misery and pain to everyone who knows you?"

"Lorelei. You can take her as payment. She's a good lay and doesn't mind being passed around."

How has this man been allowed to live and breathe the same air as normal people? "You really are a disgusting excuse for a human being, aren't you, Kendrick? Willing to do anything to save your own skin now that the game's not so fun."

"Please, Jake, we were friends. I love you and you left me for Hunter, and then that pink-haired slut."

A growl rips from my throat as I punch him in the face. "Don't you fucking dare. I'll slit your throat and let you bleed out like the animal you are."

"I'm sorry."

"Save it. There's nothing you can do to stop me from ending you. I would've walked away and left you alive after Harvard but you went after her mom, and then you went after my girl. The woman I love, and that means you get to die."

Kendrick is a weak man. He's always hidden behind his family and his money but he's pathetic and it shames me that I ever spent any time with him at all.

"You're a stain on society, Kendrick, and the world will be better off with you not in it."

I produce a small pocket knife from my pocket which Hank gave me for my nineteenth birthday, when he took me and Hunter camping.

"Lorelei is pregnant. I'm gonna be a father, Jake."

I cock my head, wanting to understand how he could think it's okay to offer Lorelei up to me as a way to keep him alive and then a second later tell me she's having his baby. Both are abhorrent to me, but then I'll never understand a man like him because he isn't really a man, he's a leech on humanity.

"Then I'm doing that kid the biggest favor of its life by ending you."

Done talking and wanting nothing more than to get back to my girl, I lift my arm and stab him in the heart, twisting the knife as he cries out in pain and making sure I'm the last thing he sees as the life drains from his eyes.

I yank the knife from his chest and Eddie hands me a clean rag. I wipe the blade and let the relief wash over me knowing that Kendrick is gone, and my Cherry Blossom is safe.

"Strip and put your clothes in the dumpster over there. The rag, too. I'll torch the lot and make sure there's no evidence we were ever here."

I follow Eddie's directions, trusting him despite knowing even less than I thought I did. He does the same with his own clothes and then throws gasoline over the top before he throws a match on the lot. Chucking a bundle of clothes at me, he starts to dress in sweats and a grey hoodie and I do the same, wondering again how he's really involved and why. He might love Cherry like he says, but this is a whole other level of protection.

"Who the fuck are you?"

Eddie chuckles. "Now, wouldn't you like to know."

"Yes, I fucking would. Which is why I asked."

"Let's just say I wasn't always Eddie Crowe, and leave it that, hey, *amico*."

A dawning realization that perhaps Eddie has closer ties to the Mancini family than I could fathom hits me, and I decide I don't want any more answers.

"Fair enough." I hold out my hand and Eddie takes it. "Thank you."

"You're welcome. Just take care of her. She's a good girl."

Still holding his hand, I pull him closer. "I will, and for the record, I don't care who you are, who you have ties with, if you ever put your hands on her again, I'll cut them off with a rusty blade."

Eddie chuckles and squeezes my hand to the point of pain before he lets go and I turn and leave. It's time to get back to my girl and start the rest of my life.

Epilogue One: Cherry

I WAKE WHEN JAKE TRIES TO SLIDE HIS ARM OUT FROM UNDER my warm body so he can shower and get ready for the day.

"Where are you going? It's still night."

Jake chuckles as I roll to look at him, with displeasure clear on my face. What I see as he looks back at me is filled with so much love it steals the breath from my lungs, and in a totally different way than when my kinky boyfriend has his hands on my throat.

It's taken us a long time to get here but today we're moving into our new home together. To think that this time last year we were fighting to save my best friend and now me and Jake are finally getting our own happy ending, makes me feel incredibly lucky.

"Hey, handsome. Happy Moving Day."

He bends close, and catches my nape with his hand, bringing me closer to his lips. "Happy Moving Day, Blossom." His kiss is quick but deep, stirring my blood to boiling as it always does. "Wanna take a shower with me and see if I can wake you up?"

I jump from the bed at his suggestion and leap towards him, knowing he'll catch me. My legs hook around his waist, and I feel the hard, blunt end of his cock against my belly. Holding my ass, in his big hands, he gives me a deeper kiss, a lazy slow morning kiss before he walks us into the bathroom as I grind against him.

"Hell, yes. I do."

Jake places me down in the bathroom and closes the door before dropping his boxers and lifting the t-shirt he gave me to wear, which has his name on it, over my head.

"God, you're too fucking beautiful. I might have to lock you up in our new house so other men can't see how stunning you are."

"Jake, you're too much." My head dips to hide how much pleasure I get from his possessive jealousy.

"I need to fuck you fast, Blossom. I can't wait."

"Then take me."

His eyes darken, the growl rumbling through his chest making a flood of heat soak my pussy. I love how much he wants me and how much he shows me and anyone else how much I mean to him. Our path hasn't been an easy one. It has been mired by lies, blackmail, attempted murder, and the destruction of his beautiful period home, but today marks the beginning. The house couldn't be salvaged, and in the end, we decided to tear it down and start again and make it into something we can both love, with none of the memories of that day.

"I don't want to hurt you, and I'm hanging on by a thread already."

I fist his hard cock in my hand, and he groans as I stroke him with a firm, practiced motion I know drives him wild.

"You'd never hurt me. Now fuck me like you hate me."

Jake would never hurt me, he's shown me in every way I could ever want how sorry he is for what happened at Harvard. Even going so far as to get me re-enrolled if I wanted to. I don't, that time in my life is gone and I'm ready to move on. I get a text from him every morning even when he's lying next to me. Fresh flowers are sent to the shop every week in every shade of pink I can imagine and better than all of that, he makes me feel like I'll always have a safe spot to land when the weight of shielding those I love becomes too much.

He's my light in the dark and the boy who showed me it was okay to be me.

Pulling my hand away, Jake spins me around so I'm facing the mirror.

"Hold onto the counter and don't let go."

My eyes meet his in the glass, and I see hunger slashed in the tight line of his marble jaw. I bite my lip and think I could come from the sight of him looking so powerful alone. Jake glances down at my ass, and I watch his expression change in the mirror, his hand moving up and down the ridges of my spine before smoothing over my ass. Running a finger lower, he dips his hand between my legs and groans appreciatively when he finds me soaked for him already.

"You are my good girl, aren't you, Blossom?"

I give him a curt nod as he spears his fingers inside me before pulling them out and rubbing them over my swollen clit until I'm forced up on tiptoes as I try to grind against his cock with my ass. The move forces my tits up, and I can see Jake's eyes on them in the glass so I lift my hand from the counter and pluck at my nipple.

"Did I say you could move your hand from the counter?"

I give him a bratty smirk. "No."

"Looks like someone wants to get her ass spanked."

"Maybe, maybe not."

I love this dynamic in our relationship. Jake allows me to be the ball buster outside of the bedroom, but in here, he gets the other part of me. The side that wants to give up all my control and trust him with my pleasure, but now and then the sass bleeds through and I think he likes that just as much.

"I'm gonna get to mark you as mine, Blossom? Make this ass as pink as your hair?"

"Yes, do it. I want to feel all of you."

"Fuck, you're killing me."

"No dying today, Jake."

His hand smooths over my ass again and he gives me a single slap that makes me moan in pleasure.

"Umm, I could do this all day, but I want inside you and it will give you something to look forward to when I fuck you all over our new house."

"Yes! Now can we please get on with it before I die from waiting?"

Jake chuckles. "Impatient brat."

He rubs the blunt head of his cock over my wet entrance before thrusting through my legs so his cock brushes against my clit. I'm sure he's trying to torture me for not agreeing to his plan to knock me up before we get married. It wasn't about the marriage but wanting us to have some time together first, but Jake is eager to put a baby in me and is using every trick he can to torture me into conceding. Little does he know I've already given in and thrown my contraceptives in the bin last week. New house, new baby, or so they say.

"Jake Marshall, either fuck me or I'll paint every room in our new house fuchsia pink."

"If that's what you want, Blossom."

I growl and he leans in and bites my shoulder lightly. "I love you."

"I love you, too. Now, fuck me."

Jake eases back and then slowly pushes into my body. I feel the size of his cock stretch me and wriggle to get him to give me more.

"Greedy girl."

"Give me everything, Jake."

Running his hand over my back, he grips my shoulder as he holds my gaze in the mirror before slamming home and giving me everything. His firm grip on my hair has me arching into him as he fucks me hard and fast. My hips press against the counter so hard I know I'll have bruises later and I know Jake will kiss them better, and I love that.

"Like this, Blossom? Is this how you want me to fuck my fiancée?"

We'd gotten engaged this last month when he'd surprised me with a trip to Yoshino, Nara prefecture in Japan. Over thirty thousand Sakura trees had bloomed with Cherry Blossoms. It had been just me and him and a carpet of pink petals as he went down on one knee and proposed with a teardrop pink diamond. It had been emotional and everything I could ever have dreamed of. I don't think I've ever seen anything so beautiful, and that he'd taken the time to plan the trip and make every detail perfect and personal showed me just how well he knew and loved me. It had been just for us, and then later he'd taken me on a bike he'd hired and we'd ridden for hours until we stopped at a boutique hotel for the night to celebrate. It was perfect, but then he was perfect for me. Not because neither of us are flawless, but because our imperfections make us perfect for each other.

"Uh-huh."

Then there's no more talking as he fucks me, watching my tits bounce as I take him.

The sounds of flesh slapping against flesh is almost as heady as the feel of his hands on my throat as I race toward my climax. "Jake, please."

He doesn't fuck around or make me beg but slips his hand to my clit and rubs hard and fast, wanting me to come before he does and knowing he doesn't have much restraint left.

I cry his name as my pussy milks his dick, and he slams into me a couple more times before he stays buried and comes hard, filling me with his seed. Leaning over, he kisses my shoulder as I turn until he can take my lips.

"I love you."

"I love you, too."

Epilogue Two: Jake

Six months Later

GLANCING ACROSS THE GARDEN THAT HAS BEEN TRANSFORMED into something from a summer fairytale, I find my new wife laughing with Lexi and Frankie. This feeling of fullness in my chest gets bigger every single day I spend loving her.

Today we exchanged vows in the garden of our home near the lake where I told her about my past. Originally we were going to get married in a hotel, but Cherry suggested we do it here, because she wanted all our happiest days to start here, and with each one, the pain of the past will fade away.

I'm not sure I'll ever forget the pain I felt that day when I thought she'd perished in a fire, but she's right. The happy memories are piling up so high that the sad ones are losing purchase on me.

"I'm happy for you, Jake."

I turn to Mac, who is beside me, my best man and best friend and brother in all but blood, and smile. "Me too. I never dreamed I'd get her back, and each day feels like a blessing."

"It is." His eyes are on his wife now, who's holding their son and I let my gaze fall to Cherry's flat tummy and hope that this month we will get our wish. Not that it matters. If I only ever get her, it will be enough for me, but I know she'll make an amazing mother one day.

Cherry turns and catches my eye and her soft look of love that she saves just for me, makes my chest feel hollow. Downing the drink Mac bought me, I cross the garden, trying to smile and keep moving as people wish me well, but all I want right now is my wife in my arms.

"Hey, you."

Slipping a hand around her belly, I press my lips to her neck. Her body sinks into mine with so much trust it makes a well of love for her rush through my veins. Her hand comes up and she strokes my cheek.

"Hey, yourself."

"You ready for the first dance, Mrs. Marshall?" God, that will never get old.

My Cherry Blossom rolls her eyes at me but nods. I've been making us take dance lessons for the past three months, even though she tried to get out of a first dance, saying it was an unnecessary tradition. I'd convinced her though, telling her that I want every tradition with her, both old and new, and then I fucked her just how she likes until she caved.

I have one last surprise for my girl today, and I know it's one that she'll like.

"Yes, I'm ready but if I make a fool of myself or step on your toes, you only have yourself to blame."

I take her hands and lead her out onto the dance floor, the mermaid train on the ivory lace dress gliding along the floor behind her. When she walked down the aisle on her mother's arm, I thought I'd fall apart. Only Mac's hand on my shoulder had kept me from sinking to my knees and weeping like a fucking newborn.

"I promise I won't make you look like a fool, and if you break every single toe I have, then it's still worth it."

"Fine." Her pout is so pretty that I can't resist pressing my lips to her mouth. Her arms come around me and her body presses to mine as if we'll never be able to get close enough. My tongue slips between her lips and my cock hardens in my tuxedo pants. Pulling away, I look down at her flushed cheeks.

"Fuck, now I want to skip the dance and find somewhere I can fuck my bride."

"Mission accomplished."

I swat her ass and she yelps, but I hold her close and bend my head into her neck as I turn her back to the band. "Then you wouldn't get your surprise."

"More surprises?"

I see her eyes dance with excitement and smile down at her as the first strains of the first dance song we picked out begin to play. *For the Both of Us* by Dan and Shay had been a perfect choice because I'd loved her since the first day I saw her.

Her body sways against mine and then he begins to sing and she stills before she turns to look up at her friend, Eddie Crowe, who is singing at our wedding. Mac had thought it an odd choice, but Eddie had proven to me that he had my back that night with Kendrick and he loved my wife. That it makes her happy is the only real reason, it's the only reason I do anything these days.

"Jake." I hear the wobble in her voice, the tears shining bright like diamonds in her eyes, and lean in and kiss her like she's the air I need to survive because she is. Without her, I'm nothing, I'm dead. With her, I'm the luckiest bastard alive and I know it and I'll spend every day from here to eternity proving it.

"I love you, Cherry Blossom."

"And I love you, husband."

Books by L. Knight

Kings of Ruin

The Auction

The Consequence

The Unexpected

The Temptation

The Enemy

Tightrope Series

Love, Honor, Betray

Love Lies Bleeding

Love Loathe Devotion

About the Author

Lia Knight is a romance author of billionaire romance with lots of angst, and heat. Her heroes are super rich, demanding and know exactly what they want, so when they set their sights on the heroines in these books you know the chemistry will explode your Kindle. Having written over forty books under a different pen name she wanted to give those rich, bossy heroes fighting for a story a chance to have their say and find their HEA.

When she isn't writing, she is binging Yellowstone, The Big Bang Theory, and Bridgerton from her home in Hereford in the UK.

You can contact me at: lknightauthor@gmail.com